"YOU'RE DRIVING ME NUTS, AMY."

"And I don't know what to do about you." Del looked at her hard. "No, I don't mean about the climb. I'm talking about us and our . . . relationship. I've got you in my head, and it's like an itch I can't get at."

"That bad?" Amy whispered.

"Worse."

"But do you want . . . do you want me to stay here tonight?"

He looked at her without speaking, yet words seemed to fly around the small tent, filling the air with an expectant thrum that made Amy's heart pound. His face was shadowed, but she knew he wanted her. The silence thickened—all those words crashing around, finding no lips to speak them. Then, slowly, his hand reached out and touched her face, moved around to the back of her head and pulled her toward him.

ABOUT THE AUTHOR

Several trips to the area near Jackson, Wyoming, "one of the last wild and woolly Western towns left in the U.S.A.," convinced Carla Peltonen and Molly Swanton, the indefatigable writing team of Lynn Erickson, that the Teton mountain range would provide an ideal setting for their fourth Superromance. Terry, Molly's husband, was able to provide technical information on climbing, and Erik, Carla's husband, assisted in the research necessary to make the Erickson blend of romance and intrigue as authentic as possible.

Lynn Erickson
STORMSWEPT

Harlequin Books

TORONTO • NEW YORK • LONDON
AMSTERDAM • PARIS • SYDNEY • HAMBURG
STOCKHOLM • ATHENS • TOKYO • MILAN

Published February 1986

First printing December 1985
First Australian Paperback Edition January 1987

ISBN 0 373 70199 3

Printed in Australia by
The Book Printer, North Blackburn, Victoria 3130

This book is dedicated to the real-life Flint Smith,
whose help was invaluable and whose forgiveness
I beg for any liberties I may have taken with his character,
to Dougal Haston, the real Lonnie Dougal,
a climber who died challenging the mountains he loved,
and to Lucy Hibberd, for her precise information
on private aircraft and flying.

Pearl Pass

PROLOGUE

Day 1 A.M.

THE TRIM SILVER WINGS of the Lear jet sliced through the frigid October air at twenty-seven thousand feet. The sun, spearing through the plane's small windows, illuminated the four men on board.

"We'll be passing over the Teton range in western Wyoming in fifteen minutes," the pilot announced to the two passengers. "It should be pretty this morning."

Roger Slavinsky, the first passenger, glanced idly out of the window, but his mind was not on the scenery. It was on his mission, his vitally important mission, which was taking him to Washington, D.C., on this elegant little plane. The second traveler was a representative of the Defense Department, sent to escort him safely from Portland, Oregon, where Roger worked for Shearing Aerospace as an aeronautical engineer.

Of course, Roger no longer worked for Shearing. He'd quit two days before and they'd taken his security pass and confiscated all his papers. Not that it mattered. Everything he needed to know was right in his head: every test and specification, every error, every computer readout that pertained to his research. Roger modestly assured himself that he was a genius, but his twin sister, Amy, had always refuted it. "You just have a good memory," she would insist stubbornly.

The Defense Department man turned to him and smiled. "Lovely country in this part of Wyoming. Ever been there?"

"No," answered Roger politely. He'd never been anywhere much. To him, scenery consisted of the inside of a test lab and the whirring of a bank of computers.

He went over in his mind what he'd have to tell the Defense Department when he arrived in Washington. His problem was to explain it all so they would understand the incredibly complicated technology involved in the president's Strategic Defense Initiative. Roger had discovered a serious flaw in the lasers that were the basis for all satellite-conducted weapons systems, the so-called Star Wars project that would take twenty years and fifty billion dollars to implement. And Shearing Aerospace had the major contract to produce it.

Roger had, naturally, reported the flaw to his superiors, but they'd pooh-poohed his findings. He'd argued with them for weeks, until he came to realize that to admit the laser system might fail to operate could cost his employers millions.

So he'd decided to take matters into his own hands. The security of his country could be in jeopardy if he let things go, and the computerlike logic of his brain would not allow him to do that.

He'd confided in his sister, Amy, because he trusted her implicitly, even though she was a bit eccentric. And besides, she wanted to scoop the story—it would be her big break. Roger was glad for her and wished her great success as a TV reporter, as long as he told the story to the Defense Department first. Once he relayed the information he was safe from Shearing. It would be too late for them to do anything about it by then. But he was quite aware, in a clinical sort of way, that he was in distinct physical danger from the giant corporation until he'd done so.

He looked out the window at the approaching wall of mountains—part of the Rockies—below them. They sparkled white in the early sun, but the valleys remained jagged black chasms. He supposed the landscape was pretty; he wondered idly what it was like up close.

"Smooth flight, isn't it?" remarked the Defense Department man.

"Very," Roger concurred.

It wasn't a minute later that Roger felt an odd vibration in the plane. He knew instantly that it was abnormal.

The pilot began touching his instruments, speaking in a low, tense tone to the copilot.

"What is it?" Roger asked.

The copilot turned around. "A little roughness in one engine. Nothing serious." He smiled reassuringly. The plane shuddered again.

The pilot switched on his radio. Roger was aware of the Defense Department man leaning forward to listen along with him.

"Salt Lake Center, this is six-one-Charlie. We're at two-seven thousand feet somewhere north of you. We have mechanical problem number two engine. Can you locate us?"

The radio crackled, but the voice from Salt Lake City was perfectly clear. "Six-one-Charlie ident."

"Rog." The pilot sounded calm, as if this sort of thing were routine. Roger relaxed a little.

Center came on again. "We have you—radar contact sixty miles northwest of Jackson VOR at two-seven thousand."

In the background the copilot swore and flipped a switch repeatedly. The plane shuddered again. Roger could tell they were descending; it seemed as if the glistening white peaks were pulling at them.

"Six-one-Charlie unable restart number two engine. Unable hold altitude. Six-one-Charlie descending rapidly. Please advise immediate airport in vicinity." The pilot's voice was tenser now. He said something in a low, urgent voice to the copilot. Then he turned to the two passengers. "Please fasten your seat belts. We're going to have to land somewhere."

Center came on. "Six-one-Charlie turn one-seven-zero. Are you in trouble? Repeat, are you in trouble?"

The pilot was too busy to answer. "Number one losing oil pressure now, damn." He did something with his controls.

The plane coughed and shivered as if it were ill. Roger could sense their forward momentum slowing. He felt every muscle in his body snap taut.

"Switch fuel tank," said the pilot. "Number one's losing oil."

"Nothing, sir." The copilot sounded scared.

"Six-one-Charlie going to try to make Jackson. May not reach it. Number one engine going," the pilot said to Center.

"We have you six-one-Charlie. Jackson directly in line thirty miles."

The plane gave a last, expiring shudder and became silent. The pilot swore again and desperately flicked switches.

"Attempt restart," he grated into the radio, and paused. "Six-one-Charlie going in. I think I see a place to put her down. There's a snowfield. I'll try to call again. Repeat. Six-one-Charlie going in."

The graceful silver bird soared downward, gliding noiselessly toward the shining, white-capped mountains that extended up to it beckoningly.

Disbelieving, frantic, Roger cushioned his head with a pillow as the pilot and copilot struggled with the controls, talking to each other in taut monosyllables. The only noise Roger could hear above their tense, disjointed words was the hissing of the wind against the plane's body.

The Defense Department man was praying out loud, but Roger didn't have time to pray. He was agonizing, with vast regret, over the certainty that Shearing Aerospace's cover-up would never be exposed now.

CHAPTER ONE

AMY SLAVIN HAD A LOT to think about that October morning. Of course, her mind was always going at full throttle, twisting and turning and wondering, but today her brain circuits were nearing overload.

"Keep it under control, Slavin," she warned herself out loud, swallowing the last morsel of last night's cold, leftover egg foo yung, then finishing her third cup of coffee.

She could feel the jitters coming on already and it wasn't even eight o'clock in the morning. "Oh, well," she mused, padding across the living room, "I'll give up caffeine next week."

She'd been awake since six, going over and over in her mind her twin brother's phone call of the night before. It had been a blockbuster of a conversation. But she had to finish something first, before she even considered Roger's news.

On the coffee table sat her best buddy—her small tape recorder. It was probably the only machine she had ever operated with any degree of success. Even screwdrivers seemed to fall apart on her. And cars—she didn't own one anymore. Four lemons in one lifetime was enough.

Amy picked up the loyal little device, sank into a chair, tucked her trim legs under her wildly colored, striped robe and began once again to put into her words her TV report exposing kickbacks and graft in the construction of the new hospital in her hometown of Rochester, New York. The story was turning into a personal vendetta for Amy. She had proof that one of the city councilmen had been paid off to direct the contract to his brother-in-law.

"It's a case of graft, typical and widespread and seemingly unstoppable. In Rochester, as in any moderate-size city across the country, it's an affront to the voters and taxpayers, and this reporter would like to see an immediate end to such corruption." Amy's smoky blue eyes grew big and round as she spoke into her recorder. "An immediate cancellation of the construction contract and a recall of Councilman Dodger are the first steps in what promises to be a war against graft in our city...."

Then she squinted, staring unfocused across the room, organizing her next thought. She couldn't see more than a blur, anyway, as she hadn't bothered to put in her contact lenses yet. It didn't matter that she was as blind as a bat without them; she had her trusty tape recorder.

She worked intensely, the way she did everything. Her parents had always termed her zeal "hyperactivity." Some of her boyfriends had been known to call it "madness." Amy preferred "purpose."

The tape was running out. Amy talked faster, gesticulating to the empty air to make a point, pushing her dark curly bangs back—an old habit. She even got up and paced the floor, immediately stubbing her bare toe on a chair leg.

A sound intruded as she hopped around clutching her foot, muttering to herself. A knock at the door.

Now who could that be?

Pulling the front of her coat of many colors together even while thinking she was too skinny to have anything to hide, Amy limped to the unlocked door.

"Ken...?" Yes, it was her boss at WYSU TV, Kenneth Lowry. "To what do I owe this immense pleasure so early in the morning?" Amy took satisfaction in the frown that pulled his brows together. Kenneth, the tall, dark and attractive station manager, had only last month ditched her for an older wealthy divorcée.

"Look, Amy," he began, "can I come in a sec? It's...business."

It had better be, thought Amy, stepping aside with a sweeping gesture. "Sure, come on in, Ken. You know your way around." Instantly she could have bitten her tongue for the catty remark; she'd promised herself to take his rejection with her head held high—another promise down the old drain....

He sat, a bit uneasily, on the wing chair opposite the couch. Amy resumed her place, taking up her coffee cup, knowing that she should offer him some but deliberately refusing to.

"I see you're working...." He nodded his dark head toward her tape recorder. "That graft report?"

"Yes." *Here it comes again,* she thought, *the "it's over your head" routine.*

"I think you're getting in over your head, Amy."

"Really?" She sat back, smiling and wishing she'd put in her contact lenses so she could see his expression instead of imagining it.

"Back off. You've got two iron-clad sources for each accusation and you can go on the air with it. Libel free."

Amy pursed her lips, her small chin pointing resolutely. "I have just a few more hours of work to do on it, Ken."

"Let the district attorney do it, Amy. It could turn out to be dangerous for you."

"What do you care?" Amy blurted out, remembering bitterly just how little concern he'd had for her feelings.

"Of course I care," Ken replied, injured.

"Oh, sure," she remarked stubbornly.

"Listen," began Ken anew, "this is strictly business, Amy."

"One more loose end and I'm through."

Ken put his head in his hands. "I get the feeling you're enjoying a bit of female revenge here."

True, thought Amy. He had, after all, dumped her, and if she felt like being contentious, she darn well would. Then she sighed, shrugging, and smiled at him. The expression on her face made her look about sixteen. "I'm just doing my job, Ken. No revenge intended. You know I've never backed off an assignment."

"You've never been on a touchy exposé before. This is Rochester, not New York City."

"You're telling me!" What she wouldn't do to work on a big city network! Oh, the hot camera lights, the reporters pushing and shoving, the glamour, the glory!

"Ken," she said, abruptly remembering her brother's phone call, "I'm going to finish this assignment and then—" she couldn't resist smirking a bit "—I've got something else in mind. A big story. The networks are going to want this one."

He looked at her keenly. "A hot story? Here?"

Amy felt excitement well up within her. "Maybe. You'll just have to wait and see, won't you?"

"Come on, Amy...."

"Oh, no! This one is mine, Ken. And I'll tell you, it's going to burn up the wire services."

"Well..."

"I'll see you at the station later." She smiled graciously. "I've got to finish this report and do the taping for tonight's spot on the news." She rose gracefully, as befitted a nationally known anchorwoman, but got snagged by her robe on the way to the door.

He got the hint but had to squeeze in the last word. "I'm going to edit this one myself, Amy. I won't have you endangering yourself."

"Sure, Ken. See you later." She almost added, "And say hello to Laura for me," but this time kept her counsel. Face it, she thought, no point making a bigger fool of herself than she already had.

Men. All she ever seemed to meet were the superficial singles with hang-ups or the nice predictable guys like Ken who were so easily swayed that women with great looks or big bucks—like Laura Reynolds—could snatch them away with a glance. Ken's mother, she thought, as a contact lens fell off her finger into the bathroom sink, must have been a real matriarch. ''Ken do this, Ken do that....''

I'm not a bad catch, Amy decided as she retrieved the lens. She knew she had an easygoing sense of humor, even if she was a touch overactive. And she was smart, had been a diligent student in college, considered alert and curious. Sure, she made plenty of mistakes, was a bit klutzy and always seemed to attract trouble. But she somehow got out of those scrapes, didn't she?

What had the jerk before Ken said about her? ''Crazy and uncontrollable.'' Perhaps there was a smidgen of truth in his assessment of her, but, then again, maybe all her men were just plain dull.

Mr. Right was out there somewhere, gorgeous and sexy, strong and gentle. He'd understand her need for adventure and that bright, romantic outlook she possessed. He wouldn't make her quit eating chocolate, give up caffeine, or dress ''sensibly.'' No. Not the guy she'd give it all up for—her career, the TV spots, her tidy, if lonely, little apartment in Rochester. Kids, a warm shining home, a loving husband—those were the things she really wanted. Maybe even a station wagon and a great, lop-eared dog who drooled on her freshly waxed kitchen floor. She walked through to her small bedroom and opened the closet doors. Her clothes were divided in two groups. There were the sensible blouses and skirts and a few pretty dresses—the chic

items she needed for news spots. Then there was the
real Amy hanging there, the clothes that made her
mother shake her head, saying, "When *are* you going
to buy something that suits your age?"

"Soon as I'm old enough to dye my hair blue,"
Amy always taunted.

She pushed a few hangers aside, deciding. Late this
afternoon, Amy knew she would be taping a spot on
the news—she was aired on Tuesdays and Fridays as
a special investigative reporter—but she could wear
whatever she pleased now, since she kept several
changes of clothes hanging in a closet at the studio.

She laughed to herself, as she always did, thinking
of the way the cameraman filming her at the news desk
looked over her outfits incredulously, ogling the styl-
ish blazers and silk blouses worn over hidden baggy
blue jeans with zippers and patches and a dozen
pockets.

"No one sees my pants," Amy always said, "unless you swing the camera behind the desk."

"Or you stand up."

She pulled out the perfect autumn outfit, something for a typical workday. No point dressing for
work *and* a date afterward, unless Mr. Right just
happened to walk into the station building and spotted her and fell head over heels in love. You never
know...

Sure, she thought derisively, tossing a few hangers
on her unmade bed.

Amy chose her calf-length gray suede skirt with the
diagonal ruffle on the bottom and a heavy white tur-

tleneck that came down over her hips. She loved loose oversized clothes because she thought they added more bulk to her boniness. She pulled on her high-heeled boots, then her puffy camouflage jacket with all those handy zippered pockets.

Her naturally curly hair she wore casually—sort of a shaggy-dog style, her mother complained—and her bangs had a way of falling down over her eyes. She grabbed her giant leather carryall and checked its contents automatically: Kleenex, lipstick, keys, spare contacts, a candy bar in case of imminent starvation, wallet, an extra cassette tape.

Then she stopped, abruptly recalling her brother's phone call with an ominous shiver.

Last night she hadn't had time to think about all the implications of his surprising accusations, but when she'd gotten up at six and made coffee, she had started to really mull them over. This, she decided, would be the big one, the story that would make her career.

As she looked out over the buildings of downtown Rochester, she wondered just where her twin brother, Roger, was at that moment. She considered for a second before deciding he must be in the air somewhere between Portland, Oregon, and Washington, D.C. Safe and sound.

"I've quit my job," he'd told her grimly. "I had to, Amy. They're crooked."

"Shearing Aerospace is crooked?" she'd asked, incredulous.

"I have proof that Shearing is covering up a flaw in the Star Wars defense system. You know, the president's pet space project."

"But that's monstrous, Roger! You mean to say the laser defense system wouldn't work?"

"Not exactly. But I found an unacceptable risk factor."

"Wow..."

"Precisely. And if Shearing has to go back into development for this tiny flaw it's going to cost them millions."

"So they cover it up and keep their fingers crossed that either the system is never used or that it works perfectly, if and when..."

"You got it, sis."

"What a story this is going to make! You do have proof?"

"In my old engineer's head, kiddo. All the government's gotta do is check the computer projections and Shearing is nailed to the wall."

"Is it real technical?"

"You wouldn't get it."

"But I do get the story. Right? An exclusive?"

"An exclusive, kiddo. By the way, I'm in a motel right now."

"Why on earth...?"

"They searched my apartment."

"Roger! They didn't."

"They're pretty sure I'm about to squeal on them. But I'm flying to Washington tomorrow with a guy from the Department of Defense. In a private Lear jet, no less. As soon as I get there and give my little speech I'll call you."

"Roger, for heaven's sake, be careful."

"Oh, don't worry, I will. I'm in this awful place. Sleazy City. They won't find me, and tomorrow I'll be out of here."

"Okay, kid brother." Roger had been born ten minutes later than Amy. "Take care. If you can't reach me at my apartment, call the station."

Amy's analytical mind was still churning with everything her brother had said on the phone. Roger was taking a big chance spilling the beans on the gigantic Shearing Aerospace Corporation; if he weren't her ever logical brother, she'd think his deed was heroic. As it was, she couldn't help but feel anxious. Nevertheless, after he got to Washington he'd be safe. Once the hoax at Shearing was uncovered it would be too late to touch Roger.

An exclusive.

She'd finish up this hospital report and clear her desk—the Shearing Aerospace exposé would take up all her time.

"Oh, Roger!" Amy breathed excitedly as she locked her apartment door, "We're going to be famous!"

Tape recorder safely in her purse as always, Amy headed down to the street. It was a bright day; leaves swirled on lawns and in the gutters and the air was crisp and smelled of autumn. She decided to walk to the WYSU office and enjoy the fantastic weather.

Suddenly, as a light wind whipped her dark brown hair into her eyes, she was seized by a mental image.

She envisioned herself standing in front of the Pentagon, a new, soft suede coat draped around her, microphone in hand. The TV camera lights were focused on her, hot and blinding; the air was pulsing with excitement, and somewhere a voice called to her, "You're on in three, two, one...."

"Good evening. This is Amy Slavin reporting from the Pentagon...." She grinned at the picture she'd concocted, mentally exulting, *eat your heart out, Barbara Walters!*

DEL PARDEE was glued like a fly to the vertical face of rock. He stood in his *étriers*, or stirrups, hammered in a piton and raised himself another two feet. The hot October sun pressed like a hand on the back of his plaid wool shirt and sweat beaded his forehead.

The rock was a physical and mental challenge, an exercise to keep his mind and body poised and sharp and ready. He found a crevice for his fingers but hesitated a fraction of a second too long, and the hold drew back, vanishing. In his mind he had to overcome the fatal indecision and fear: there had to be another move immediately...and then another.

The vertical face was inflexible in its demands. Yet in his extremity Del emitted a kind of power, as if he himself were holding up the rock. He was filled with freedom, like a sailor on the bosom of the ocean.

He paused, panting, held only by his toes and fingers, as he abruptly became aware of the sound of a jeep below.

He twisted his head and saw his brother pulling up in a cloud of dust and hopping out of the vehicle.

"Hey, Del!" his brother yelled, cupping his hands around his mouth.

"I can hear you!" Del shouted back.

"Come on down!"

Del sighed, his concentration broken, and slid down the fixed rope that the Pardees left on the face to aid the students of their Moose, Wyoming, climbing school. He hit the ground lithely and walked over to Rob, slapping dust from his clothes. "What's going on?" he asked, squinting up at his brother, who was even taller than his own six foot one frame.

"Dad got a call this morning about the crash," he said excitedly.

"Yeah, I know...."

"Well, there's another call. It was from Shearing Aerospace."

Del cocked his dark head in question.

"That big company in Oregon that does all the defense contracts. Anyway, it seems one of their employees was on board that plane." Rob permitted himself a wide grin. "They want us to do the rescue."

"Why can't they send a helicopter?"

"I guess it's too windy up there. There's a front moving in. The Lear went down near Pearl Pass."

"How do you know all this?" asked Del, retrieving a canteen of water from his van and taking a long gulp.

"The sheriff in Jackson called again. He wants you to get in touch, pronto."

"Does he know if anyone's alive up there?"

"The Flight for Life chopper made it over the site but only got in one pass, then had to head on in to base. Couldn't get near enough to tell. The plane's reportedly in one piece, though. And there were three other men on board besides the Shearing guy."

Del whistled between his teeth, then ran a big, calloused hand through his curly brown hair.

"This could be a tough one," Del mused aloud. "Guess we've got our work cut out for us."

"Hey, that's our job, Del," replied Rob, slapping his older brother on the back so hard that dust rose from Del's plaid shirt.

As he drove back to the Pardee Climbing Ranch with good old Sally—the Pardee's golden retriever—sticking her yellow head out of the van's window beside him, Del began making mental lists. He was experienced enough at thirty-five not to go off half-cocked, and he knew the importance of good organization: food, gear, climbing paraphernalia, backup help, radios—the whole complicated mess they would require.

He lived in rough country, at the base of the much photographed Teton range. He loved his home and recognized its wild beauty, but he never made the mistake of underestimating it.

It was big country, all right, and it took a singular kind of man to survive in it. Nothing, in this land of dry, sage-dotted expanses and purple mountains straining to pierce the azure sky, was forgiving. Before the Pardees there had been the Indians, then the stalwart mountain men and finally the lonely cow-hands riding the tall-grass prairies. Del often felt humbled by the sight of the mountains, just as he did that crisp autumn morning.

When he climbed out of the van, he could hear his mother, Hilkka, in the lodge, scolding Rob. He grinned to himself. As if Rob weren't half a foot taller than his statuesque mother, outweighing her by fifty pounds! But she treated all three of her boys like kids, alternately nagging and pampering them.

There was Rob, the middle brother, weighing in at two hundred pounds, burly, loquacious and outgoing. Jay, the youngest and the biggest, was shy and as gentle as a kitten. Del frowned. He needed Jay on this climb, but his youngest brother had taken a nasty fall last year and had shied away from anything too technical since then.

With Sally loping dutifully behind him, Del strode through the kitchen door of the main lodge, the log and stone building that functioned as the heart of the Pardee Climbing Ranch. It was a venerable, rough-hewn structure, built of native pine and river rock by Del's grandfather in the 1920s, and had sheltered three generations of climbers from all over the world, as well as innumerable neophytes who sought an initiation into the mystique of climbing.

"Hi, Mom," he said.

"Better get busy," was her tart reply, issued with her hands immersed in dishwater.

The Pardee Ranch thrived on the combination of climbing and location. There was nothing like the

Snake River Valley and the wild West atmosphere of
Moose, Wyoming, for captivating people's imagina-
tions. Scenic beauty, physical exertion, danger, adventure, experience—these were the attractions that
Del offered to all comers.

He was rewarded, often enough, with a compli-
ment. Countless numbers of visitors had remarked,
"Wow, it must be great to live here, stress free, without constant pressure and the big-city crunch."

Without pressure. Del wondered often why none of
the summer folk ever realized the effort that went into
making their stay stress free. Didn't they know what
it took to keep a place like this running? There were
twelve cabins to maintain, the horses to take care of,
miles of fences to mend or replace, paths to be graded
after the fierce mountain winters, roads to level and
patch, over and over. Did they ever wonder why Rob
and Jay were unmarried? Or how about Del himself?
When was there time for romance?

Oh, it was true their father took life easy these days.
He was one of the old school: a hard day's work, a
good solid diet, a few kids to bounce on his knee. But
Oliver Pardee had never worried about expansion or
bank loans or mortgages to keep it all running and
properly maintained. And nowadays the tourist
wanted it plush—no outhouses or trudging across
rocky fields to dine up in the main lodge. They wanted
air conditioning, health food and indoor plumbing.
Plumbing that worked.

Stress free? Hardly. So here Del was, almost thirty-
six. No wife, no kids. Sometimes he wondered if he

was truly a hardened bachelor, or if he was really using his busy life as an excuse not to get involved with the perfect woman, if or when she came along.

Del shook his dark head and marched over to his mother. What the devil was he doing thinking about an imaginary woman when there was a plane down and his services were needed? "You heard," he commented to her.

"Your father told me all about it. At least it's off-season, so we won't have a houseful of dudes to take care of." She shrugged capable shoulders. "Also, the sheriff called and so did Shearing Aerospace from Portland. They both want you to get in touch as soon as possible."

"So Rob said," he replied absentmindedly, already busy deciding who he wanted on the rescue team.

He poured himself a cup of coffee and searched out his address book from a drawer. He'd take only the very best climbers on this one—he knew exactly who to contact, who would drop whatever they were doing and come immediately. Rescuers were like fire fighters; their employers and family understood the emergency nature of volunteer services.

"What about Deborah?" asked Hilkka while she bustled efficiently around the large, warm kitchen.

"I'm going to call her," answered Del over his shoulder.

"It would be nice to have her back . . . only for the climb, of course," mused Hilkka.

And, thought Del, his mother would love it if he and Deborah Brewster renewed their relationship.

Hilkka didn't care that the passion had ended ten years before or that a marriage between them would have been disastrous. No. His mother wanted grandchildren.

By midday, Del had reached three of the climbers. Two would fly in from various parts of the western United States; one, Flint Smith, would drive up from Colorado and be in Moose by morning.

That was six definite climbers: he, his two brothers, Flint, Lonnie Dougal from Taos, New Mexico, Swede Björkman from Seattle. He knew Deborah, the seventh, would fly her own plane up from Los Angeles immediately, the minute she heard. They needed eight climbers. If anyone was alive up there in the pass, it would take eight skilled hands to carry four litters. Even if Deborah made it up, there was still a vacancy on the team. Del would have to fill it locally. But no real problem there.

Finally he took the time to return the call to a Mr. Gerhunt, the vice-president of Shearing Aerospace.

"Mr. Pardee," Jack Gerhunt said, "this is an honor. I saw your picture last year on *National Geographic*'s cover. Fascinating life."

"It's different," replied Del, feeling a little uncomfortable with the fanfare.

There was a short pause on the line. "Roger Slavinsky's welfare is very important to us here at Shearing, Mr. Pardee. He was in possession of vital information."

"I know there was a pilot and copilot and Mr. Slavinsky aboard. Was another Shearing employee on that Lear, too? There were four people reported down.''

Gerhunt was silent on the line for a long moment. Finally he said, ''There's a representative of the Defense Department on board. That's all I'm at liberty to say. I'm afraid it's a matter of national security.''

Touchy situation, thought Del. ''Well, Mr. Gerhunt, we'll do all we can to get to the site as soon as possible.''

''It's a difficult climb?''

''In a few places. It's a matter of time right now. There's a storm moving in. Bad weather can take a hard day's climb and turn it into three or four days. More sometimes.''

''Listen,'' said Jack Gerhunt, ''I'd like to send along a representative from Shearing....''

''Not on the climb!''

''Oh, heavens no! Our Mr. Pereira would merely fly into Jackson to be on hand. You understand.''

''Of course. That's fine. He's welcome here at the ranch. The cabins are empty now. Off-season.''

''Good. Good. Then I'll have Frank on the next available flight.''

''Have him phone the ranch and one of us will pick him up.''

''That's very hospitable. Now if you need anything...''

''Thank you, but by tomorrow we'll be all set. I hope your people are safe up there, Mr. Gerhunt.''

''Yes. We're all praying, too. And Mr. Pardee, I want you to know that Shearing will cover the costs of this rescue. And there'll be a big bonus for you, as well."

"It's strictly volunteer, Mr. Gerhunt."

"I realize that, but I'm sure a donation to your ranch wouldn't hurt—for equipment or the helicopter time or something."

"Well, no, it would be much appreciated."

"Mr. Pardee, finding those men is imperative. Do you understand?"

"Of course. We'll do our best, sir."

"Vice-president of Shearing, huh?" observed Jay Pardee as he sauntered into the kitchen. "Big time."

"Largest aerospace contractor in the country," put in their father, Oliver, as he came in behind Rob.

"They're real concerned about this Roger Slavinsky. He must have been on some sort of business for them," said Del. "They offered to pay for the rescue, but I don't think they realize that money can't buy them their employee's survival."

"Do you think those poor men have a chance?" asked Hilkka.

Del poured the rest of his cold coffee down the drain and then braced himself on the counter. He was frowning. "There's always a chance. At least the plane's reported to be in one piece."

The wall phone in the kitchen rang then. "What now?" muttered Hilkka as Del picked it up.

"I want to speak to a Mr. Pardee," came an authoritative voice.

Del rolled his clear blue eyes. "Which one? There are four."

"Delwood Pardee, I believe."

"Speaking."

"Name's Kirklaw, Mr. Pardee, I'm with the United States Department of Defense." Del sat up a bit straighter—next, it would be the president! "And I'm given to understand that you will be leading a rescue attempt for a downed plane up on an area called Pearl Pass."

"That's correct, sir."

"I did some checking while trying to get through on your phone line, Mr. Pardee, and you sound like the man for the job."

Del did not answer that statement.

"I'd just like to say one more thing and I won't take up any more of your time," continued the decisive voice. "This rescue mission involves national security and it is vital that Mr. Slavinsky—should he be still alive—be handled with the utmost care. I assume that the sheriff in Jackson will contact me as soon as the rescue is complete?"

"If that's what you instructed him to do," returned Del with growing impatience. First Shearing Aerospace, now the government. Del didn't give a hoot about either of them or national security or the fact that for some unknown reason, the Defense Department had been using a private Lear jet to escort this Roger Slavinsky to Washington. Del did care about those men up there.

"I'll say goodbye, then," said Kirklaw. "And if there's anything you need..."

"I'll get in touch," finished Del.

There were myriad chores left to do in preparation for the climb. Del still had to contact Deborah, meet all the flights at the Jackson airport in the morning and find yet another good man to complete the climbing team. He walked outside with Sally at his heel and leaned up against a fence rail, thinking, stroking the dog's ears and forming more mental lists and contingency plans. A cool October wind stirred his dark hair even as the sun warmed his back through his shirt. He put his hands in his pants pockets and studied the mountains.

Del's gaze followed the stretch of flat river valley to the upsweep of the surrounding heights. He loved the familiar profile of the three Grand Tetons, the famous needle-pointed peaks named "the great breasts" by some long ago poetic French fur trapper. Their glistening white summits had beckoned many men. Some had succeeded in climbing them; some had been left with wounded bodies. And some had forfeited their lives in their attempt to conquer the three silent ladies.

The sky above Del was sapphire blue, the trees lining the river golden, the wide prairie brown and the mountains stark black and white. It was beautiful country, calm now with autumnal serenity. Only the wisps of clouds forming way off to the northwest threatened the peacefulness.

Del shivered inadvertently as his eyes strayed from the tall craggy peaks northward to Pearl Pass. For experienced climbers it was an easy assault. But there was always the weather...

Somewhere up there, crushed, its silver wings broken, lay the Lear. Del envisioned the possible spots the pilot might have put her down. Was anyone still alive? The odds, of course, were not good for those poor souls. Nonetheless, Del whispered up a silent prayer as another stronger gust of wind reached through his clothes with cool fingers.

CHAPTER TWO

Day 1 A.M.

AMY HAD JUST REACHED the steps of the WYSU building, when suddenly she felt bitterly cold. Strange...the day was still beautiful. There was no wind, not a cloud or even a change in temperature.

The chill she was feeling, curiously, was groping at her from within, causing goose bumps to rise on her arms beneath the sweater, surprising her. She pulled open the glass doors a little breathlessly, trying to warm herself as she pushed the elevator button.

"Weird," she whispered.

Her mind was filled with busywork: she had to type up her report from the notes on her recorder, get it to Ken for editing, make the taping schedule for 4:00 P.M., then go on the air at 6:20 and again at 11:00. Hectic!

Amy was greeting fellow employees and heading toward her desk, when she spotted Ken motioning to her through his glassed-in office window.

"Amy...come in here a minute, please." His voice sounded terse to her. Was he going to start that business again about her putting herself in danger? Oh, no....

"Ken," she began impatiently.

He held up a hand. "Amy, just sit for once. *Please.*"

She looked quizzically at him.

"I tried to get you at your place, Amy, a few minutes ago."

"Sorry. I walked."

"Listen," he said carefully, "I just took a call for you from Jackson, Wyoming...."

She stared blankly at him. "Jackson, Wyoming? Isn't that a ski resort or something?" All the while she pondered the oddity of a phone call from somewhere out west—near Yellowstone Park and Old Faithful and all that stuff, wasn't it—a small bubble of alarm formed in her breast.

"I'm not really sure," said Ken, avoiding her eye. "Look, Amy, I don't know how to tell you this..."

Something was wrong. The bubble swelled into full-fledged apprehension.

"There's been an accident...."

The knowledge burst within her. Roger! She should have known! It had always been like that between them. Twins—one knew when something happened to the other. "Tell me," Amy whispered. "What happened?" Dread clutched her heart with an icy hand.

"There's been a plane crash, Amy," he said softly as he reached out to take her hands in his.

KEN HAD DRIVEN HER straight from the station to her apartment, and all the while he'd been asking her pointed questions.

"Amy, why was your brother going to Washington?"

"Oh," she'd replied absently, "he was on some kind of business, I guess."

"For Shearing?"

"I really don't know, Ken. What does it matter now?"

"Sorry." He'd glanced over at her carefully. "I was just thinking, flying in a private jet and all. Must have been sensitive business."

Amy had looked at Ken thoughtfully for a moment. "Why would you say that?"

"Well, you told me a while back that Roger always had his nose buried in a lab. The sheriff out in Jackson led me to believe that Roger was traveling with a government representative. That's not lab work."

"Look," Amy had put in impatiently. "It makes no difference whatsoever now what his business in Washington was. I don't really know and I don't really care. All right?"

"Sorry... guess my reporter's instincts get away from me at times."

Distracted, she'd rushed to pack a small suitcase: makeup, extra blank cassettes for the tape machine, blow dryer, underwear, a warm shirt, her favorite sweatshirt and jeans. Ken had promised to finish her report on the hospital construction and to air it in a few days. He'd also taken her apartment key in order to water the plants and had driven her to the airport for a flight to Jackson via Denver, Colorado.

Amy's flight would land in Jackson, Wyoming, at 5:00 P.M. mountain time. Besides the instant decision to fly to Wyoming, Amy had been forced to make one more: not to call her parents, who were on a second honeymoon, *Love Boat* style, in the Caribbean. Until there was definite word on Roger, it was both pointless and heartless to alert them.

When she'd had time on the airplane to think, she'd had to really search her mind for the reason for her first decision. Why exactly *was* she traveling to Jackson?

It had come to her somewhere over the buff-colored expanse of the Midwest: she was going to that godforsaken Timbuktu of a place because she *knew*, inexplicably but positively, that her brother was still alive. If he was—she put it delicately—gone, she assured herself she'd know.

No one in Jackson expected her, and all she had was the number of the sheriff's department there. The only facts she possessed were that Roger was somewhere in the mountains and that a rescue had not yet been undertaken. As the Frontier Horizon plane touched down, her mind buzzed with a million questions and too much coffee. A terrible anticipation made her heart pound.

She'd call the sheriff from the terminal. No. Better yet, she'd take a cab straight to the sheriff's department. There wasn't a moment to be wasted.

The terminal was smaller than she'd expected. The passengers even had to walk across the runway to the building. A quick impression of space and sunlight and distant mountaintops struck Amy, but she was more interested in collecting her small bag and finding some sort of transportation.

She had to wait a few minutes in front of the terminal and it was then, even through her desperate worry, that the total strangeness of the place assailed her senses—its high altitude, its cool, clear, dry air emptied of all smells but those of nature: sagebrush and dead leaves and earth and sunlight. There were tall lanky men—ranchers?—in jeans and pointy-toed boots and wide-brimmed cowboy hats, and jeeps and pickup trucks encrusted with mud. There was the wide flat valley that rose gracefully to mountains, which should have been on a postcard.

Jackson, Wyoming. Of all the places in the good old U.S.A., Amy would never have figured she'd end up here.

The cabdriver was polite and friendly—too friendly. Amy didn't want to talk, feeling herself on the verge of desperation. She clenched her teeth and endured the five-mile ride into Jackson.

The actual sight of the dyed in the wool Western town made her sit up a little. False-front buildings, saloons, and everywhere she looked there were arches and gateways made of... It eluded her for a time, but then the driver explained what they were... elk antlers! How peculiar!

Just as they pulled up to the Victorian-style city hall where the sheriff's office was located, Amy's driver remarked, "We had an airplane crash near here this morning. Got the whole place upside down."

Amy's heart gave a dread-filled leap. She'd forgotten for a second. "Have they reached the crash yet?"

"Don't know, but the sheriff can tell you that, ma'am."

Ma'am. Was this a Western movie or real life? Was John Wayne going to stride out onto the sidewalk any moment, thumbs hooked in his belt and boot heels clicking?

The receptionist, at least, looked ordinary. "May I speak to the sheriff?" Amy asked, trying to conceal her impatience.

"Sheriff Conger's gone home for the day," said the girl pleasantly.

"Well, is there somebody I can talk to? My name is Amy Slavin...Slavinsky, actually. My brother was on that plane that crashed. I've come all the way from Rochester, New York—"

But she didn't have to say another word. The receptionist's eyes widened and she jumped up. "How did you get here so quickly? I mean...our department just finished contacting the next of kin—" She caught herself. "I'm so sorry. I'm sure everything will turn out all right, Miss Slavinsky...I mean, Miss Slavin." The receptionist walked around her desk. "Hold on a minute. I'll get Glen. Please, just sit down. I'll be right back."

Amy sank wordlessly into a chair, dropping her bag with a thump. Who was Glen? She hoped he wouldn't be long, whoever he was. A hard, cold coil of anxiety writhed in her stomach.

What if Roger was... No! He couldn't be. No!

"Ma'am." A soft low voice made Amy look up. "I'm Deputy Glen Shepherd, the undersheriff of Teton County. I'm real sorry to hear about your brother."

Deputy Shepherd was a revelation. She gasped and popped up out of her chair so fast he had to step backward. He was long, lean and handsome in an understated Western way: Gary Cooperish but younger. The weather crinkles in his face showed just the right amount of concern for her brother's plight. On both sides of his thin, wide mouth were vertical lines that deepened when he smiled.

Wow, thought Amy. *Can this be happening to me?*

Then he was shaking her hand gravely, and she stared at their clasped palms in a state of near paralysis.

"Did you find him yet?" she finally blurted out, her throat nearly closing on the words.

"No, ma'am. But the Flight for Life helicopter flew over the crash site. The plane was in one piece. Somehow the pilot put her down like a champ."

She merely stared at him, mutely observing the Adam's apple in his strong neck; her smoky blue eyes were huge and round.

"What that means is, there's a much greater possibility of finding them alive," Glen said gently. "Now why don't you sit down, Miss Slavin. Gerty, get the lady a cup of coffee."

Amy sat back and felt, suddenly, that she was missing something. There was an unformed question floating around in her head, obviously something about the accident. But what?

Come on Slavin, she prompted herself. *Who, what, where, when, why....*

Perhaps it was ... why?

An accident. But had it been an accident? Roger had clearly told her that his room had been searched. Shearing had suspected him, then. Had Shearing—her mind worked feverishly—been somehow involved in the crash? It could be....

"Deputy Shepherd?" she asked cautiously. "Does anyone know how the accident happened?"

He rubbed his jaw for a moment. "Don't rightly know, ma'am. Seems the pilot radioed Salt Lake City Center and reported engine trouble." He shrugged apologetically.

"I was only wondering..." Her voice trailed off. Engine trouble. Could Shearing have been involved? It seemed so unlikely. For a moment an image teased at her: she could see some man dressed in dark clothes dumping sugar—or was it salt—into the gas tank of the tiny jet. Wasn't that how a person wrecked an engine? Ridiculous, decided Amy. Giant corporations did not hire ugly little men in dark suits to go around dumping sugar into tanks! No. But the plane had crashed. Whatever was wrong with the aircraft must have been very unnoticeable to the naked eye. From what Amy did know about planes—which admittedly was scant—they were checked out thoroughly by a mechanic and, of course, by the flight crew before takeoff. Actually, she thought, it was all very academic, anyway. The fact was that Roger's life was in peril, right now.

It only mattered that she knew he was alive and somehow *someone* had to save him.

"You've got to get to that plane," breathed Amy, her gaze pinning Glen Shepherd in desperation.

"Now you must relax. Everything possible is being done. I must say, Miss Slavin—"

"'Amy,'" she corrected automatically.

"*Amy*, then. I'm real surprised that you got here so fast. We weren't expecting anybody."

"It was a pretty quick decision," she admitted. "Can you tell me what's being done to rescue Roger and the others?"

Gerty came back with a mug of coffee, which Amy grasped and hugged to her.

Glen Shepherd took her elbow. "Let's talk in my office. I'll give you a complete update, Amy."

He seated himself in the oak swivel chair across his desk from her. "Well, Amy, there's bad weather expected and the crash site is in rough country. It's at about ten thousand feet near Pearl Pass. Unfortunately a helicopter can't land, so a rescue party is being formed."

"I don't understand." Amy shook her head. "Can't a helicopter get in somewhere nearby?"

There was a map on the wall behind Glen Shepherd. He unfolded his lean form from the chair and stood. "Here's Pearl Pass." He pointed with a slim finger. "As you can see, it's surrounded by high peaks, and believe me, the weather would have to be perfect to get anywhere near that site." He turned, placing his hands on his narrow hips. "It looks like a great day in Jackson, I know, but up there at ten thousand feet, it's gusting up to forty knots right now." He smiled at Amy grimly. "It was dangerous for the chopper to fly over once this morning, but now I'm afraid it would be suicide to try another pass at it."

Amy sighed in resignation. "You said a rescue party is being formed. Just how long would it take them to get to the site?"

"Again it depends on the weather. It looks nice and mild now, but October in the Tetons can be downright terrible."

"Where is this rescue party? I'd like to talk to them. You see, I *know* Roger's alive. He's my twin brother. I'm absolutely sure. They have to hurry!" She could hear her voice growing more and more frantic but was unable to control it.

Glen Shepherd looked at her assessingly for a moment. "The rescue is being organized out of the Pardee Climbing Ranch."

"Where's that?"

"It's in Moose, about ten miles north of here."

"Moose? You mean like the animal?"

"It's a small town, ma'am."

"How do I get there?" Amy demanded purposefully, standing up and grabbing her bag.

"Hold on there." Glen thought a moment. "Tell you what, I'll call out there. It's off-season, so they'll have a room for you. You can stay there."

"Oh, would you? Thank you so much." Amy hesitated. "Could I use the ladies' room? Too much coffee...."

"Sure, just ask Gerty."

It didn't matter that her brother was stuck up on a ten-thousand-foot mountain or that she'd just met the sexiest man she'd seen in a while. No. Trust her! She always had to go to the bathroom right in the middle of everything!

When she emerged from the rest room, Glen was holding her overnight bag. "Let's go, Amy, I'll drive you to the ranch. I wanted to talk to someone out there anyway."

It would have been kind of fun to ride in the Sheriff Department's Blazer, if Roger hadn't been waiting up on some godforsaken pass—Pearl Pass—to be rescued.

As it was, she was only vaguely aware of her surroundings. The interior of the vehicle and the scenery speeding by the window seemed to her illusive impressions. It was not like Amy to be so unobservant; normally she would have been pressing her nose to the window glass, taking it all in, pulling her tape deck out and talking rapidly into it.

Mountains. Boy, did Wyoming have mountains! Somehow she had always thought of the state as being prairielike. But that must have been another part of Wyoming—where the deer and the antelope play... A plaintive tune, a lonely whistle, a cowboy riding the empty, wide-open range. Ah yes, thought Amy, the wild and romantic West.

She tried hard to adjust her mind to the here and now. She was in Jackson, Wyoming, driving north along an arrow straight highway that cut through a breathtakingly beautiful valley—a valley that evidently saw an early autumn, because only a very few trees near a winding river to her right still held golden leaves. Perhaps those were the famous aspen trees. And she thought she recognized cottonwoods near an isolated log house.

The silence in the big patrol vehicle was companionable. Glen certainly knew how to treat a girl. She glanced over at his strong capable hands on the steering wheel and adjusted her skirt, crossing one leg over the other. Did he think she was attractive?

It was then that her stomach growled, a long rumbling noise. Darn her rebellious gut! How humiliating!

But Glen merely grinned and asked, "You hungry, ma'am?"

"No, really, it's just..." But her mind refused to find the right words and her voice died a sad little death.

She sat there, holding her breath, tensing her stomach muscles against another growl and rolling her eyes at the gorgeous scenery rushing by the window.

"What is this Pardee Climbing Ranch?" she asked finally.

"Well, the Pardees teach in the summer. Sort of a dude ranch for would-be climbers. Oliver Pardee used to be quite well-known, but he's a bit arthritic these days from a fall."

Amy gasped. "How awful!"

"Del Pardee, his son, runs the place now. He's the one who'll head up this rescue."

"Is he any good?" asked Amy bluntly.

"They say he's the best."

"Do I detect a note of doubt in your voice?"

Glen was quiet for a time. "Del is a good climber, yes, but I, for one, don't think much of him. He's a fast man for a buck. Always seems to need money for something."

"You mean he's only doing this for money?" Amy was aghast.

Shepherd shrugged, his silence as eloquent as words.

"That's awful," Amy breathed, picturing Snidely Whiplash himself.

"Yes, ma'am," Glen replied laconically. "But don't you worry yourself over this. We'll get them all out. Why, did you know those folks at Shearing Aerospace have promised to back the whole operation? They're even sending their own man out here to help. Pretty good company your brother works for."

It was on the tip of her tongue to cry, "But Roger doesn't work for them anymore. He quit!" Then the ramifications of Glen's news struck. Shock hit her and dropped to her stomach like lead.

Amy looked at Glen Shepherd in horror. Her voice barely squeaked when she asked, "A man from Shearing is coming *here*?"

"He may already be out at the Pardees'. I know you'll want to talk to him, ma'am."

Her heart jumped like a wild thing. If Shearing was sending someone to "help rescue" Roger, it could only mean one thing: Shearing wanted to silence him before he could divulge his damaging information!

They wanted Roger dead! Oh, how fortunate they must consider themselves, in the plush Shearing boardroom, that Roger's plane had crashed! They must be hoping he had died in the accident. But they had to know, they needed positive proof that their secret would be safe.

It was tempting to tell the whole story to Glen. She would have liked nothing better than to dump her awful suspicions into the lap of this tall, friendly Westerner, especially since he was a sheriff's deputy, a man who stood for law and order.

Boy, Amy thought, looking at Glen's handsome profile as he drove, she sure could use somebody on her side!

But something made her hesitate. Some indefinable feeling that she should bide her time and weigh the situation and see everything for herself stopped her. Her quick mind cried, *wait ... what if ...*

It could be, outrageous as it seemed, but it *could* be that Shearing had already enlisted local help to silence Roger.

If they were completely desperate, and had billions at risk... Why, people—and corporations—had done worse for lower stakes. Shearing would probably lie, cheat, steal, even kill to protect itself. It could also afford to bribe or buy off absolutely anyone it wanted.

She felt adrenaline surge through her veins again. Anyone? Glen Shepherd, for instance?

Or what about Del Pardee, the "fast man for a buck"? Wasn't he the most obvious person for Shearing to approach? And Glen had said the man from Shearing might already be at the Pardees'—planning Roger's very convenient demise, no doubt!

Oh, Lordy, but she'd adore to confide in Glen! But she wouldn't—not yet, at least.

And besides, since when did Amy Slavin need help from anybody?

"Lovely country," Amy said ingenuously, steering away from anything touchy.

"Sure is," agreed Glen. "I just wish you were out here on a happier mission."

"So do I," murmured Amy pensively.

They turned off the highway. "This is Moose," Glen said.

Amy looked around in amazement. "I'm glad I didn't blink." She saw a store, a gas station, a couple of houses.

"There's a little museum over there." He pointed. "It has a bunch of relics and pictures from the old rustling days. You know, the Hole in the Wall Gang. Butch Cassidy and the Sundance Kid."

"They lived here?"

"Sure. This valley was home to all the worst outlaws."

"It was?" She instantly decided she had to record everything Glen told her. Background for her exposé.

Glen turned again and they bumped along a dirt road for about half a mile, eventually driving under a Western-style archway that read Pardee Climbing Ranch.

"Just about there," said Glen, smiling at her.

They were much closer to the mountains than they'd been in Jackson. Looming peaks closed the sky off on one side of the valley, cutting off the sun. It was dusk at the Pardees', just as it would soon be dusk in the rest of the broad valley. A gloriously picturesque log home nestled at the base of the mountains, surrounded by huge old spruce trees.

"That's the main lodge," explained Glen, pointing, "where everyone eats. Hilkka Pardee's a great cook."

Amy recalled her stomach's awful treachery and said nothing.

"And I guess they'll put you up in one of the smaller cabins."

Stiffly Amy climbed out of the Blazer while Glen got her bag. She took a deep breath, inhaling the biting evening air. So this was the abode of the mysterious and mercenary Del Pardee, climber *extraordinaire*. Well, he'd met his match in Amy Slavin, investigative reporter. She wouldn't let him get away with anything.

She turned from the car and wrapped her camouflage jacket tightly around her against a sudden sharp blast of wind, all the while aware of the darkening sky and Glen coming around the car with her bag. An owl hooted softly somewhere. Then the door banged open.

Amy glanced toward it, seeing only a lighted rectangle at first. Then she blinked her eyes and the bright rectangle was filled, as if by some curious conjuring, with the silhouette of a man.

Amy's first impression was of the sheer size of him: tall, broad, *big*. He walked toward them, moving with supple grace for his size, and his face finally emerged from the darkness. It was a warm face, square and solid, with lines of good humor etched on it and a lovely cleft in the strong chin. He had curly brown hair, heavy dark brows over brilliant blue eyes, a thick mustache. There was even dark curly hair bursting out from the V of his plaid wool shirt, as if the energy in him could not be contained. He stood over Amy finally, a head taller, dwarfing her.

She found herself looking up at him, a little awed.

"You're Amy Slavin," he said in a deep, warm voice. Amy's stomach tingled, reverberating to the timbre of it. "I'm Del Pardee, ma'am."

CHAPTER THREE

Day 1 P.M.

AMY FELT HER SMALL, finely boned hand encased in Del's large one and wondered if everything and everyone out West wasn't just plain *big*. She looked up and met his eyes and sucked in a deep breath, momentarily forgetting Glen's warning as she lost herself in Del Pardee's cobalt-blue gaze.

She'd been instantly taken with men before and this was one of those rare and thrilling times. His blue eyes met hers with utterly sincere concern, sending electric currents tingling all the way to her toes. He was smiling a little, just enough to deepen the dimples in his cheeks. She thought she'd never seen such adorable, manly dimples.

Wow, Amy thought, willing time to stand perfectly still as she clung to the wonderful sensations.

Then he was disengaging his hand from hers and Amy grudgingly came back into the real world. Her mind shifted into gear sluggishly, and she really looked at him, noting a powerful, tanned neck and a definite five o'clock shadow on a strong jaw. Somewhere in a far recess of her mind a notion teased: she'd seen that forceful, robust face before. But where? She shook off the thought.

Stop standing here like a moonstruck kid, Amy chided herself, *and remember Glen's assessment of this fellow.*

"I've got your bag for you," said Glen from behind Amy. "Which cabin is Miss Slavin's?" He looked at Del with a studiously expressionless face.

"I'll show her," replied her host rather coolly, hefting the small bag. "It's over this way." He nodded to a tiny wooden cabin about fifty yards down a sloping meadow from the main lodge. "Watch your step on the path, Miss Slavin. It's uneven."

"I will," said Amy, as she found her voice and turned back to Glen. "Thank you so much for all your help."

"No trouble at all. And don't go worrying too much about your brother. I'm sure everything's going to turn out okay." He touched her arm for a moment and gave it a reassuring squeeze. "Maybe I'll see you later up at the main house?"

"Well . . ."

Del Pardee eyed Glen. "Are you staying?" It *wasn't* an invitation.

"I'd like to talk to you for a few minutes," answered Glen, equally as curt.

"Have it your way." Del began to lead Amy toward the cabin.

Those two, she thought as she followed his broad back, sure don't get along. Why, she wondered. Glen had said that Del Pardee was a fast man for a buck. Could that be it? No, she decided, there must be more. Curiosity itched in her brain.

"Is there any news about my brother?"

"Nothing, I'm afraid."

"Why is it taking so long?" She didn't want to nag, but for a moment her anxiety got the best of her.

"I'm waiting for the team to get here. The cardinal rule for an expedition like this is not to endanger the rescuers. I know it's hard to wait, Miss Slavin, but we're doing all we can. By the way, is it 'Slavin' or 'Slavinsky'?"

"I use 'Slavin' professionally, but just call me 'Amy.'" Then she blurted, "I know Roger's alive up there and here we are safe and sound.... It seems awful."

"I agree," he said solemnly.

They were about ten feet from the cabin, when suddenly a dark scurrying thing rushed across the trail in front of Amy. "Oh!" she cried, tripping on a stone and stumbling. "Oh!"

Del was at her side in an instant. "Are you all right?"

"Did you see that ... *creature*?" she gasped.

"You mean that little chipmunk?"

"Whatever.... It looked like a rat or something...."

"Chipmunks," he said in a patronizing tone, "do *not* resemble rats, Amy."

"They all look the same to me," she said with a grimace.

"You're quite the naturalist," he commented. She couldn't tell if he was being friendly and understanding or downright sarcastic.

She shrugged and followed him the rest of the way, but kept her eyes scanning the sides of the path carefully.

Del switched on the light. "Are you going to be okay down here, alone in the cabin?"

"Of course I am," Amy said with conviction. "I've lived alone for years—in the *city*."

"There are rooms in the lodge, too."

"I like this." She looked around the small but cheery cabin. There was a double bed, a dresser and a rocking chair. The wooden floor was covered with a Navaho rug; the curtains over the two windows were homemade of a plain coarse material. It was a rough-hewn but welcoming place, and Amy instantly felt comfortable.

"When do we eat?" she asked.

Del looked surprised by her frankness. "Are you hungry?"

"I'm *always* hungry, Mr. Pardee...Del, if you don't mind. When things get rough for me, I soothe myself with food."

"That's honest." He was standing quite close to Amy, with his booted feet apart and his hands on his lean hips, and he was undeniably assessing her. Of course Amy returned his appraisal. She couldn't help but notice that despite his height—at least six-one—and his weight, which she judged to be around a hundred and ninety or more, he had a dynamite build. Trim hips, shapely thighs, a very hard-looking stomach, a wide chest and shoulders, sinewy forearms covered with dark curling hair. His face was rugged and handsome with those great blue eyes, an ample, manly nose, humor-quirked lips below the thick mustache and those wonderful dimples that appeared when he smiled.

He could have stepped right off a Western movie set. She tried to envision him climbing those mountains of his. She could almost see the muscles of his arms and back flexing, straining, slick with sweat....

"Up at the main lodge," he was saying.

"What?"

"You eat up at the lodge. My mother does all the cooking around here."

"For everyone? I mean, you must get crowded here in the summer."

"We do. But she has a helper then. And besides, nobody cooks in Hilkka's kitchen but Hilkka."

"Oh, I see."

"Not yet you don't."

She could hardly wait to meet Hilkka Pardee.

"If you like, you can come on up to the lodge now. Dinner is around seven-thirty, but if you're hungry..."

"Oh, I'll wait." Besides, she had that candy bar in her purse.

"Well, I'll be going." He opened the door and stepped out into the dusk. "Come on up when you're ready."

"I will. Thanks." She leaned out, one hand resting on the doorframe, and studied his outline against the ghostly whiteness of the dusk-shrouded Tetons. It was all so *big* here, big and slightly intimidating. "Do you sleep in the lodge?" she called to his retreating figure.

Del stopped and turned on his heel. "No. But why do you want to know that?"

"Oh," said Amy offhandedly, "just in case one of those rats sneaks into my cabin."

She could almost see the tilt of his lips. "That's my place." He pointed to a larger cabin a few hundred feet below hers. "Just in case . . ."

"Umm," said Amy, "I see it," adding, "you live alone?"

He threw back his head and laughed. *You've gone too far this time,* she told herself.

"Yes," Del called over his shoulder, "I do live alone."

She grinned wickedly to herself.

When he'd finally disappeared from her sight, Amy closed the door firmly and settled back down to earth. She scanned the small one room cabin once more, and then used the bathroom. The plumbing was what she'd call Early Depression—a tub on feet, a sink with chips and rust stains, a wobbly handle on the toilet—but it all worked just fine. Besides, she had little use here for the creature comforts.

She unpacked—it took her all of two minutes—placing her meager possessions in the sturdy oak dresser. Then she sat on the bed and crossed her legs, leaning against the two fluffy pillows. Searching through her purse, she found the tape recorder and switched it on.

"I could spend this whole cassette describing two of the best-looking men I've ever seen, Glen Shepherd and Del Pardee, but more important, it looks as if Roger's plane went down in a really remote area. Which is putting it mildly." She thought a moment. "Tall, white-capped mountains. The Tetons. Look like shark's teeth. Jackson—a tourist trap, maybe. Moose, where I'm staying, is the old Hole in the Wall Gang's hideout. Must explore that angle more one day. Aspen trees and white-water rivers and lots of evergreens. Remember to buy postcards. Roger, is he safe?"

There. Amy stopped and switched off her recorder to save tape. She tried to feel Roger's nearness, to sense his well-being. It came to her slowly, grudgingly, since her mind was too consumed with worry, but it was there. Roger—he *was* alive.

She switched the trusty little machine back on. "He's okay," said Amy. "I had this thought today. Did Shearing somehow tamper with the Lear? No way of telling, of course, but I suppose that next spring when the snow melts, the FAA will investigate. It's likely that no one will ever know, but I won't miss putting the question—stated properly, naturally—in my exposé." She turned off the tape recorder and relaxed against the pillows for a minute, doing a bit of abdominal breathing to soothe her raw nerves.

An image appeared in her mind's eye: Del Pardee. All sinew and muscle and dark curling hair. As if she didn't have anything better to think about! Still, what a hunk he was. She wondered, fantasizing, what it would feel like to be held in those mighty arms, to put her head against his wide chest, to lose herself in the irresistible male aura he projected.

Ah, well, Slavin, Amy mused, good luck finding out....

The main lodge was essentially a tremendous hall with vaulted, beamed ceilings, a gathering area containing four large comfortable-looking sofas and a huge hearth and eating alcove where twenty or more could sit at a trestle table. It was, despite the echoing size, a wonderful room, made homey by a sizzling, crackling fire.

Amy stood viewing it with Glen. "So this is a ranch house."

"Yep," he replied as his eyes held hers. "Just like the old days."

"Not in my family." Amy was thinking of the Slavinskys' middle European background, the low, thatched-roof farmhouses that must have sheltered them.

"So you're Amy!" exclaimed a woman's voice from the kitchen door. "Come on in here while I get dinner ready." To Glen, she said, "Del'll be here in a minute." Then she turned on her heel, shooed away a big golden retriever and disappeared through a swinging door.

"That's Hilkka," explained Glen, "the mainstay of the Pardees. Don't mind her frankness. She means well."

"I'm frank, too," Amy said over her shoulder. "See you in a minute."

Hilkka's aromatic kitchen was as large as the woman who ruled it. It was equipped with everything: copper pots on a rack, a huge worktable in the center, an iron stove, myriad cupboards and the dog, Sally, who crunched on a bone at Hilkka's feet.

"Is that Brunswick stew?" asked Amy, her nose twitching, her stomach growling loudly.

"'Brunswick'?" Hilkka said with a laugh. "Out here we call it like it is—chicken stew. You know, a little of this, a little of that—all in one big iron pot."

"Smells great."

"You should eat more." Hilkka put her big hands on her wide hips and studied Amy. Her graying head was cocked to one side. "You do eat?"

"Constantly," replied Amy crisply. "In fact, I'll bet I eat more dinner tonight than any of the men."

Hilkka turned back to her oversized Vulcan stove. "Not more than Jay," she mumbled. Amy guessed Jay to be one of the Pardee brothers. How big was he? And then Hilkka brought her a mug of coffee.

"Great! How did you know it's just what I wanted, Mrs. Pardee?"

"You look like you drink too much coffee," the older woman answered with a shrug. "And please call me 'Hilkka.' Everyone does."

In a minute Amy had drunk the coffee and was starting on a thick slice of freshly baked bread with butter and home-canned jam.

Hilkka finally finished bustling around and sat down across from Amy. "Do your parents know about the crash?"

"No." Amy put her second cup of coffee down. "They're on a vacation. I just couldn't tell them."

"Ah." Hilkka nodded, then put her big knuckled hand on Amy's. "My boys are the best, Amy. If your brother can be rescued, they're the ones to do it."

If. Amy's heart sank. Suddenly she was close to crying; the day's tension had overwhelmed her.

"There, there." Hilkka patted her dark curly head. "Don't you fret now. It's out of your hands. My boys'll take care of everything. Have a good cry, if you want. Here." She handed Amy a giant red bandanna from her apron pocket. "There, there, child."

It did feel good to let it all out. Finally Amy sniffed and wiped her eyes. "Do I look awful?" she asked.

"Sure do," replied Hilkka matter-of-factly, and they both smiled at each other, instant allies. "Now splash some cold water on your face and go on out and keep Glen company. I've got dinner to get ready."

In the cavernous living room, Amy paused when she saw a stranger sitting by the fireplace, head to head in conversation with Glen. Immediately Amy guessed who this man must be—the representative from Shearing Aerospace. At least, he didn't look like a Pardee....

"Amy." Glen rose. "I want you to meet Frank Pereira. He's from Shearing."

Frank Pereira stood, offering his hand, which Amy shook as nonchalantly as she could. She certainly didn't want to arouse his suspicions.

"Rob Pardee just got in from the airport with Frank here," explained Glen. "The rest of the team members should be arriving tomorrow morning."

"*Rest* of them?" questioned Amy.

"The other climbers. Mr. Pereira here is an onlooker, I guess."

"I'm no climber, Miss Slavin. I'm here only as support, you might say," Pereira elaborated, smiling.

"'Support,'" murmured Amy. Then he would definitely require local help. Good thing she'd kept the secret to herself.

Pereira went on for a few minutes, waxing eloquent over her brother and his many fine achievements at Shearing, while Amy sat studying him. Frank Pereira was about five foot five, slightly overweight, dark and overdressed in a three-piece suit and shiny loafers. A thought kept beating at her mind: there sat the man who wanted Roger dead. Dead and forever silent.

Rob and Jay Pardee arrived for dinner. They, too, had their own cabins near the lodge, and both had evidently just showered, as their dark hair was still damp.

Rob, Amy discovered, was outgoing. He threw Sally's tennis ball while chatting away with Pereira as if they were old buddies. Jay, on the other hand, was even bigger, but shy, and stood alone near the hearth. Once he smiled at Amy, then looked away quickly.

Del strode in shortly. He, also, had just showered, and Amy could imagine Hilkka chasing her three dirty-necked boys around when they were small—*if* they were ever small—and sticking them all in a hot bath and scrubbing their ears. Wouldn't it be lovely, she thought, to have three strapping boys, a kind husband, a warm home?

It struck Amy that Del had been purposely ignoring Glen. What was wrong between them, she wondered again.

"Anyone want a beer before dinner?" Rob asked cheerfully.

"Sure," Glen said.

Del shot him a measuring glance.

"Hilkka asked me to stay," Glen said disarmingly.

Del grumbled something under his breath. Amy squirmed uncomfortably as Glen shrugged and turned away tactfully.

Taking her life in her hands, Amy mustered the courage to approach the glowering Del. "That Frank Pereira isn't going along on the climb, is he?" She had to hear it from Del's lips; he was, after all, the leader.

"No," replied Del, "that Frank Pereira is staying here."

"Good," Amy pronounced. "He'd be a detriment to your team."

"Oh? Would you mind qualifying that statement?"

Amy thought quickly. She couldn't. She didn't dare say anything to Del—or anyone.

In answer, she replied, "I'm an excellent judge of character and I just don't like him. That's all."

"I see." He looked at her curiously. "Tell me, what do you do for a living?"

"I'm a reporter. You know, TV news spots. In Rochester, New York."

Del gazed at her with new interest. "You are? That must be very stimulating work."

"It is. But in no way does it equal climbing. I mean, really, crawling up those rock faces. Gives me chills just to think about it." Suddenly Amy's back straightened, and she looked at Del keenly. "That's it!" she cried. "The cover of *National Geographic*!"

Del had a sheepish expression on his face.

"That *was* you," Amy pressed.

"Yeah, it was me."

She had to rearrange her thoughts quickly. So Del Pardee really was one of the best.

"I'm impressed," Amy said frankly.

"No need for that." Del smiled. "I'm just a working man."

Working man, indeed, thought Amy. And then, crashing on the heels of that thought, came another. Shearing would have known of Del Pardee. Why, he was famous. They would have known—and contacted him immediately....

"I guess I'm lucky to have you leading this rescue," Amy said hastily to cover the awkward silence.

"Thanks," Del said quietly. "I only hope—" He stopped himself abruptly.

"That's okay," Amy breathed. "I know my brother is going to be okay."

They all sat down to dinner, Glen included, by eight. Amy was out of character during the meal, immersed in thoughts about Roger, feeling his danger, his cold as if he were a part of her.

After dinner, as Amy helped Hilkka and Oliver to clear the table, Glen finally got Del aside to talk to him. Amy tried to listen. It wasn't difficult; Del had a voice that matched his size.

"Over my dead body you are!" he said once.

Then Glen. "I'm as qualified as anyone, and you know it! Sheriff Conger wants me along. I say let bygones be bygones."

Their voices lowered.

Hilkka stood at the kitchen door, dwarfing her husband. "That Del better watch his temper," she told Oliver. "Glen's only trying to help."

"You know how they feel about each other," put in Oliver.

Hilkka shrugged. "There are lives at stake here. Feelings don't count. Del needs another hand and Glen is good. You trained him yourself, Ollie. Maybe you should step on over there and talk some sense into Del's head."

"Come on, Del," Glen was saying, "you know you need me. You know I'm one of the best."

They faced each other in tense silence. Everyone stopped what he was doing and watched. Finally Del shook his head angrily and ground out, "Okay, be ready tomorrow. But one false move, Glen, and you're out."

"Sure," said Glen, taking up his Stetson. "Anything you say, Pardee." He approached Amy. "Sorry about all that." He nodded toward Del, who was still standing near the fireplace, watching them. "Now you get some rest, Amy," said Glen. "You look pale."

"It's only my city pallor," Amy replied, trying to return his smile.

Glen nudged her softly on the chin with a fist. "There's a good girl. See you in the morning, Amy Slavin. Sweet dreams."

She couldn't help herself as she watched him leave; her heart quickened just a tad. Then she glanced toward Del, who looked away quickly.

Frank Pereira approached Amy, smiling ingratiatingly. "I'd hate to see our Mr. Pardee really mad." Then he changed his course. "I understand you're an investigative reporter for a TV station."

"I am, but who told you that?"

"Del Pardee, Miss Slavin. Why, is it a secret?"

"No, of course not."

"It must be a very interesting job," he said smoothly.

"Not nearly as interesting as yours, Mr. Pereira," she couldn't resist saying.

"Mine? Why I'm just a plain old corporate employee. Nothing special about my job."

"I see."

"I can't help but wonder, though, why you've come so far, Miss Slavin. I mean, what can you really do?"

"The same thing you can, Mr. Pereira," said Amy coolly.

"Not as much as I'd like to, unfortunately." He spread his hands deprecatingly.

Innuendos, thought Amy, they were speaking in innuendos.... Did he know she suspected him? Or was
he only trying to feel her out? All he could sense, she
was sure, was her hostility. It was stupid of her to show
how much she disliked him, but she couldn't help it.
Amy was the worst liar in the world.

"Excuse me," she finally said, trying to smile, and
went into the kitchen.

Hilkka allowed her to help with the dishes. Mostly
she carried them from the long trestle table and
cleaned up the crumbs as Hilkka very efficiently
stacked the dishes into a giant dishwasher. There was
time for Amy's mind to ramble, to begin digesting all
the new impressions which she'd been bombarded
with.

First of all, she had to suspect each person until he
proved himself innocent. Pereira, she knew, was a bad
guy from the word go. But he wasn't going on the
climb.

There had to be someone on the climb itself, someone who could silence Roger before he was rescued. It
would be easy to fake a mishap on the descent.
Everyone knew climbers had accidents. Or maybe
Roger would conveniently die of exposure or starvation or whatever injury he might have suffered. It
would look perfectly normal under the circumstances. But the death would really be caused by
smothering or untraceable poison or an air bubble in-
jected into the bloodstream—hadn't she read about
that somewhere?

The next step in Amy's logical progression was obvious: *she* had to go along on the climb.

There wasn't a soul she dared trust. Mentally she went over everyone she'd met that day: Glen Shepherd, Del Pardee, his brothers, Jay and Rob. Frank Pereira. Hilkka and Oliver she put aside as only remote suspects. Then she made three columns in her mind: good guys, bad guys and not-sure-yets. Pereira went squarely under bad guys; all the rest were not-sure-yets.

She'd made up her mind what she had to do. And when Amy made a decision, she implemented it immediately. Usually her decisions were right. *Usually.*

Purposefully she left the kitchen and sought out Del, who was discussing the supply list for the climb with his brothers. The three men kept talking, however, and Amy stood near their seats, shifting her weight from one foot to the other nervously. Why hadn't she asked Hilkka for a cup of decaffeinated coffee with dinner?

They were talking about the team. Presumably that meant the climbing party, the rescuers. Who were these people, some of them with odd foreign names? Were they, like Del, world renowned climbers who had their pictures taken with ice hanging off mustaches and faces haggard with strain and exhaustion and bitter cold? Did they have all their toes? Why would someone, *anyone*, want to climb a mountain? The old adage was, of course, because it was there. Bunk, thought Amy.

Del looked up at her finally. "Would you like to sit down?" He began to rise politely, indicating his own chair to her.

Amy shook her head. And to think she was contemplating climbing a mountain herself! But not because it was there!

"Sit down, Amy," Del repeated, breaking into her unsettling reverie.

"Oh, no, thanks," she said, smiling tentatively. "Can I talk to you a minute?" she asked. How to broach the subject, wondered Amy, remembering Del's reaction to Glen's going on the mission.

"What is it, Amy?"

"Privately?" She nodded toward the front door.

Del looked at her a bit curiously for an instant but then did get his jacket. They walked outdoors. The cold mountain air buffeted her and Amy shivered inadvertently. "It's about the climb Del. I . . . look, it's my brother up there and . . ."

"What?" Automatically he took off his jean jacket and draped it over her shoulders.

"Thank you," she said. "I guess what I'm getting at is . . ." Why was it so hard to ask him? Of course he'd say no at first—she knew that already. But she could convince him, couldn't she?

Whose side was Del on? Was he the "support" man? Certainly logic pointed a finger in his direction. And Amy suddenly recalled, it was Del who had told Pereira about her job. Why had they been discussing her, anyway?

Oh, my, thought Amy, if it was Del, she was sunk. She knew he'd *never* let her go along.

"Amy." His voice reached through the darkness. "You wanted to talk?"

"Ah..." She hesitated. "Well, I guess I just needed some company...."

"You've had a bad day," said Del sympathetically. "You can tell me about it if you want. I'm a good listener."

They made their way toward a now empty corral. Then they both stopped, as if by silent agreement, and leaned against the railings.

"I don't really want to think about it anymore," said Amy.

"I understand."

Oh, but he didn't! She would have loved to tell him everything, but she couldn't. It hurt physically to hold back all her awful suspicions and fears.

"You know, I never got it straight," began Del, "but if 'Slavin' is your professional name, is it Miss or Mrs.?"

"Miss," said Amy firmly, her heartbeat elevating a smidgen.

"And you are from western New York State?"

"Uh-huh." *Keep talking,* thought Amy; the deep timbre of his voice in the darkness was vibrating in her belly and massaging her taut nerves.

"A reporter..." he mused aloud. "Were you always interested in TV?"

"Yep. When I was younger, I used to pretend I was Barbara Walters. I guess I still have the same dream."

He laughed gently. "Don't we all."

"You had a dream, too?"

"Just climbing."

"I see. It must take up all of your time, then. I mean the ranch and the climbing."

"All of it," he replied.

Did she detect a wistful note in his voice? "No aspirations then of . . . well . . . a family life?"

"A family?" he said. "My, you're a curious one, aren't you?"

"Always."

"Well, Miss Reporter," he replied levelly, "sometimes there isn't time in life for everything."

Amy wanted to tell him that his explanation sounded like a cop-out, but she held her tongue. One thing these bachelor types with cold feet didn't want to hear was the word "cop-out."

"How about you?" asked Del. "No prospects back in New York?"

"No. My work keeps me too busy . . . just like you, Mr. Del Pardee." And she thought then that as long as they were getting along so companionably, maybe now was the right moment to ask him if he'd take her along on the rescue climb. But, no, she would have to plan her speech a little better and rehearse those pleading lines until she had them right. If she blew it . . . But Amy knew she had to persuade him somehow. She *had* to be there when the climbing party reached Roger.

"I suppose I should get a little work done," she said aloud. "I've got some recording to do."

"Some what?"

"On my tape recorder. I record everything. It's a habit."

"You know," he said as they began to walk again, "you're a crazy kid. I can't quite figure you out."

"I am *not* a kid."

"Excuse me. A crazy lady, then."

"Why, thank you. But I'm not sure if you're insulting me or complimenting me."

"Neither am I." Del laughed. "Come on, I'll walk you to your cabin, Amy."

"You don't have to."

"It's because of the rats."

"Oh . . . them."

They reached her cabin.

"Well," Del began.

He loomed over her, so tall she had to tip her head back to look at his face. His nearness suddenly took her breath away, while questions writhed in her mind, making her singularly vulnerable. She only knew that she desperately needed to be comforted because she could no longer bear the constant, appalling worry. Here was a man who, she knew instinctively, could hold her and make her forget.

It would be so easy to let go, to rest her head on his broad chest.

Instead she shrugged off his jacket. "Thanks," she said in a muffled voice, aware that she was doing a lousy job of covering her distress. She turned away to unlock the door and was surprised to find Del's strong hands turning her to face him.

"We'll get your brother out," he said in a soft, husky voice.

Amy tried to read his expression. He sounded concerned, but the darkness obscured his expression from her. She was about to say thanks again—for this was a gentle side of Del that Amy had not seen before— when he leaned toward her, a mere suggestion of movement, and her throat closed over the word.

Slowly, as she felt the moment's struggle in his body, he bent his head and his lips brushed hers lightly. The sensation took her breath away; it was as if the entire world had been emptied of air in a big whoosh. She could feel her pulse jump and her stomach flutter in exhilaration.

He pulled back and they stared at each other wordlessly for a moment, held in a hush of expectation. Amy could still feel the touch of his lips on hers, warm and tingling and slightly shocking.

"Amy," he whispered, then stopped as if there was nothing more he wanted to say.

Amy recovered first, taking a step backward. She felt for the door behind her, suddenly afraid of her reaction to him. "Well," she murmured, "good night."

She pulled the door open and stepped inside. Then, when it was safely closed behind her, she drew in a deep, quavering breath and sagged against the small barrier.

CHAPTER FOUR

Day 2 A.M.

DEL PARDEE WOKE UP, as usual, before the alarm went off. It was a game he played with himself, setting the alarm clock every night. He hadn't been awakened by its shrill buzz once in five years.

Automatically he turned on the radio for the early weather report. Today, however, the gesture was of more than usual importance. He listened carefully as he shaved. He'd shaved before dinner the evening before, but, damn it, his beard was so heavy he had a five o'clock shadow at three!

His razor stopped short at the announcer's words and he nicked the cleft in his chin. Blast it! The weather report bothered him even more than the cut, though—windy, cloudy, possibility of snow showers in the afternoon. A bad forecast for a rescue attempt.

He even wondered if all the team members could get in. If it got bad, they'd close the airport.

He shook his curly head, worrying. If the weather worsened, those men up there in Pearl Pass would die of exposure—that is, if they weren't dead already. And that was in addition to the increased danger for his own party. Del pictured the route up to Pearl Pass. In

snow it would be difficult, but there was one dangerous traverse that would be downright scary.

It was still partly sunny out that morning as he
walked up to the lodge, but the wind was picking up,
twirling dust devils and rattling the dead leaves on the
trees.

He glanced inadvertently toward the pass. Up there,
several thousand feet higher, it would be like December, not October. There was snow already....

His pace picked up. No time to lose, he thought.

"Good morning, Del," someone said behind him.
He turned and saw the little Slavin girl puffing up the
path toward him. "Wow, you sure walk fast," she
said, smiling, her waiflike face scrubbed and clean.

She looked to be in better spirits than last night,
thought Del. She'd been real down, not that he blamed
her, and it had gone straight to his heart. He couldn't
bear to see anyone suffer. Especially not a girl—lady—
with the spunk of Amy Slavin.

Then abruptly he was remembering the feel of her
lips—soft cool silk. He'd wanted to pull her to him
right there and kiss her hard, feel those delicate hands
of hers on his skin, but of course he couldn't.

Every so often over the years, Del had met a woman
like Amy—someone who brewed up that certain
chemical reaction in him. But he'd always let the moment slip by. Was he *really* too busy, or was he a
chicken at heart?

Ah, hell's bells, he thought, there was no point
hashing it over. He'd chosen his way—climbing—for
better or worse...and there weren't many women

who'd put up with a man whose life was so involved in something dangerous and not particularly lucrative.

He'd believed once that he had found someone special and different, but they'd both been so young. It could never have worked out. Yet for almost twenty years he had wondered what would have happened if Glen Shepherd hadn't stepped in and destroyed everything.

And then there had been Deborah, but that hadn't worked out, either....

"Mornin', Amy." He nodded. Then he noticed the curious way she was walking. Well, no wonder. She had on those silly, ankle-high pixie boots with pointed toes and skinny high heels that wobbled on the rough path. Amazed, he glanced over the rest of her. What an outfit! She had on baggy jeans pegged at the bottom, so that he wondered how she got them on, though he noted in passing that she had nice little feet. A gray sweatshirt with pink hippopotamuses on the front hung all the way to her knees, and the hippos were dancing in shiny toe slippers!

"That's a cute sweatshirt," he said, smiling uncertainly.

"Thanks," she replied brightly, "I like it myself. It's cheerful."

"Sure is."

"Is it time for breakfast? I'm starved," she was saying. "Are we starting this morning?"

" 'We'?"

"You," she amended hastily.

"I have to pick up the rest of the crew at the airport and get supplies. I'm shooting for dawn tomorrow."

She stopped short on the path in front of him and staggered a little on those heels. "Tomorrow?" she gasped. "But Roger's up there!"

"I know, Amy," he said, feeling sudden helpless sympathy for her. "But believe me, your brother would be the first one to feel guilty if we weren't organized properly and someone was hurt because of it. This is not a little Sunday jaunt we're going on. Don't underestimate the danger, Amy. I don't," he continued gravely, "and it's kept me alive."

He could see her smoky blue eyes cloud over. What was going on in that head of hers? Didn't she believe him? Or was it just disappointment?

The lodge was saturated with the aromas of bacon and toast and maple syrup and coffee. Amy went straight into the kitchen. It was good for her to have another woman to talk to, Del guessed.

He sat down at the long table, nodding to his father and Jay. His youngest brother had already eaten and was sipping coffee from his giant mug, his head sunk between his brawny shoulders. Del shot a questioning glance at Ollie over Jay's back.

"He says he isn't goin'." Ollie sat there stolidly, swallowing a bit of toast.

"What?"

"I am not going on your rescue mission," corroborated Jay, finally looking up. "It's too dangerous."

"For Pete's sake, Jay, I need you. You know that!"

Hilkka came in and plunked down a plate and mug in front of Del.

"Mom, tell him he's got to go," implored Del.

"He isn't ten years old anymore, Del. I can't order him around," said Hilkka.

"The heck you can't! You do it every day!"

"Not in this matter, son." She pursed her lips and went back into the kitchen.

Del began to eat, not enjoying his breakfast as much as usual, since Jay's statement had really rattled him. He only finished two of his eggs and half the biscuits.

"Dad, talk some sense into him."

"An unwilling climber is an unsafe climber, Del," said Ollie.

"And Sue-Ann doesn't want me to go," put in Jay.

Del took a deep breath. He would not let his temper get the best of him. And he truly felt for Jay. It was hard to clamber back on a snorting bronco that had just tossed you into the dust, but it had to be done.

"Jay, I know how you feel."

"The hell you do," muttered Jay.

"Hey, remember the time I fell on Devil's Steps? I busted my knee up good and limped around for six months. And I'll tell you, I was scared when Ollie took me back up there. But I did it. And you have to do it, too, Jay."

"Why? People live without climbing."

"Not the Pardees," said Del decisively.

"Maybe this Pardee will."

"You know how much you'd miss it? The thrills, the challenges? The summits? Do you remember, Jay, what the valley looks like from the top of the Grand Tetons?''

"Yeah," mumbled Jay.

"Leave him alone, Del. He's got to make up his own mind," said Ollie.

Del shot his father a hard look. He *needed* Jay along.

"This climb is easy. There's only that one short icefall. We'll do it on fixed ropes. It'll be as safe as climbing out of bed."

Jay raised his head up and met his brother's frank gaze. "There's *always* a risk, Del. Don't patronize me."

"Okay, I'm sorry. A tiny possibility, then. But Jay, I need you. I can't get anyone else on such short notice. I trust you. You're good, Jay. I need good men on this rescue."

"Sue-Ann..."

"Sue-Ann," said Del in exasperation, "is not running your life.... Or is she?"

Jay's jaw set in a hard line. "I'm my own man, Del. Lay off. And besides, it wouldn't hurt you or Rob to have a woman around to care about you. Maybe," he added heatedly, "that's your problem!"

Del shook his head. "I don't want to argue, Jay. I didn't mean to insult you or Sue-Ann. She's a fine woman...the best there is."

"Darn right she is," muttered Jay.

"I only meant that some things in life have to stay the same, marriage or not. You were born a climber. I honestly don't think you'd be happy as anything else."

"Yeah . . . well . . . I'll have to think about it. I don't like going back on my word to Sue-Ann."

"I'd never ask you to. But just remember one thing. Sue-Ann may be worried about you now, but don't you think she's wondering just as much as you, what could happen to your life if you didn't meet this one challenge? Think about it, little brother. If you go on this mission now, then never climb again, at least you'll have given it every shot."

"Maybe," mumbled Jay.

"You gotta do it, buddy," said Del with intensity.

"Oh, I'm sorry!" They all looked toward the end of the table, where Amy was dabbing up a splotch of spilled coffee.

Ollie rose and excused himself; Jay sank his head back between his shoulders, and Del groaned. Just what they needed in the middle of a family crisis: Amy Slavin, investigative reporter. She fitted in about as well as a sheep in a pack of wolves.

But she looked so ill at ease, dabbing uselessly at the brown spot, probably embarrassed as the devil, that he relented. "Sit down and eat," he said gruffly. "Don't mind us."

"Okay." She tried to grin. "If you say so."

Frank Pereira arrived then, having traded his three-piece suit for brand-spanking-new jeans that could have stood on their own, a perfectly laundered shirt and a cashmere sweater.

Del greeted him politely. Why in God's name was he burdened with all these city folks? Why didn't they just let him to his job without their well-meaning help?

Then he remembered. Shearing was paying for this rescue. A few extra bucks wouldn't hurt the ranch, not a bit. "Sleep well, Frank?" he asked.

"Like a baby, thank you, Mr. Pardee," Pereira said, nodding. "And how about you, Miss Slavin?"

"Oh, me? I slept pretty well. I thought I heard some noises in the night, like an animal scratching around. Probably rats," she said pointedly.

"'Rats'?" repeated Pereira, puzzled.

"Oh, sure, there are lots of them around here," she said, staring so hard at Frank Pereira that the man dropped his eyes uncomfortably.

Del bristled. Why had she developed this crazy dislike for a man she didn't even know? It wouldn't do the Pardee ranch any good to have its benefactors insulted.

"She means chipmunks, Frank," explained Del carefully.

"Oh." Pereira smiled tentatively.

"I know a rat when I see one," Amy insisted.

Del rolled his eyes heavenward, swallowed his last gulp of coffee and excused himself.

Flint Smith from Colorado arrived around nine o'clock in the morning, bursting in the front door with a huge backpack slung over one shoulder and a head of curling bright red hair.

"Where's Ma?" he yelled. "I want Ma Pardee!" He marched straight to the kitchen, dumping his pack on the floor and hugging Hilkka.

"I'm starving, Ma!" he said. "Lord, I drove all night to get here in time for breakfast!"

Del popped into the kitchen a minute later. "Heard you were here, buddy," he said, slapping Flint on the shoulder.

"Haven't seen you in a while," said Flint with a grin as he ruffled Sally's fur and grinned from ear to ear.

"I think the last time was on Mount McKinley in a blizzard. We were stuck there for three days," said Del. "I saw plenty of you then."

"Yeah, you were ripe enough to pick, as I remember."

"Flint!" admonished Hilkka. Then, turning to Amy, who was helping peel apples for pie, she told him, "This is Amy Slavin. Her brother's one of the men in the plane."

"Oh, I'm sorry, Amy. But we'll get them, won't we?" The redhead took Amy's hand, pumping it enthusiastically.

"Flint," said Del, "is a paramedic."

Del sat with Flint as he ate breakfast, and explained the whole situation. Flint nodded, commenting between mouthfuls. The worst problem, they both agreed, would be the weather. Del was aware of Amy still drinking coffee, paying close attention to the conversation. Once one of her big shiny earrings somehow fell into the apples she was cutting, and there was a flurry for a moment. But she retrieved it, hooking it back on with an apologetic smile. "Sorry," she mumbled, cutting uneven lumps of apple furiously.

"I'm all thumbs myself," put in Flint, grinning sympathetically as if he were already infatuated with Amy.

First Glen, thought Del, and now Flint. One might think she was the only game in town.

Amy, however, was not all thumbs. Oh, Del could see she could spark that protective instinct in a man, but underneath the girlish demeanor, Amy's mind was always clicking furiously. She started in on Flint Smith as soon as Del had finished going over a few details with him.

"So you're a paramedic?" Amy asked.

"Yep." Flint reddened a little, while Del sat back in his chair silently.

"And what sort of drugs are you allowed to administer?" Amy fetched her big floppy purse from under the table and searched out the small black recording device. "Do you mind?" she asked Flint. "I have a dreadful memory." Very sweetly executed.

Flint looked at Del, who shrugged. "She's a reporter," Del quaiified.

"Oh," said Flint, sitting up straight as he began to rattle off the long list of drugs he could administer in a life-threatening situation. Then he went on to tell Amy—or rather, thought Del, to brag to her—about his medical skills.

"You aren't a doctor," Del mumbled once.

"No, of course not," said Flint hastily.

"But very knowledgeable," Amy was saying, as if Flint's medical experience were of the utmost importance to her.

Finally Amy put away her recorder. "Well, thanks," she said innocently. "You never know when you'll need all this stuff for a good story."

"Flint, you rest up now, and I'll go on in to the airport and pick up the others." Del rose from the table.

Flint stretched and yawned. "Okay, see you later. Ma, that was the greatest."

"Don't they have good cooks in Aspen?" she asked.

"Not like you."

Del was on his way to his cabin to pick up the keys to the van, when he heard Amy calling his name. She was hurrying along the path, trying to catch up to him, her ankles doing curious things in the high-heeled boots.

"You certainly do walk fast," she puffed.

"I think you said that once already."

She stopped short and looked up at him with narrowed eyes. "You're still mad I said that stuff about the rats, aren't you?"

"Don't be ridiculous. I'm just in a hurry."

"Go on, admit it." She paused. "But there's something much more important I have to discuss with you." She looked as if she were going to burst with some momentous secret. She practically danced from one foot to the other.

Del folded his arms across his broad chest. "What is it?"

Her mouth opened. Then, as if she'd thought better about the matter, it closed. "You *are* mad. Well, maybe I can just ride with you to the airport."

"Amy, what is this important thing you want to discuss?'

"Oh, nothing," she said airily. "I just want to go to the airport with you."

Del gave up. "Okay, I have to get my keys."

"I'll wait," she said demurely.

She sat beside him in the van, asking questions about the scenery: what was the name of that mountain and how high was it? What kind of tree was that? Was that really an elk herd over there? She looked not a day older than sixteen, he thought once, and couldn't help asking, "How old are you, Amy?"

"Twenty-eight," she said offhandedly. "Why, are you afraid I'm under the age of consent?"

She was a bit wacky, as bouncy as a jack-in-the-box, all motion and gestures. She had a vivid, carefree smile and a quick alertness about her. Strangely enough, Del had the feeling that she was judging him, and weighing his responses.

She *was* nutty and hyperactive, but underneath it all there seemed to be a kind of unaffected sweetness and that ever questioning mind.

A curious girl. . . .

Del gave her a sidelong glance and saw her digging through that huge purse of hers. Finally she pulled out her recording device.

"Ah, here it is," Amy said cheerfully. "Mind if I ask you a few questions?"

"About what?" Lord, how he hated fanfare, photographers and the like. What *was* she up to?

"Oh," replied Amy, "nothing specific. Climbing, I suppose. You know—" she switched on the tape machine "—where you got your experience, what mountains you've climbed, rescues. . . ."

Del scrubbed a hand across his whiskers. "I'll answer anything you like," he said, "but not on tape. Those things make me edgy."

Reluctantly she turned the device off and dumped it back into her purse.

"You're going to bust that thing," said Del offhandedly, "if you don't quit tossing it around like that."

"It's little, but it's tough," she said, "like me." And then she went on, "Tell me about yourself. Everything. From the beginning."

Del did tell her a bit more about the ranch and how his grandfather had started it all. "I've been climbing since I was four," he admitted.

"Four?"

"Yep. Started right here in the Jackson area. I did the Grotto Wall when I was nine...."

"The what?"

"Never mind. I'm just explaining that we Pardees have pretty much always climbed."

"Then Jay would really miss it if he quit?"

Del nodded. "But he's not quitting."

"He might if his girlfriend tells him to," murmured Amy, before catching herself and shooting Del a sheepish smile. "So tell me about Nepal," she rushed to say. "I assume you've climbed there."

"Umm..."

"Tell me, then."

With Amy's constant prodding, he did. She had a way of nosing around, putting in questions that seemed curiously irrelevant. What kind of accidents could happen on a climb? How long did it take to become a weekend climber? Did frostbitten toes hurt terribly? What did they wear on a climb—say, one like this rescue?

It seemed as if she had some ulterior purpose in asking a few of the questions, but for the life of him he couldn't figure out what it was. She was just nosy, he supposed.

"I'd love to do some climbing," she began after a rare spell of silence.

"In that?" he gestured at her outfit.

"I could buy some climbing gear, couldn't I?"

"Sure, but it's the wrong time of year. Come back in the summer."

"You're going on a climb," she said.

He chuckled indulgently. "True. But hardly a beginner's attempt. And it's my job, Amy."

"Well, it's my brother up there."

"Don't worry. I have the best crew in the business lined up."

"I want to go along," she burst out.

"You *what*?" He turned to look at her in mild amazement.

"I'm tough."

"Why in hell would you want to go along?"

"For the experience."

"Amy, do you have any idea what a climb like this entails? No, don't answer me. I'll tell you. Hard labor, cold, discomfort, danger. Possible injury, frostbite." He shook his head in disbelief.

"I want to go," she insisted stubbornly. "It's *my* brother."

"Well, you can't," stated Del.

"You're still mad at me," she pouted.

"I am not!" His temper was beginning to flare. "For Pete's sake, Amy!"

"Then let me go."

"No!"

She subsided, but somehow Del had the distinct feeling that she hadn't really given up. She was just withdrawing her forces to rest for another onslaught. She was a little unusual, but not that off kilter. What reason could she possibly have to go on the rescue? It wasn't as if she could help her brother. Heck, no, she'd just be a hindrance.

He glanced over at her, but she was turned away from him, watching the mountains slide by the car window. Vague suspicions began to crawl around in Del's mind. His instincts told him that Amy was not leveling with him. There was some reason she was keeping a record of her trip out here and an even better reason she wanted to go on the climb.

A thought came to him then. He remembered Jack Gerhunt of Shearing Aerospace making an allusion to—what was it? "Important information in Roger Slavinsky's possession. Vital to get to it. To do with national security." Kirklaw had mentioned it, too.

He looked over at Amy again, then ran a hand through his hair.

The airport was busy, as if everyone wanted to get in or out before the weather socked in. To the west, clouds were building up in a gray line, like an army massed, waiting to advance. Fitful gusts of wind whipped leaves and scraps of paper across the runway.

A plane taxied up and emptied. Del picked Lonnie Dougal out from the crowd without hesitaton. He was dressed as if ready for the climb—heavy boots, sweater, corduroy knickers. But that's what he always wore.

Lonnie was a quiet and intense man, a soul turned inward, Del often thought. But a good man to have at your back. Totally fearless.

"Lonnie, this is Amy Slavin. Her brother's one of the men who was in the crash."

Lonnie looked at Amy, a hint of a sympathetic smile on his lips, but he merely nodded and said to Del, "Let's get my gear." There was still a touch of a Scottish burr in his speech.

They loaded Lonnie's gear into the van while Amy drank coffee in the cafeteria. Then it was time for Swede Björkman's flight to arrive from Seattle.

No one could miss Swede. He was a true, flaxen-haired Viking, hugely tall and boisterous, with a full blond beard. They could hear him yelling *sköl* to the stewardess the minute the plane door opened.

Del introduced Amy to Swede.

"Ah, the poor little t'ing, what with her brother up dere and all!" boomed Swede, crushing Amy in a bear hug.

More gear was stowed in the van. The clouds advanced, shrouding the Tetons in mist. Del began to get nervous. Would Deborah make it from L.A. in time?

Swede and Lonnie retired to the bar to wait. Del stood with Amy at the big glass window, watching the runway. Inevitably he glanced over at her, and their eyes met. He felt her tension as if she were vibrating all over; she shivered, and Del wanted to put an arm around her skinny shoulders and comfort her. How did she manage to change from one extreme to the other so fast? It had only been a short while before that she'd aggravated him beyond words.

"Amy?" he began.

She tried to smile at him, but her eyes, fixed on the mountains, began to fill with moisture. "He's alive, Del. He's cold, but he's alive. We have to hurry...."

He felt his heart go out to her. He didn't even bother to correct her statement, "*We* have to hurry." That could rest for now. Poor kid. He put one of his large, rock-scarred hands on her shoulder, wanting to cuddle her like a kitten, wanting to stroke away the worry lines on her face and the haunted look in her eyes.

"We have to hurry, Del," she repeated as her huge dark blue eyes implored him.

CHAPTER FIVE

Day 2 Noon

AMY HAD A WORD for this kind of moment—a happening. It was one of those times when everything between a man and a woman clicked.

Del's hand still rested on her shoulder, big and warm and strong. A shiver of excitement ran down her side, electrifying her skin and making her yearn to lean even closer to him. He must have sensed her feelings, because the pleasant pressure of his hand changed in some subtle fashion to an insistent telling squeeze.

He felt the attraction, too—she was sure. Should she move and break the spell? The situation was ridiculous, yet as real as the mountains around them.

Had it been less than twenty-four hours since she'd met him in the dusky evening? Impossible. When his hand lifted from her shoulder, she felt a circuit being cut.

"I wish," Del was saying, "I could snap my fingers and have your brother back safe and sound for you."

She turned her head and looked up into his eyes. "So do I," she managed.

And then, for a very long time, even after he had turned his attention back to the tarmac, Amy watched him. Del Pardee, she thought a dozen times, was everything a woman would want.... But then she'd remember, *take care*. He was a suspect, possibly a criminal.

"Ah," Del said finally, pointing toward the end of the runway, "there's the plane now."

Amy tore her eyes away from him and looked across the runway.

"Safely down," he said with satisfaction. "We're a full team now."

They stood together and watched the light, twin-engine model that was taxiing up to a parking spot. Lonnie and Swede appeared at his shoulder.

"She's going to kill her-rself in that thing one o' these days," commented the Scotsman glumly as he nodded toward the plane.

She?

Amy saw the pilot climb out. Then the long-limbed female waved at the group and began striding in their direction. Amy was immediately struck by her ease of movement, by that look of natural health and strength.

A woman? And what a woman! Amy instantly detested her, knowing that her reaction was catty and immature but still irked that even while Del had kissed her the night before and pretended concern, he had been expecting this Amazon beauty.

The female seemed to grow in stature as she approached, and Amy swore the girl possessed the longest legs she'd ever seen. The lady pilot was stunning.

Her blunt-cut honey-blond hair swung at her shoulders, her long face was split in a beguiling white smile, her ample breasts swayed gently beneath the pigskin flight jacket—which would have cost Amy two month's salary—and her firm rounded butt filled the western-cut jeans alluringly.

"Hi, Del baby!" the lady cried as she stepped up her pace and finally leaped into his outstretched arms. They even twirled around together.

Amy watched the scene, wondering if the two had rehearsed it: girl rushes to man's arms, they spin in slow motion, eyes are locked in sensual embrace.

Yuck, thought Amy. Then, naturally, the blond dynamo put her capable hands on either side of Del's face and kissed him soundly. As if that weren't enough, she proceeded to give Lonnie and Swede a big hug, too. At least, Amy observed, the poker-faced Lonnie Dougal didn't pant like a puppy dog when she kissed him.

"Oh, I'm sorry," Del finally said as he remembered Amy's presence. "This is Amy Slavin. Deborah Brewster. I'm afraid Amy's brother is one of the men stranded up there."

"Amy!" said Deborah, turning to her. "So glad to meet you!" She took both of Amy's cold hands in hers. "I *am* sorry about your brother. But don't worry, we'll find him."

That did it, thought Amy as she quietly disengaged her hands. To top it all off, this Deborah appeared sincere and nice!

Amy followed the group toward Del's van. Watching Deborah's beautifully developed backside, Amy wondered morosely if she should start pumping iron. Deborah had her arm locked with Del's, not Lonnie or Swede's, and Amy decided that the great-looking couple had once been, if they were not currently, lovers.

"Here, Amy," Del said as they all began climbing in, "sit up front."

"That's all right," sulked Amy, "I'll get in back." She saw the exchange of glances between Del and Deborah. Oh, so what, Amy thought, feeling totally unbalanced by this unexpected aspect to the puzzle that was Del.

On the drive back, Amy sat mutely absorbing the conversation, which was technical and intent. Obviously the team members had a lot of catching up to do. Amy sat alone in the very back, listening with undisguised disinterest to chatter about exposures, crampons, glacier routes, icefalls and cold fronts. "Who cares," she felt like crying. What they needed to discuss was the crash site and just exactly when they expected to reach it!

Thoughts of the crash site reminded her that Amy Slavin was going along on the climb. Maybe she should pay closer attention to the conversation. Then a thought struck her. She needed clothes to accompany them. Where was she going to get outfitted? Oh, my...

"Del!" She leaned forward purposefully. "You have to go back!"

Suddenly the van was silent. All eyes were turned, pinned on Amy.

"What's that, Amy?" called Del over the heads.

"You have to stop in Jackson. I need to go shopping."

"You what?"

"I have to buy some clothes. Some climbing stuff."

"Forget it. You are *not* going climbing," he called over his shoulder.

"No! Please! Just stop for a few minutes.... You can all eat or something. I ... I really do need to get some, you know, feminine things."

That shut him up. Del shot her an incredulous glance, but what else could he do? He turned onto the main street of Jackson and pulled into a small parking lot.

"The van will be right here," Del said as he climbed out. "I guess we'll grab a quick sandwich while you get your ... er ... stuff."

"Thank you," gushed Amy.

She left the group and headed determinedly down the street, which was lined with those false-front stores and arches made of elk antlers. She was distracted immediately by a Western gunfight that was being staged for the tourists right in the middle of the street—shooting, an outlaw, a good guy in a white hat, the works. Even a vintage stagecoach that the outlaw was robbing. Amy applauded along with the other onlookers when they were finished.

She walked on, marveling at the show, remembering Glen's telling her that outlaws had made the valley their home. Then she remembered what she was there for.

She was moving past a sporting goods store, barely noticing the tents and Coleman stoves in the window, when abruptly she stopped. Amy turned and went back, entering the store, thinking that she must have really lost her mind this time.

The clerk, because it was off-season and slow, was on Amy in a flash. "Somethin' I can show you, ma'am?"

Amy met his gaze squarely. "I want to look at a gun."

Immediately the older man scanned her with a disbelieving eye, his stare resting for too long on her hippo-covered chest.

"A gun?" A chuckle gurgled in his throat.

If that's the way you want it, thought Amy. "Yes," she said, "just a little thing I can hold in my hand. It's for those wild chipmunks y'all have out here."

She shivered as he showed her several "pocket models." They all looked the same. Ugly and deadly.

"So which one, ma'am?" He shifted his weight from one foot to the other.

"This." She pointed. "No, that one. It's the cheapest, isn't it?"

"Yep. But it ain't as reliable."

"I'm not going to *fire* the thing."

He raised a bushy brow. "That right? Then you won't be needing bullets, either."

"No," Amy said, taking up the challenge. "I won't." She might wave it under some as yet unexposed assassin's nose—but actually use it?

Amy paid with her charge card, knowing that the purchase would just slide by when the clerk called in for authorization. Someday she was going to cut that card into a thousand pieces...someday.

She slipped the little weapon into her purse and felt its weight, which was both reassuring and scary.

A clothing store, she decided, must be just nearby. She started down the street, wondering if her charge card could bear any more purchases, when she heard her name being called.

"Amy!"

She turned toward the direction of the voice, squinted, and saw the Sheriff Department's Blazer.

"Glen," she said uncertainly, while trying to make out the blurry face.

"Hop on in. Where're you going?"

Amy climbed in. "I'm looking for a clothing store."

"Oh, yeah? What kind?"

She glanced over at him, was once again taken by that sexy smile and the wonderful grooves bracketing his curved mouth. Would he have the same reaction to her pronouncement as Del?

Here goes. "I need some climbing stuff."

"But you're not going climbing...."

"I am. I'm going with the team."

Glen brought the Blazer to a screeching halt, then turned and looked at her in amazement. "Amy...you can't be serious! Why…why I *know* Del Pardee would never let you do such an insane thing."

"I *am* going." She pushed open the door and jumped out before he could stop her. "Thanks for the ride," she bit out, and began to walk along the sidewalk, her too high heels clicking loudly, her ankles wobbling.

Glen drove the Blazer slowly alongside her. "Amy," he kept pleading, "stop this nonsense."

She bit her lower lip. "Leave me alone, please."

Finally he stopped the car several yards ahead of her and reached across the seat, opening the door. "Get in," he said. "I'll take you to Jackson Mountaineering."

Amy smiled winningly. "Thanks, Glen. You're a real pal."

He helped her with every last detail: the right knee socks, ungainly climbing boots, a puffy red parka, hat, gloves, even corduroy knickers. "You realize all this is a waste," he kept saying.

"Now, Glen," Amy replied, "never underestimate the power of a woman."

Then came the bill. Four hundred eighty-nine dollars and twelve cents. The twelve cents, she could manage.

"I didn't know this was Saks Fifth Avenue," she muttered helplessly. Maybe, Amy thought, the clerk wouldn't call for authorization....

"I'm dreadfully sorry." He came back, handing her the plastic albatross and looking down at his feet.

"Oh, my," said Amy as she almost died on the spot. "I...I didn't know...." She tried to gather her thoughts while Glen stood looking at her with embarrassed curiosity. "Would you take a check?" she ventured.

"We don't take out of town checks," the clerk began uneasily.

"Oh..."

"I know," suggested Glen. "I can cosign it for you."

"Oh, Glen! Would you?"

"Sure, Amy." His smile made a sigh bubble up in her.

As they walked out of the store, Glen carrying two very full sacks, Amy wondered just how in heaven's name she was going to cover that check.

"Where's Del's van?" asked Glen as he tossed her bags in the back and started up the Blazer.

"That way," directed Amy, pointing while she leaned forward and squinted.

"It's not in this lot," said Glen when they stopped.

"Oh, my," breathed Amy, casting around hopelessly and wishing she'd noted the exact spot, the name of a store, anything. "Well, it's got to be down that street over there." She pointed once more.

Glen drove around the streets. And around.

"Oh, no," Amy gulped. "It's probably down there. Oh, my...."

Finally he stopped and parked in front of the Million Dollar Cowboy Bar. "It's all right, Amy. Del will drive back to Moose and wait for you to call."

"But I'm holding everyone up!" she said, frustrated. "It's all my fault. Oh, poor, poor Roger...."

"There, there," soothed Glen, leaning across the seat and putting his strong hand on her shoulder. "It's not you holding us up. It takes time to collect all the equipment and supplies. Besides, there's a storm brewing up there. You're not holding anyone up."

"Are you sure?"

"I'm positive."

He locked the vehicle—thank goodness, because Amy's valuable purchases were still inside—and they began to walk together toward the bar. Amy was feeling dreadful, despite Glen's assurances.

He stopped her in front of the entrance. "Hey," Glen said, "try to cheer up. Everything's going to turn out okay. Besides, your hippos are frowning."

"My what?" Then she remembered and looked down at her sweatshirt. "Oh." Amy sighed. "Glen," she said, "these past two days have been the pits."

"Yeah, I know." He smiled and pushed open the swinging doors. Then he did a sweet thing; he put both his hands on her waist from behind and held her motionless for a moment. His light yet intimate touch caused Amy's skin to tingle all over. He seemed to be such a nice guy! Yet, with her reporter's instincts, she couldn't help reserving judgment.

Glen telephoned the Pardee Ranch from the saloon while Amy found the ladies' room, as usual. She was assailed by the authentic Western atmosphere of the combination restaurant and saloon. The place was huge, with two long bars on either side of the building, a wooden dance floor and bandstand. She noticed a few lunch customers and a number of grizzled old-timers leaning against the bar, each with a heel hooked over the brass rail.

On her way back from the rest room, she heard a distinctive, loud ping and looked down to the base of the bar. There sat a real spittoon. Ping! Ping!

"Would you like a drink and some lunch?" asked Glen as he nodded toward a booth near the front window.

"Well . . . sure. I'm always hungry."

A waitress in jeans, a plaid gingham shirt and a cowboy hat seated them. She was wearing tall boots over the outside of her pants—white rhinestone boots! She snapped her chewing gum. "Somethin' to drink, folks?"

Amy ordered a white wine. Glen passed. "I'm still on duty."

"I'm awfully sorry to take up your time like this."

"No problem. I was only getting ready for the climb, anyway."

"Do you get paid for the climb?" Amy asked, always curious, always questioning.

"Well, the department pays me, but a rescue is volunteer."

"Then why did you say Del is doing it for money?"

Glen hesitated a split second. "There's usually a donation, Amy. The family of the victim or the employer. . . ."

"Shearing Aerospace, in this case," Amy said.

"Well, yes, I understand they offered Del quite a bundle for his time." He smiled charmingly. "I guess they wanted the best."

"And they got it," suggested Amy.

"It seems so."

Amy's brain shifted into a higher gear. So Del had been offered a "donation." She looked across the table at Glen. She really could use someone on her side. But how could she be sure, absolutely positive, Glen was not involved with Shearing? Maybe she should feel him out out a little, find out what made Glen Shepherd tick. And just why didn't Glen get along with Del?

Amy sipped on her wine pensively. "Were you born and raised here?"

"Yep. A dyed in the wool local."

"Are your parents still living?"

"My dad is. He's a rancher."

"Oh," said Amy, "that must be lucrative."

"Not hardly!" Glen laughed. "You're thinking of the movies, where a ranch spreads for miles and has its own airstrip and all. That isn't ours."

"I see. Did you ever want to move away... say, live in Denver or Phoenix or some big city?"

"You bet. When I was a kid, I used to dream of being a big city detective."

"Can't you be one?"

"'Fraid I lack the education to really move up. Jackson is just fine, anyway. As I get older, I realize that a small town can offer just as much as any big city. The grass really isn't any greener, no matter where you are, Amy."

"Yes," Amy agreed, "I feel the same about Rochester. It's fun to dream, though. . . ."

They talked some about Roger and how he had gotten all the brains in the family.

"I'm pretty smart," admitted Amy unabashedly, "but Roger is a genius."

"He must have been—" Glen suddenly caught himself. "I'm sorry."

Amy felt those blasted tears burn behind her eyelids again. "That's okay. I know everyone thinks those men don't have much of a chance, but if you can understand, I just *know* Roger is alive."

Glen nodded kindly. "You're twins, you said?"

"Yes. But we don't look all that much alike. Roger is quite tall and his eyesight is perfect and his hair is real kinky."

"I like your hair," Glen said in a deep, manly voice, and immediately continued, "Sorry. I didn't mean to come on that way."

Amy, however, was warmed by his words.

"And I like your mouth, too." He reached over and took her hand in his. "In fact, Miss Amy Slavin, I like an awful lot of things about you."

Wow, Amy thought, always happy to accept flattery. And then she had another thought on the heels of the first: she wished, somehow, that it were Del sitting across from her, gushing with compliments that made her stomach tingle deliciously.

"Do you think," Glen was saying, "that you might stay after the rescue? I mean, you don't have to rush back to New York, do you?"

Amy sat quietly for a minute. Lord only knew what the future held. There was Roger's imminent welfare to consider, and if and when they did get him safely back to civilization, there was the exposé of the monstrous cover-up at Shearing. She recalled her thoughts about standing in front of the Pentagon, airing the shocking story. Somehow it seemed terribly trite at the moment.

Where was her life headed? After the ordeal with Roger—and God knew *that* wasn't over—what did she really want?

"I might be able to stay for a bit," Amy replied slowly. "But a lot depends on Roger."

"Just keep believing that everything's going to be all right."

"I am. God, I am." She looked up from his hand, which was still covering hers, and met his brown eyes. "You've been a good friend, Glen. I've known you less than twenty-four hours and you've really come through. You won't try to stop me from going on the climb, will you?" Her tone was imploring.

"Amy. I want to be your friend. Your close friend. But friends don't lie, do they?"

She shook her head.

"Then I've got to tell you how dangerous it would be. It would make me breathe a whole lot easier if you were safely back at the Pardees' with Hilkka."

"So you'll agree with Del when the showdown comes."

Glen paused thoughtfully. "I should," he said simply.

"Then you haven't made up your mind yet." It was not a question.

"No, I haven't. I can only advise you to stay below. I'd hate to order you around like Del very well might."

Several thoughts flitted through Amy's mind. Glen would not try to stop her and he really seemed to care about her safety. What was more, he'd just opened a door in the conversation.

Amy leaped in. "Why do you say Del would order me around?"

"He pushes everyone around. Sure, he seems mild mannered on the surface, but you ought to see his temper." Glen hesitated. "I imagine you will see it, Amy."

I already have, she thought. "Glen," Amy prodded gently, "why don't you two get along?"

He studied her face for a moment. "You really are a reporter, aren't you?"

Amy smiled. "You could say that."

"Well, Del and I go a long ways back. Actually, to grade school." He stopped. "You really want to hear this?"

"Yes."

"Well, Del always seemed to want a competition of sorts between us, you might say. Right from the first grade—alphabet recitals to spelling bees to the football field in high school.'' Glen shrugged, remembering. ''Never knew why he had it in for me.''

''And girls?'' Amy ventured.

''Girls, too,'' he said with a nod. ''I recall a pretty little thing in seventh grade.... Anyway, I was the first to get her to go to the movies. Del was madder than a hornet. He started a fight one day and got us both suspended.''

''I see,'' Amy mused. ''So you two never did get along.''

''Nope, I suppose not. Del just had to be the big man around campus. He couldn't take criticism—always had to run the show. I even remember him as captain of our football team. Bossy as all get out. Just like now....''

Glen's dark eyes held Amy's for a time. She could see a tight muscle ticking in his jaw and was almost ashamed of herself for dredging up the past. *Almost*.

Finally Glen leaned forward a little, conspiratorially. ''There were other things, too.''

''Can you tell me?''

''It's not a pleasant story.''

''Glen,'' said Amy, ''I'm a reporter. I've seen and heard a lot.''

''Okay,'' he said in a low voice. ''Guess you have a right to know, what with Del leading a rescue involving your own brother.''

He paused, taking a deep breath. ''There was this Indian girl in high school—from the local reservation. Del was dating her hot and heavy. Anyway, the poor thing got ... pregnant, Amy, and our great hero,

Del Pardee, dumped her flat and denied the whole thing. The real sad part is that I still see her around town with that kid—well, a grown kid now—and no one ever married her. She's lived on welfare ever since then. It's pathetic.''

"Wow," breathed Amy. "That is, well, cruel. It's so hard to imagine Del doing that."

"He did it all right. Ask anybody around here. He was going with her at the time."

"I'm sure that's true, Glen," said Amy, "but perhaps it wasn't actually Del."

"You aren't defending him!"

"No... how could I? I'm simply saying that from what I've seen of Del, it's hard to believe. I guess, though, you're sure of the facts."

The grooves in his face deepened. "Of course I'm sure," he said. "I'm not in the habit of making things like that up."

Amy decided against pressing it further. "No, I'm sure you aren't."

Glen smiled at her. "Look, I didn't mean to snap at you like that. I apologize."

"Accepted."

"But promise me that what I told you goes no farther than this table. Okay?"

She didn't really want to, but there seemed no other choice. "I promise. You have my word." Then she decided to feel him out on another question he had raised in her mind. "Yesterday," she said, "you told me Del was a fast man for a buck."

"That's right."

"Well . . . why?"

"Say, is Del all we're going to talk about, Amy?"

She shook her head. "Last question. It's just that Roger's life is so important to me and I feel as if I should know all I can about Del."

Glen smiled at her, relaxing. "I was only referring to all his money talk about expansion at the Pardee ranch. Then every time we have an auction around these parts . . ."

"An auction?"

"Horses. Del always makes it a point to outbid everyone. You can't get an even break around the guy."

"Has he gotten a horse that you were bidding on?"

Glen frowned slightly. "Not me. My dad. Several times, in fact. We could've used one in particular . . . a real fine piece of horseflesh, Amy. The stud fees sure would have helped. . . . My dad's been having some problems lately. And his problems are mine. Know what I mean?"

"Umm," said Amy thoughtfully, "I understand."

My, but she'd love to hear Del's version of these stories. Somehow she sensed that they might be quite different. Amy was not a bad judge of character . . . oh, sure, outbidding someone on a horse—no big deal. Business was business. But her instincts told her that there was more to this Indian girl story than met the eye.

"Another wine?" The waitress snapped her chewing gum again.

Glen looked up at her. "I'll have more coffee with lunch. You ready, Amy?"

"Yes. I'll have a hamburger and fries and lots of mayonnaise, please. And yes, I'll have another wine, too." She mused aloud, "Getting lost, ruining everyone's schedule...what's another wine? I'm in enough trouble as it is...."

CHAPTER SIX

Day 2 P.M.

"DEL!" HILKKA CALLED. "I'm glad you're back. There was a message from Glen Shepherd. He's with Amy at the Million Dollar."

"Where?" barked Del.

"You know, the Million—"

"Yeah, all right, I do know where it is. How in the devil did Amy end up there, with him? For Pete's sake...."

"He really didn't say, son. What's the matter?"

"We do have a rescue to put together, Mom. And somehow little Miss Slavin disappeared in Jackson."

"So you drive back in and fetch her." Hilkka turned to her sink. "Did everyone get in all right?"

"Yeah." Del picked up a plum from a kitchen basket and popped it in his mouth. "They're in their cabins."

"Deborah, too?"

"Yes, Mom, Deborah, too. I suppose I have to go now to get Amy. Boy, that girl.... And why didn't Glen just drive her back himself?"

He heard his mother mumble, "Maybe he likes her company."

It was a twenty-minute drive back to Jackson. Del seethed as he pushed the gas pedal to the floor. How dared she pull a stunt like this? A rescue took an impossibly long time to organize as it was—the team didn't need a nosy, inept flatlander like Amy holding it up.

On the other side of the coin, he suddenly realized, the unfortunate odds were that it might make no difference whatsoever when they reached the plane.

He wondered then, did Amy realize what the statistics were? Sure, she professed to have an inner knowledge of Roger Slavinsky's safety, but was she merely retreating from the facts?

Poor kid.

He caught himself. Kid nothing! She was a nuisance. A skinny little crazy lady from the city.

He could see her in his mind's eye: the funky outfit she was wearing, the way those innocent smoky blue eyes of hers could turn shrewd and calculating at the drop of a hat, the slightly upturned nose and pretty pink mouth, which set determinedly at the corners.

Generally Del was attracted to a more substantial woman. Amy was a bit bony for him, practically chestless. Yet he hadn't failed to notice that she had *something* beneath those dancing hippos on her sweatshirt. She'd be the type of woman you'd handle carefully in bed. Or...would she? Would Amy Slavin be wild and passionate, all movement and impatient hands?

What are you thinking, Del asked himself sharply. Her nuttiness must be infectious. He was furious with her. Yet paradoxically he was envisioning sleeping with her!

"Get your act together," he chided himself under his breath.

There were no parking places near the Million Dollar, naturally, so Del pulled the van into a lot two blocks away. His stride was long and impatient as he approached the saloon. Glen couldn't possibly have given Amy a ride home. No. He'd just sit and chat, maybe over a drink, until good ol' Delwood got there.

What the devil had come into his life with this girl— a tornado? First the Lear jet crash, then that curious talk of national security, and then Amy had stormed into the picture. She shied from scurrying, harmless creatures, yet squared off to Frank Pereira like David to Goliath. And why didn't she like Pereira? Then she wanted to go on a dangerous rescue mission when she could barely walk along a dirt path without tripping!

If Del hadn't sensed a purpose behind her madness, he'd have thought she was a bungling, inept female. But obviously she wasn't, and as the hours since she'd arrived ticked by, he was becoming more and more convinced that she had a secret, some knowledge about this national security business and her brother's role in it. Perhaps she'd spoken to her brother before the plane had crashed and found out something that way.

Why was Roger Slavinsky flying to Washington with a Defense Department official? And why did Amy feel she had to be there on the rescue?

Maybe, Del thought as he pushed his way through the swinging doors, he'd just shake some answers out of her!

He walked up to their table and saw that Amy pulled her hand out from under Glen's when she noticed him.

Was that what this whole episode was about? Not female necessities but a prearranged rendezvous with Glen Shepherd?

Anger ignited within Del. How dared she inconvenience him like this!

"Come on, Amy," he commanded, "we're leaving."

Glen tipped his wide-brimmed hat and settled back into his seat. "What's with you, Pardee? Cool off there."

"Don't pull that macho deputy sheriff stuff on me, Shepherd," snorted Del.

Glen narrowed his dark eyes and tensed while Del fastened his stare on Amy, who was sliding under the table.

"Del," she gulped, "please. I got lost...."

"My foot you did!"

"I did! And Glen here..."

Del glared at her. "Glen what? Made sure you were well taken care of?" He eyed her half-empty wineglass. "Don't take me for a fool!"

"Del," she said defensively, "you're very wrong...."

"Yeah? Well why didn't Shepherd drive you to the ranch himself? Tell me that?"

Amy looked uncertainly from Del to Glen. She shrugged stiffly. "I . . . I guess he has to get back to work. . . ."

"Don't be so naive."

"That's enough!" Glen rose and stood eye to eye with Del. "You wanna take this outside?"

"With you?" Del frowned, a flashing memory of the last time they'd come to blows washing over him. The whole sad, sordid mess. . . .

"Thay!" came a shout from behind Del. Surprised, he spun around. A wizened old drunk was staggering over from the bar. He recognized Fred Walker, a rodeo clown. "You botherin' the deputy and his gal?"

"Ah, no," Del grumbled, wishing he'd just walked in, taken Amy's hand and carefully pulled her out. Too late now.

"Oh, my . . ." Amy drew in a breath. "Let's just go now, can't we?"

Glen put his hand up to the swaying cowboy's chest. "Hold it right there, Fred. There's no problem."

"Oh, yeah?" slurred Fred. "I 'member when them Pardee boys was meaner than a den a' grizzlies . . . lemme at 'em!"

"Fred," warned Glen, "mind your own business before I run you in for disturbing the peace."

Del watched the scene unfolding with disbelief. He hadn't been in a fight since his teens; he was too old for this stuff.

Amy was trying to get up from her seat in the booth. Del took her hand. "Can we go now?" he asked as his heavy dark brows drew into a frown.

"Of course." She looked tentatively from Del to Glen and back. "I'm really sorry..." Suddenly one hand flew to her cheek...what? And then she groped with both hands around the front of her sweatshirt, crying, "It fell out!" Quickly she bent over, as if she were falling or fainting or Lord knew what.

"Amy?" said Del, bewildered.

"Oh, my!" was all he could get out of her.

The drunk pushed past Glen abruptly. "Del hit that gal! Let me attem!"

Del was aware of Fred lunging at him, but he had reached down to keep Amy from bumping her head on the edge of the table. Suddenly he felt a blow to his side, and before he could recover, Fred caught him with a glancing left on his lip.

Del reacted instantaneously and grabbed Fred's buckskin vest, shaking him. "You old goat!" he shouted, "I should plaster you all over this bar!"

Then suddenly they all heard a shriek. "Don't move a muscle!" It was Amy, desperate, and half wailing. Like a bunch of disobedient kids, they all froze guiltily—even Fred.

"It's my contact lens!" she was crying. "We have to find it!"

Her contact lens? Del, who had one hand still poised to strike Fred, looked at her in amazement as realization flooded him.

"Help me find it!" Amy looked up from the floor, where she was on her hands and knees, to Del to Fred to Glen. "Please!"

Del would never know how, but it was Fred, as drunk as a skunk, whose rough old splotched fingers stumbled onto the tiny lens beneath the booth.

"Here it is, missy!" he sputtered proudly, swaying, his breath assailing them.

"Oh, thank you," breathed Amy as she wet her finger and took it from Fred gingerly.

"Are you all right, Amy?" Glen was asking and Del thought, *I don't believe this....*

When Amy's contact lens was back in place, they finally escaped outside. Glen was telling Amy how sorry he was that she got mixed up in that mess.

"I shouldn't have taken you in there," he stated. "Del was right."

"They have good hamburgers." Amy smiled tentatively.

Del watched as Glen held her arm for a moment too long, then leaned down and kissed Amy's cheek. "You go on back to the ranch with Del. Wait a minute. I'll get your stuff out of the Blazer, okay?"

"All right." She carefully kept her eyes on Glen, who was striding over to his vehicle and pulling her parcels out, but Del could feel the tension that held her. He wondered briefly what was in the bags, but childish pride stopped him from inquiring.

Glen handed the bags to her. She thanked him. Then he tipped his hat and was gone, and she stood alone on the pavement with Del and the two mysteriously heavy sacks. Finally she had to turn and face his black scowl.

"I'm really sorry..." she started to say. She looked so young and so upset that Del almost forgave her on the spot. But he remembered Glen's kissing her and the way she'd pulled her hand from his with guilty haste and he got mad all over again.

"Don't say it." He put a large hand on her back and started guiding her down the street, intentionally letting her lug the two bags. It was about then that he noticed his side and jaw were beginning to really hurt.

"Del," she said sheepishly once they were in the van, "are you all right?"

"I'm perfectly fine. I just don't want to talk." He knew exactly how he sounded, adolescent and wounded, but he didn't give a hoot.

They were five miles from Moose when Amy tried again. "I really got lost...I never did have any sense of direction."

Del kept his eyes pinned on the straight ribbon of road, wishing she'd shut up and wishing he had a bag of ice to put on his lip.

"Please talk to me," she finally implored.

Del sighed. "What's there to talk about? You want to discuss meeting Glen Shepherd for lunch or maybe letting him fondle you out on the street?"

"It wasn't like that!"

Del shot her an incredulous, sidelong glance. "It wasn't? What do you think I am? Blind?" He could see Amy's back stiffen.

"Really," she said angrily, "you are the most ridiculous man I have ever met! Why...why, you sound as if you're jealous!"

Del felt embarrassed anger seize him by the back of the neck; a lump formed in his throat. He could feel heat rising up out of his shirt collar and a vein throbbing in his temple. "Jealous?" He tried to laugh it off. It came out choked. "That's crazy."

But she only sat there, eyeing him narrowly. He felt like a fool. He just couldn't get the hang of her game. What in hell did Amy want from him?

"Why don't you believe me?" she demanded. "I got lost, I met Glen by accident. He helped me out, for goodness' sakes!"

He tried a new tactic. "I'll believe you when you start telling me the truth, Miss Slavin."

"You are evading the point," she said angrily.

"So are you." He glanced sideways at her again. She looked so darned mad. Flustered and pink cheeked and about sixteen years old. Her eyes were storm dark; her mouth was set stubbornly. Del suddenly noticed that her eyebrows were very black and that they swept back in swallow's wings. He forgot what he was going to say. Then, with a rush of irritation, he remembered.

"Okay. Let's say I believe you about Shepherd. Now your turn. Talk, Amy. Tell me. What's this national security stuff? Why was Roger on his way to Washington in a private government jet?" He looked over quickly to catch Amy's expression. She was shocked, but hastily turned her head to look out of the window, hiding her reaction. He fixed his eyes back onto the road. "What I'd really like to know is how come you want to risk your neck to go on this climb? What's up there, Amy, besides Roger?"

Silence pulsed in the van's interior. Del shot Amy another quick glance; her face was set obstinately.

"I think," he said more softly, "you would be wise to confide in me, Amy. For all our sakes."

But she said nothing.

Del pressed on. "What's really in those bags you were carrying?"

This time he caught her eye. "Clothes, climbing clothes."

"I see." He thought hard a moment. "Then you haven't gotten it through your head that you are *not* going on this climb?" His tone was firm. She wasn't really a bad sort. It was just that trouble seemed to follow her around like a pet dog. What he ought to do was ship her straight back to Rochester. Yet somehow, and the reason remained a puzzle, she had touched him, gotten inside his head and twisted his feelings. No one, not even Deborah, had ever done that.

With Deborah it had been plain and simple passion. Del had been twenty-five, Deborah twenty-one. They'd taken one long panting look at each other and fallen head over heels. The affair had lasted—what? A year, he recalled. And like a candle, it had burned down, slowly, smoothly, inevitably.

And yet, Del thought back over the years, they had never fought. It was, frankly, that Deborah was too footloose and fancy free with her trust fund and he was stuck, albeit contentedly, on the ranch. Their goals differed. They'd agreed to split up because marriage wouldn't work. And then had come the friendship, lasting, solid and dependable.

Now Amy was a horse of a different color. She aggravated him, lighted his short fuse and somehow kept him on edge continually. There was a charge there between them, all right, but he was afraid it was explosive. If he were smart, he'd avoid her like the plague. If he were smart . . .

They drove under the arch and headed up the sloping road toward the main lodge. Del tried hard to concentrate on the many details of packing up the supplies. By morning, he hoped they would have a good forecast and be able to head out. If those men were alive, they couldn't last up there forever.

He parked the van in front of the lodge. Swede was sitting on the porch in the cold, blustery wind, negligently smoking a pipe, his wild blond hair whipping in his eyes.

"I like your friends," Amy said as she reached for the door handle.

Del turned toward her. "They're a good lot."

"Even Deborah seems okay."

"'Even Deborah' is it?"

"Well, for a woman."

"That's a strange thing for another woman to say."

Amy eyed him keenly. "It's not at all strange." Then abruptly Amy's brow knit and she let out a small gasp. "Your lip! Oh, my gosh, he really did hit you!"

"Hey," said Del, reddening, "it's nothing." But she had scooted across the seat and put her small, delicate hands on his shoulders. "Stop this, Amy...." What could he do, shove her aside?

"Hold still," she ordered softly, and then turned his face toward her. "Oh, gosh, it's still bleeding a little. Here." She began groping around the huge purse of hers. "I know I have a handkerchief. Here it is!"

"Amy, quit it." He fidgeted, but she only put more pressure on his chin with her hand while he watched her big blue eyes moving over his face.

Then she wet her hankie with her pink tongue and began dabbing carefully at the cut. "You've even got blood in your mustache." She blotted away. "Am I hurting you?"

"You're murdering my pride," Del grumbled.

"Sorry," she said, smiling, "but I always mend my fences. Habit."

"I'll bet it keeps you busy."

She was rubbing away at the side of his lip. "Don't you shave?"

"Every morning. Now will you stop it?"

"Every morning? My, oh, my...." She finally took her hand away. "There, but keep the handkerchief and maybe put some ice in it. Okay?"

"Sure," Del muttered, thoroughly done in. Then he watched as she moved back over to her seat and opened the door, stepping out into the biting wind.

"I really do feel awful about today," she managed to say as she dragged the bags out of the back seat. "I'm sorry for everything and wish none of this had ever happened." She looked at him with a question in her eyes. When he didn't answer it, she set her chin steadfastly.

"I'm sorry we've been thrown together like this—at odds, it seems—but if you'd give me a chance, you'd see I'm not really a scarlet woman or a liar. Or incompetent."

"Look," he began, but she'd already given her door a slam shut and was heading down the path toward her cabin.

Del sat for a moment with his hands on the steering wheel, watching her. The wind picked up her dark curling hair and molded her sweatshirt to her slim back as she struggled to haul the big shopping bags. Her small derriere swayed as she fought to beat a path away from him in those punk boots. In one hand he still held her hankie. It was soft and warm. Her flesh would be as soft and warm....

Del lifted the little scrap of fabric to his nostrils and let the aroma touch his senses. It's odor was flowerlike and natural. Like Amy. He felt his heart beating against his ribs rapidly, as if he'd just assaulted a summit and were standing scanning the world from above, alone with creation.

A sharp rap at his window startled him. Del saw Swede standing there. He opened his door. "What is it, Swede?"

"Yust vanted to know if you were okay?"

"Now that," Del mused aloud, "is a darn good question."

CHAPTER SEVEN

Day 2 P.M.

DISCRETION BEING THE BETTER PART of valor, Amy prudently retired to her cabin.

Was she in trouble now! How had everything fallen apart like this? And Del with that nasty cut on his lip. She paced the perimeter of the tiny cabin, squeezing her eyes shut in mortification as she recalled scenes from the afternoon. Why did such things always happen to her? She supposed there were women who sailed through life smoothly, like ocean liners on a calm sea. Women like Deborah Brewster, for instance.

Why did Amy have to paddle through life like a rickety dinghy whose rower got tired arms?

Then she remembered. Sticking her arm into her big purse, she felt around, finally locating the thing. Gingerly she pulled the gun out, holding it as she would a dead mouse, then looked around. Where should she hide it?''

In movies they hid things in the toilet tank, but she was sure the gun would get wet and rust. Under her pillow? Oh, my, no. Eventually she just stuck it under a sweater in the bottom dresser drawer. It was ridiculous to hide the darn thing, anyway.

Then she started thinking about how she'd break her story to Ken and how his eyes would widen with respect. How impressed he'd be that Amy had done the whole thing herself, even climbed a grandmother of a mountain to get her story! Of course, there would be no story if they didn't get to Roger....

Then she pulled her tape recorder out. Therapy. Unloading the soul was healthy, wasn't it?

"Del Pardee is the most contradictory man I've ever met. He looks like a lumberjack. He has a hair-trigger temper, but he's like a little boy when he's hurt. And everyone seems to love him, except Glen Shepherd. There must be more to Del than I've seen so far, but I have a feeling his bark is worse than his bite.

"I wonder what they're all going to think of me now. Del is no doubt telling everyone the whole story. Oh, Lordy! I got lost, practically started a barroom brawl, upset the leader of the rescue mission and wasted half the afternoon. Not to mention sticking that well-meaning Glen Shepherd with a rubber check!

"I bought a gun. Ridiculous. I keep thinking this whole affair is a figment of my imagination, something out of a Ludlum novel. But then reality hits again—Shearing has covered up a flaw in the defense system. Shearing did search Roger's apartment. Shearing has sent a man to Wyoming. Logical progression stands: Shearing cannot allow Roger Slavinsky to spill the beans. Thus my purchase of the gun. One last thought—what is Del's version of his relationship with Glen and what's the truth behind Del's Indian girl? I haven't known Del very long, but still...I have a real strong feeling that he wouldn't get a girl pregnant and then drop her. I don't know why I have this feeling, but I do. So why would Glen lie? He seems a real decent guy, too.''

She ended her talk feeling not much better. She could have used some company, but she was afraid to go up to the lodge and face the flak.

Sighing, she began to pace again, but stopped at the little curtained window to look out. Leaves and dust were chasing one another across an empty corral and lowering gray clouds hung over the mountains, obscuring the needle-sharp peaks.

Amy shivered. Roger.... All thoughts of her own troubles dissipated and she could think only of her brother. Her sufferings were nothing compared to his! How dared she wallow in self-pity? He was freezing up there—and hungry and possibly hurt. Maybe he was even completely alone if there were no other survivors. ''Roger,'' she called silently, ''we're coming! Hang on!''

She considered, briefly, changing into her new climbing gear, so as to look ready for anything. Also, to steer attention away from herself, her *old* self that was. But the ploy was too transparent, she decided. They'd have to take her as she was.

Once more into the breach. Amy dragged on her camouflage army jacket and stepped briskly out of her door. She'd just have to tell them all to hurry now that the whole party was here.

And besides, she could really use a cup of Hilkka's coffee.

She clenched her teeth and squeezed her eyes shut again as she paused before the thick oak door of the lodge. Then she pushed it open and walked in, head held high. Would they all laugh? Or ostracize her? Okay, she could take it. She could take anything but pity.

However, nobody seemed to notice her at all. A few hellos, a smile or two. Rob and Jay grinned and waved beefy hands from where they sat over a checker-board. Del and Deborah were nowhere to be seen. She made her way into the kitchen, feeling relatively secure encased in its warm aromas.

"Amy," Hilkka said, beaming. "Just in time to help peel potatoes."

She wasn't mad! Thank heavens Hilkka wasn't mad at her! Amy sat and peeled and sipped coffee and listened to Hilkka's chatter. A few well-placed questions and she had everyone's history, from when and where they'd been born to the last article in *Climbing* magazine about their daring exploits.

"Now Deborah Brewster," Hilkka was saying wistfully. "There's one fine girl. She has a trust fund from her family—very wealthy folk out there in L.A. But she's not spoiled, not a bit. Came out here one summer to climb and she and Del…well, nothing came of it. At least not yet. She flies that little plane of hers all over. She's done every peak over fourteen thousand in the country. Goes to Europe a lot, too. Hand me that pan, will you? Thanks.

"Deborah offered to lend Del the money he needs for expansion of the ranch, but he said he was too proud. Frankly, I think he should have done it. Now he's wrangling with the bank to get the loan, and the interest rates are awful. And Deborah put all of her money in long-term oil leases.'' She shook her head. ''Del's a real worrier. You'd think he was president of some big corporation the way he talks about loans and expansion and profits. I don't know. Ollie never bothered much about that stuff.''

Amy listened carefully. Glen had indicated that Del needed money. Oh, my. Very interesting.

''Then there's Lonnie,'' Hilkka continued. ''Lonnie, of course, is a little hard to know. Darn Scotsman. But he's done Everest and all the big ones. He's been on every major European expedition that's been mounted in the past ten years. Quiet, but you know what they say—still waters run deep. His eyes are weird, you know what I mean?

''Okay, I'll take those potatoes now. Swede Björkman has a weakness for drink. He's strong as a bull. I'd say he was a little . . . well, naive, immature. But happy and full of fun. A little loud from time to time.''

Hilkka wiped her hands on her apron and sat down across from Amy. ''Flint is a good boy. He's a ski patrolman in Aspen. Also a paramedic, and he teaches climbing and first aid. He's got so many irons in the fire I wonder he knows where he's at. He'll be handy if there are any injuries—oh, I'm sorry, Amy.''

''No, it's all right. I know Roger could be hurt.''

''You'll know for sure soon. It's this awful waiting. I know. That day I waited for them to get Ollie down...believe me, Amy, I know about waiting. And then last year there was Jay's accident. But that wasn't quite so bad.''

''Why do they do it?'' asked Amy, leaning forward over the table.

''Climb, you mean?'' Hilkka shrugged heavy shoulders. ''I don't understand it myself, but I've stopped asking. It's something bigger than they are, a challenge. One of the few left. Man's mind is a dark, uncharted place, Amy. Women are much simpler.''

''Deborah climbs.''

''For thrills. All that money and nothing to do with it. Same reason she flies. Oh, Deborah will settle down someday, I suspect.'' Hilkka smiled, showing strong teeth. ''You know, Amy, climbers are all nuts. They have to be.''

Amy looked thoughtfully at Hilkka. ''Well, it's a nice sort of crazy. After all, they don't hurt anyone but themselves.''

''Saints preserve us!'' breathed Hilkka.

''Sorry.'' There she went again, putting her foot in her mouth.

But Hilkka didn't seem to mind. ''Del has made climbing into his life's work, Amy. He's doing what he loves best. They all are. You'd understand if you stuck around for a while,'' she said.

''Not much chance of that,'' mumbled Amy darkly. She lost herself in a jumble of thoughts for a time, vaguely hearing Hilkka humming a tune in the background. ''Jay's getting married?'' Amy finally asked curiously.

"Umm," said Hilkka. "Most likely. Sue-Ann is a nice girl. Oh, she's possessive, but Jay is a touch—how should I say it—slow to make any decisions."

"Not like Del."

"No. Del has always been the decisive one around here. Maybe it comes from being the eldest. Rob is too wild, although he's settling down some these days."

"Any marriage prospects for Rob?" asked Amy, but her thoughts were really on Del. Why hadn't he met anyone since Deborah? Or was that still on?

"No, deep down I think Rob's scared of women. But someday he might get caught."

"And Del," Amy ventured. "You'd think he and, well, Deborah would have tied the old knot by now."

"You'd think so." Hilkka shook her head.

"Maybe Del's got someone else. In Jackson or somewhere."

"Don't think so," said Hilkka. "He's been so busy around here what with his expansion plans and all that he doesn't take much time for himself. It's a shame."

Eventually Hilkka shooed her out of the kitchen and Amy wandered into the big living room, where everyone was gathering for dinner.

Jay was carefully winding a bright red rope over his arm, loop after smooth loop.

"Are you going along, Jay?" Amy asked hopefully.

"Yeah." The youngest Pardee looked down bashfully. "I decided I needed to."

"I'm so glad," said Amy. "I know you'll be a great asset."

"Maybe. I sure had a humdinger of a fight with Sue-Ann. But a woman's got to learn her place."

Well, thought Amy. She wouldn't begin a women's lib argument at the moment, but Jay might have to change his tune eventually.

Frank Pereira ambled in, having added an elegant tweed shooting jacket with a leather shoulder patch to his ensemble.

"Good evening, Miss Slavin. Have a nice day?" he asked pleasantly.

"Just great," she answered. "Going shooting, Mr. Pereira?"

He appeared bewildered. Then his swarthy face lightened. "Oh, you mean this," he gestured at his jacket. "Not really, it just seemed appropriate attire."

"'Appropriate,'" Amy muttered under her breath, meeting the mildness of Pereira's glance with a fierce one of her own. "Just make sure you shoot the rats."

"Rats? Oh, yes." Pereira smiled uncertainly.

Swede Björkman came in with a bottle in one ham-sized hand. "Yust a little cocktail," he said. "Vant one?"

"No, thanks," Amy declined, smiling.

"Do you good, a little skinny t'ing like you," he remarked.

Lonnie, as usual, said nothing but sat in a corner sharpening his Swiss Army knife, stroking it precisely, carefully, patiently, over and over on a whetstone. His pale eyes were like empty holes through which the sky showed. Silently he accepted a glass of whatever was in Swede's bottle.

Flint Smith arrived, his red hair still tousled from sleep, his shirttail hanging out. "I'm starved! Where's Ma?"

"Give her a break, Flint," said Rob. "She cooked for you all day."

Amy wondered if she was imagining it, but she thought there was a kind of tension pulsing in the room. A suppressed thrill of the unknown, a question that superseded all others: how would they meet the challenge? She felt a little of it in herself, along with the anxiety over Roger and her most immediate worry—how to convince Del to take her along.

Amy sat in an overstuffed armchair, leafing through a climbing magazine, listening to the conversation wafting around her.

"That ascent of the Grandes Jorasses in France."

"Froze his toes so bad one fell off like an ice cube."

"Hundred yards of nylon rope and two dozen pitons."

"Rotten snow up to my ears."

"Crampons wouldn't hold. I'll tell you . . ."

"I was so scared on that traverse . . ."

She didn't understand many of the terms, but one thing struck her: they were all facing something huge and frightening and risky and needed to talk about it with brave profanity and a kind of obsessive infatuation.

She got up restlessly, walked to a big window and stared once more out at the mountain. It looked as if it were already snowing there. Somewhere in those heights Roger was frightened, waiting, endlessly waiting. The wind, ominously warm and moisture laden, whipped around the stout corners of the lodge, moaning and rattling loose boards.

Amy was only too aware of the silence that fell in the room as they all watched her, of the glances that met meaningfully, then fell away.

They thought Roger was dead! She wanted to turn and rage at their blindness, but they couldn't know...so she bit her lip, blinked back tears and turned with a smile on her lips. "Hey, Swede, maybe I will have a swig of that poison."

"Sure t'ing, little lady." The big man grinned.

The glass of aquavit was upended, and the liquid was burning her throat like fire when the door banged open and Del entered, ushering in a gust of wind. Deborah followed, her shining honey-colored head reaching Del's ear.

"Howdy, folks," he said. "Things shapin' up?"

Amy took a breath, strangled on the sharp fumes and went into a spasm of coughing. Flint slapped her back and Swede deftly grabbed her glass before it sloshed over. "Easy there," he said. "That's strong stuff."

When she finally got the fiery liquid out of her throat, her eyes were tearing and one contact was sliding around, out of place.

"You all right, Amy?" Del asked, concerned.

She noticed immediately the scabbed-over cut on his lip. It looked sore. She wanted to cringe. "Yes, sure

I'm okay,'' she sputtered. She bet Deborah never choked on aquavit.

"Listen up, everybody," said Del then. ''We're going to try to start tomorrow morning early, so get a good night's rest. This'll be your last night in a warm bed. Deborah and I have been going over the supplies. We're hoping for a quick ascent, so the food we'll be carrying is minimal. We'll set up a base camp at the point where the jeep road gives out. Ollie will man the radio from there.''

The group applauded. A catcall was heard. Oliver Pardee rose and held up a restraining hand, grinning. Obviously he was pleased to be going along.

"The rest of us will be in close contact with base. Weather permitting, the helicopters can help us out.''

Del didn't remark on the worsening weather, but he may as well have. Several heads craned around to look out of the window. Isolated raindrops were spattering on the big plate-glass windows. A few eyebrows raised; a few pitying glances ricocheted off Amy's back. She could feel them.

Del certainly did have charisma. The feeling of tension as he spoke metamorphosed into group energy, a combined will to succeed. The job was no longer fearsome but routine. Amy looked at Del with new respect.

Hilkka came out of the kitchen. ''Half an hour,'' she called.

"Aw, Ma, I'm hungry!" complained Flint.

"Hold your horses, sonny," she admonished, then disappeared into her domain again.

The group split up into gatherings of two or three. Del's head was bent close to Deborah's over a list he'd pulled out of his shirt pocket. What were they talking about so intensely? Amy wished she were an expert on the subject of climbing. She'd love to go right over there and say something stunning, such as, "The exposure is too dangerous unless we use..." What was the word? "Carabiners." Or some such thing.

Feeling fidgety, she stood up and walked to the hearth. The fire needed another log, didn't it? She picked one up and tossed it on; a large ember popped out and landed on the floor, sizzling and filling the air with smoke. Grabbing a poker, she began trying to push it back onto the stone hearth, all the while crying, "Gosh. Oh, gosh!" Then Deborah strode over and deftly kicked it back onto the stone. "There," Deborah said, "it's all right."

"Thanks," murmured Amy.

Before dinner she had time to watch this group of people, strangers really, but individuals who would be vitally important in her life for a short while. Maybe they'd save her life on the climb—for she *was* going— or maybe she'd save theirs. Whatever the circumstances, they would all be exceedingly close—companions on a dangerous mission.

All except at least one of them. One of them—and she looked around the innocent scene once more—was a bad guy, and he—or she—was going to be a traitor to his country. A murderer, probably, and a saboteur.

Which one was it? Which one had smooth Mr. Frank Pereira paid off?

Was it Del himself, the obvious choice? As leader of the rescue, he was the one who could most easily sabotage the mission. And he needed money....

Or Lonnie Dougal, the dour silent Scot, thin, wiry, totally unreadable, his pale eyes seeing farther than those of a normal man. Seeing great riches after a job well done? Jay and Rob Pardee—seemingly uncomplicated. But Jay and Del had quarreled.... Good guys or bad guys? Flint Smith, wildly red haired, talkative. Trying—too hard?—to be everybody's friend. She'd heard him telling Ollie that his Annapurna climb was off due to lack of funds. Deborah Brewster. She was terribly rich. No monetary motive there, but could she be after a different kind of thrill? Swede Björkman, a loud sportsman with a boisterous facade. Was it a cover-up for some deep, hidden motive?

Then there was the only absent one, Glen Shepherd. Charming, handsome, sincere. Not quite reconciled to being a small-town cop, despite what he said. And some family problems a little extra money might solve? Certainly he'd been in a convenient position to talk to Shearing before anyone else.

It was a regular Agatha Christie gathering, thought Amy. Only the butler was missing. One of these people was going to try to kill her brother and make it look like an accident, all in order to bury a vital weakness in the nation's defense system.

Ollie Pardee interrupted her tortuous musings. "Now where did you say you were from?" he asked, sitting down across from Amy.

"Rochester, New York."

"That near New York City?" he asked.

Amy laughed. "About five light-years away—in upstate New York."

"So you climb there?" he wanted to know.

"Only stairs."

Ollie thought that was funny. He slapped his knee, then winced. "Durned leg," he complained.

Amy regarded him questioningly.

"Just that blasted fall I took a few years back. It gave me the rheumatiz. This kinda gray weather makes me feel crippled up like an old codger."

Amy remembered Glen's telling her something about Ollie Pardee's fall.

"Tried everything," Ollie was explaining earnestly. "Aspirin, all sorts of prescriptions. But it's the weather today. The barometer's low as a hog's belly." He shook his head in disgust. "Only cure I can find is that stuff of Swede's. It sure takes the edge off. But here I am talking about myself. You doing all right, Amy?" His strong featured face was drawn in lines of concern.

"I'm fine."

"It's the waiting, I know. We've had our fair share of rescues in these parts and it's the poor family that always suffers."

She nodded.

"Your folks know about the accident?"

"No. They're on vacation. Until I have definite word ... Well, there's nothing they can do to help." She shrugged.

"Sensible decision, although if I caught one of my kids doing it I'd have a fit. There was that rescue back in '52 where something like that happened...." And Oliver Pardee went on to tell Amy about every climbing accident he could recall, circling back around to his own. "Of course," he said, "it sure made my arthritis worse. Can't hardly climb at all these days."

"You miss it, then?"

"Sure do. But I can sit and watch the boys and teach in the summer. There's lots of work to be done around the ranch. I stay busy. I breed a few horses, you know." Off he went, telling Amy about his stud. It was sweet of him, but Amy was far too distraught to really listen.

"I went riding once," she replied vaguely. Finally he went off to get another glass of Swede's "cure," and Amy felt in her coat pocket for the tape recorder. It was a perfect time to enumerate her impressions; no one was paying the least bit of attention to her. She pulled her legs under her and curled up like a cat in a big overstuffed chair in a corner, trying to keep her voice low. If anyone noticed, so what? She was a reporter and had every right to talk into her machine. It was her way of taking notes.

She told her story, naming each suspect, getting her feelings off her chest. When she'd finished, she clicked the machine off and sat thinking for a minute. Then she pushed the On button. "I really don't think it's Ollie or Hilkka, because they aren't going along on the climb, but everybody else is a possibility. I'll just have to keep watching them very carefully. Someone, sooner or later, will slip up and give himself away. And I'll be there to see who it is. Roger's life depends on me.'' Her voice subsided; her finger automatically found the Off button, stilling the whirling tape.

She sat silent in her big chair for a long time, her tape machine lying in her lap, as she searched every face in the room, probing, scrutinizing each expression. Surely her instincts would tell her who was guilty.

All her instincts told her, however, that it wasn't, it couldn't be, Del. *Please don't let it be Del,* she prayed.

CHAPTER EIGHT

Day 2 Evening

FINALLY THE STRAIN of Amy's speculations proved too much for her. She couldn't bear to sit in that room for another second. She jumped up, noticing a few surprised faces glance in her direction, and went into the kitchen. Hilkka at least was completely trustworthy; she'd bank on that.

"Can I help?" Amy asked.

"Oh, sure. Thicken the gravy, will you? I'm still mashing the potatoes."

Thicken the gravy? "Sure," said Amy, looking at the bubbling concoction in a huge cauldron. "How?" she wanted to ask, but didn't dare. She took a big spoon and mixed diligently. *Thicken the gravy.* She turned the heat up under the pot. If it boiled down some, it'd thicken, wouldn't it?

"How can I convince Del to take me along on the climb?" she finally asked, shielding the pot with her body, *willing* the gravy to thicken.

"You can't," stated Hilkka flatly.

"I've got to," Amy said vehemently.

Hilkka turned around and put her hands on her hips. "Poor thing. I know how you feel. All this waiting. But you'd still have to wait there."

"Where?"

"At base camp. Well, you'd have to wait, but at least you'd be busier."

"Busier doing what?"

"Cooking. You can cook, can't you?"

"Cook?" squeaked Amy. "Of course, I'm a great cook. Strictly gourmet."

Hilkka laughed. "You won't need those recipes at base camp. Just heavy hot food and lots of it."

"Simple," said Amy, snapping her fingers.

"He might let you go if I ask," mused Hilkka, "but just to base camp as a cook."

There were ten people at the long trestle table, Hilkka at one end and Ollie at the other. It sort of reminded Amy of a dinner scene in the Great Hall of a medieval castle. Everyone talked and ate hugely. The scene lacked only the wolfhounds growling over bones under the table. Sally merely munched docilely.

"Del," called Hilkka, "you're going to take Amy along to base camp."

Amy's fork froze in midair and a piece of food fell off onto her plate, kerplunk. She braved a look at Del. He was scowling, glaring at her with narrowed eyes, his heavy brows meeting in a black line of anger. "I am not," he said.

"You'll do what I say," Hilkka said calmly. "She's going to be the cook."

"Ollie can cook," growled Del.

"His grub is lousy," said Rob. "You know that. Let her come."

"It'll be easier waiting up there," chimed in Deborah.

"What's this?" asked Del. "A convention to elect a cook?"

"Please," breathed Amy, her voice purposely small and thin. "I can't bear waiting here anymore."

"Can you cook?" challenged Del.

"Yes," Amy replied firmly.

Del shook his head doubtfully. "I don't like it. First you buy those clothes, now this. It's like you planned it all along."

Amy said nothing. This was one time to keep her big mouth shut.

"Then she can go," pressed Hilkka.

"All right," grumbled Del, "but only to base camp and *only* to cook."

Amy smiled tremulously, gratefully, at Del. She was going along! At least to base camp. Relief swamped her. She wouldn't even think about the cooking part now. No, she'd think about that tomorrow.

Suddenly Amy was starving. She began to chew vigorously and fork up big fluffy mouthfuls of mashed potatoes.

Then she heard Rob complaining from the other end of the table. "Ma, your gravy's too thin. What happened?"

She never said a word, but just kept on eating as if she hadn't even heard him.

She consumed a mountain of dessert, too—hot apple pie à la mode. The talk around the dinner table was still animated; only Lonnie Dougal was quiet. Hilkka had already told Amy that he was introverted, and she decided that he was just plain strange in addition.

She finished, sipped her coffee, then sat back in her seat for a minute. It was then that she noticed that Del was staring off into middle space somewhere. Even his dessert sat untouched in front of him. What was he thinking?

Amy couldn't keep from looking at him. The constant chatter around her receded. The room seemed somehow warmer and too close; she was vaguely aware of the wind blowing outside, of the dust clicking against the windowpanes.

Then Del seemed to shake himself out of his reverie. He leaned back in his chair, folded his arms across his chest and glanced around the table.

Their eyes met. Boldly Amy held his gaze. It was like a dare, a child's game full of unspoken rules and covert significances. If he looked away she lost.

But he didn't look away. His sky-blue eyes studied her from under thick, dark brows. His regard was like a touch—she felt it acutely, quiveringly. Conversation eddied around them like warm water in a bath, unimportant yet comfortable. The pungent aroma of coffee touched her nostrils; the table under her elbow felt reassuringly solid and smooth. The dog's tail thumped on the floor.

It was all only a stage setting, a background for their game. Her eyes dropped to his folded arms, to the dark crisp hair on his forearms and the sinewy cords of muscle. She tore her gaze back up to meet his. Yes, she thought, there's something there, something bonding them—a tension, a charged wire between the two of them. And Del felt it, too.

How had it happened? Chemistry? Or the intensity of the situation?

Del, her mind asked, *what's going on?*

"More coffee?" A voice crashed in her ear. "Amy? Would you like your coffee warmed up?"

She sucked in a breath, forced her gaze away from Del and looked up over her shoulder. It was Ollie, steaming coffeepot in hand.

"Sure . . . thanks," she managed.

After dinner she helped Hilkka with the dishes; she didn't dare show her face in the living room again, in case Del might change his mind about her cooking in camp. When they were finished, she hung her apron over the back of a chair, said good-night to Hilkka and left by the back door.

Hugging her arms around herself against the cold, she walked along the dark path. She'd left her jacket in the lodge, but never mind, she'd get it tomorrow. She wasn't going to remind Del again that she even existed, not tonight. She'd just show up in the morning, all ready to go.

A blast of frigid wind from the snowfields of the Tetons buffeted Amy; dust hit her face in tiny stinging particles and a ghostly bundle of tumbleweed rolled across the ground, startling her. She looked up at the mountains. Even in the dark she could tell that the sky was threatening and that the peaks were hidden in clouds. She shivered in the eerie wind of the approaching storm.

What was it like four thousand feet up in Pearl Pass? "Roger," she whispered, a gust tearing the word from her lips, "I know you can hear me, Roger. We're coming. Tomorrow...."

Then, in the darkness behind her, Amy heard the click of one stone against another. Her heart leaped into her throat. Another wild animal? She whirled around, losing her balance. Her arms flew out automatically and one of them struck something solid. She gasped.

"Amy?" came a familiar voice.

"Del?" she breathed.

"You want to hit me again?" he asked, his words filled with humor.

"I'm sorry... I didn't meant to. I was just trying to catch my balance," she said a little breathlessly. He hadn't changed his mind, had he?

"You forgot your coat," he said, his tone low and soft, "and it's starting to snow."

"Oh." Her voice sounded very small in the rush of wind.

He put the jacket over her shoulders tenderly.

"Thanks," she whispered.

"You're freezing," Del said. "You'd better go in."

"Yes." But neither of them moved. The silence stretched out between them for too long, like an extenuated thread of glass that might break at any moment. Amy looked up at Del's face, shadowed in the blackness, his features blots of dark, and her heart thumped in a heavy rhythm.

"Well," he began, "you should get some sleep. Tomorrow's the big day."

Was it possible that the sincere concern she detected in his voice was false? Did this man really want her out of the way and Roger dead? Her instincts told her no, but her mind whispered, *take care....*

A sudden gust bearing a load of wet snowflakes shuddered against Amy, pushing her toward Del. His hand went to the small of her back, steadying her. Something melted in Amy and she felt all the tension of the long, difficult day drain away as if a plug had been drawn. It felt so good to be close to this big substantial man. If only she could really trust him, open her heart to him.

But it didn't matter at the moment. Nothing mattered. They could have been the only two people in the world. She felt the land's wildness, its call to adventure. And she felt a breathless primitive urge to be enfolded in Del's arms.

Then the night wind heard her silent yearning, spattering them with snow and wrapping itself around their bodies, as if to press them closer. She was in his arms, arms stronger and gentler than she could have imagined. The wiry hair where his shirt was open tickled her cheek. Then he was tilting her face up and his lips were closing over hers.

She shut her eyes, lost in the wonder of the kiss, sagging into his embrace. His mouth moved over hers, tender, caressing. He smelled of wool and leather and a sweet man-smell that was his alone. Her hands pressed into his back, kneading the muscles that moved under his skin.

Then abruptly he pulled back. Amy drew in her breath sharply, as if thrust naked into the cold.

"I didn't meant to do that," Del mumbled, embarrassed.

"Neither did I," whispered Amy.

"Well." His big shadowed form shifted nervously. "I'd better go...." His hand inadvertently touched the cut on his lip.

"Yes," she said breathlessly.

"You going to be okay?" he asked.

She couldn't bear to let him walk away. Her craving to touch him again, to be close to him, overwhelmed her. "Well, maybe you could walk me to my cabin."

"The rats?" he asked dryly.

"Yes, the rats . . . or something," she fumbled.

"Sure," he said, taking her hand in the darkness.

Wordlessly she gave him her key, and just as silently he opened her cabin door. There was an unspoken promise between them, something expectant and provocative. Amy knew Del felt it, too. She was tense with anticipation, so excited her throat was tight and her pulse hammered in her ears.

He flicked the light on and turned toward her. It was then that Amy knew she wanted this man. She wanted his strength and warmth, the closeness of his powerful body, the feel of his skin against hers, the sound of his voice in her ear. It meant less than nothing to her, at that moment, that he might be dangerous to Roger—or to her. She only felt need flood her with sensation as she stood motionless, her heart pounding and aching with mindless desire.

"Del..."

He turned toward her slowly and their eyes met. The tiny room seemed filled to bursting with their longing to go to each other, to hold and touch and feel.

Amy felt perspiration dampening the back of her neck. All Del had to do was make a move in her direction.

"Come here." He unfolded his arms and stood waiting. Amy began to move toward him slowly, then faster, and he reached out and pulled her up against his chest.

For glorious moments Del held her that way, pressing her to his hard body, stroking her hair. Then he tipped her chin up with a hand and their eyes met.

"Kiss me," Amy breathed. "Just hold me, Del."

His mouth descended slowly, slowly, until it touched hers. Inevitably he parted her lips with his, and the kiss flared with passion. Amy felt her stomach roll over and her knees give way. Then, as if a flash flood had suddenly swept them both away, their hands roved over each other in a desperate search. Clothes gave way to impatient fingers; their lips met and locked once more.

They were naked finally, and Amy was gasping as her hands moved urgently over the long muscles of his back, down the hard spine and across his firm buttocks while Del crushed her to him and opened her mouth with his tongue.

He leaned over suddenly and swept her up into his arms as their lips lingered. When he placed her on the bed he moved next to her, and reality receded.

It seemed as if the room were on fire and her flesh were burning. Perspiration beaded her skin and made their bodies glide together like silk on silk.

"There's no turning back now," came Del's thick voice.

Amy rolled her head from side to side as Del's mouth covered her breast, his hands kneading her flesh, moving quickly up and down her limbs, her buttocks, leaving a trail of fire behind each touch.

She'd never wanted a man like this. She'd never unashamedly let herself go before, taking what she wanted, pressing a knee between his legs to feel his hardness, searching, desperately, every sinew, every hard muscle and bone and hair on his body.

She was wild for him.

"Oh, Del! Please!" Amy moaned.

He sucked on her nipple, still teasing, his hand moving to the soft inner flesh of her thigh.

Amy pressed herself against his hand, the blood in her veins pounding as he sought her inner flesh. Then he was on top of her, his eyes dark with passion, searching her face.

"Yes . . . oh, yes, Del!"

She felt his hardness pushing against her, seeking her warmth, her core, wanting the promise of pleasure.

He entered. Amy arched up in longing as her nails dug into the unyielding flesh of his back.

He filled her; he left her empty and burning. And then slowly, with sweet desperation, he filled her again and again until she clasped him to her and cried and tossed her head as the fire exploded within and without, as if molten lava rushed through her blood.

It's so beautiful, she sang inside. *Oh, Del!*

He shuddered above her finally, his hard male body rocking, releasing, loving. And then he held her to him and softly kissed a breast before his head rose to her lips.

"I wondered," he said much, much later, "what it would be like with you."

Amy smiled in contentment. "Don't tell me it was 'good.' I'll scratch your eyes out."

"How about 'the best'?"

She shook her head.

"The truth, then?" Del smiled down into her eyes. "You haven't got a shy bone in your body and no one has ever made me feel so damned great."

"Now that," she said, "is more like it."

CHAPTER NINE

Day 3 A.M.

AMY REACHED OVER in the darkness; the bed was empty next to her. So Del had left. She'd been so tired and slept so deeply she'd never heard him get up. Of course, maybe he hadn't actually been there. Maybe she'd imagined the entire dazzling, magnificent night.

Her body felt relaxed and drowsy, as if their lovemaking had drained away her tension and incessant worry.

But the anxiety, still lurking in the corners of her mind, was recalled in sudden terrible clarity.

Amy felt abrupt irrational anger toward Roger. He had to be a big shot, to expose Shearing all by himself. And she'd been the starstruck reporter who'd pictured herself making it to the top.

"You want this story, Barbara Walters?" Amy whispered. "Well, come and get it."

But she had met Del. Strong and handsome Del Pardee. A man who could make her blood boil and desire pound in her veins.

Del. Her mind, as she showered, began to churn. How could she have gotten so...so involved with him? Darn her foolhardiness! She had made love to a man whom she suspected of being a possible criminal! And she'd adored every minute of it—even had nice big whisker burns on her cheeks to prove it. She'd actually forgotten all about Shearing and Roger and national security!

What kind of woman was she?

But her emotions defended themselves with tenacity. Her judgment couldn't be that bad, could it? Sure, Del needed money to expand, and no doubt Shearing Aerospace had offered him a handsome donation. But there was nothing wrong with that. It was his business.

So what about Glen's assessment of him? The overzealous competition and the story of Del's relationship with an Indian girl? Fantasy or fact? As they had during her conversation with Glen, Amy's instincts still told her Del was not the type of man to have done such an awful thing. Yet the tale lurked in her mind uncomfortably.

Oh, forget it, Amy scolded herself. There was probably some perfectly simple explanation. Of course there was. Del had to be one of the good guys. He had to be, because Amy was falling head over heels in love with the big, growling bear.

She looked out the window as she dressed in her layers of new climbing clothes. The sky was just beginning to brighten, but she could see that there were two or three inches of snow on the ground.

Amy thought a minute: she had gotten the okay to go along as far as base camp, but how in the dickens was she going to persuade Del to take her on the climb?

She checked her parka pockets for her money and those little essentials: a change of underwear, a toothbrush, even a mirror and her tape recorder. Then she remembered. The gun. She dug under her sweater in the bottom drawer and stuck the thing deep into a pocket. She still quaked to feel its cold, impersonal metal and tried to imagine waving it under someone's nose. Who was that someone, that ally of Pereira's? Which one of the eight team members would go to desperate lengths to stop Roger? And what, wondered Amy, would happen if, by some miracle, the helicopter could fly that morning and execute a rescue? Had Frank Pereira covered that base, too?

When Amy locked her door and began hiking up to the lodge she could see two jeeps and a pickup truck already loaded to go.

Thank God! One more hour of waiting might kill her, not to mention her courageous brother.

Stopping suddenly on the dark path, Amy tried to feel Roger's nearness. Yes, he was there; he was still there. Cold and hungry, but still alive. Was he the only one?

Glen, who was carrying a backpack out to the vehicles, greeted her. "Good morning, Amy. I hear you're coming with us. Did you sleep all right?"

Amy swallowed hard. But, no, Glen couldn't possibly know about Del. Would he notice the whisker burns on her face? Glen looked different this morning in his climbing gear; Amy had only seen him in the sheriff department's garb. Today he was wearing a dark wool cap, much like hers, pulled down over his forehead, and a puffy dark green parka.

"I slept okay," she mumbled evasively, then looked up at the brightening sky. "It's clear out at least."

"Let's pray it stays this way."

Amy looked dubiously at the backpack. "Do I get one of those, too?"

"Yep, sleeping bag and all. Ever camped out before?"

She shivered. "Only in Girl Scouts."

"You'll like it. And the cooking won't be hard, you know. Canned goods and packages of dried fruits and nuts."

"And coffee?"

"That, too."

"Speaking of which," she said, "I really need a cup right now. Is there time?"

"Sure. Fifteen minutes, anyway."

She excused herself and walked toward the lodge, wondering what Glen would think if he knew she was carrying a gun along.

Her backpack was ready, sitting in a corner near the front door. Amy kneeled down and began putting her things in the zippered pockets of the pack. Her loaded tape machine and two blank cassettes nestled nicely into the sleeping bag. She promised herself to keep a close eye on her precious recording device. Someone would just love to know what was on the tiny, innocent-looking cassette inside.

The gun she kept in her pocket; it gave her a perverse feeling of security that she recognized as ridiculous, but there it was....

Then she went to eat while the vehicles were being loaded. Even Frank Pereira was up early that morning, helping the men pile gear in the jeeps. Trying to be one of the guys, Amy thought in derision.

She had coffee and three huge buckwheat pancakes.

"Eat up," urged Hilkka. "You never know when you'll be able to fix lunch."

"Fix lunch," Amy mused. "You know what? I will have another pancake, please."

She had a mouthful of syrup and buttered pancake when she looked up to see Del approaching the table. She'd told herself to stay cool when she saw him, but unexpectedly Amy's stomach gave a great leap. What a gorgeous guy he was!

He seemed distracted and terribly busy, however, and only gave her an absentminded greeting. Her heart plummeted like a rock.

How could he act like that after last night? Or had the whole thing merely been a ploy to throw her off guard? If only, Amy mused miserably, she could be sure of the man she'd given herself to with such abandon.

Great, she thought. Del no doubt saw her as one of those women who "did it" with every man she could. Terrific. She was right in there with the poor little Indian girl, though perhaps a bit smarter.

Amy set her chin firmly and looked at Del. The rat. Glen was probably perfectly correct in his opinion of him. Del, preoccupied, was standing at the far end of the table, eating a roll with one hand and holding a coffee mug with the other.

"Good morning," Amy said loudly.

He glanced over at her and nodded, indicating that his mouth was full. Then, after he'd swallowed, he managed, "Good morning. Are you all ready?"

"Oh, my, yes," Amy said. He was talking to her, anyway. "I've got everything I need."

"Umm...let's get a move on, then," said Del, turning away and heading toward the front door.

So he wasn't talking to her, after all. Oh, blast it! She'd ruined it. She'd managed to come off as one of those loose types, and Del had obviously no more use for her. Men! They only saw exactly what they wanted. And to think she'd really believed he liked her. The cad.

Abruptly her appetite fled, and she sat looking at her plateful of soggy pancakes and syrup. She felt slightly nauseated.

Hilkka went outside with Frank Pereira and the dog to see the party off. She hugged Amy to her, while Sally whined her distress at being left behind. "Take care, and remember, just open the cans and heat them. It's as easy as pie."

Amy nodded and tried to return her confident smile, all the while thinking, *pie, how do you make pie?*

She rode in one of the jeeps with Rob and Glen and Lonnie. Del, Deborah and Oliver drove the pickup and Jay, Flint and Swede followed.

How had Deborah ended up with Del? Jealousy, green and ugly, gnawed at Amy. Maybe it was Deborah's job to see that Roger never made it down....

It was a bumpy eight-mile ride to the end of the road. From there, Rob explained, they would go on foot.

"Pearl's at ten thousand feet," Rob said. "The road ends at seventy-five hundred."

"That's not so bad," said Amy optimistically. "I mean, a twenty-five-hundred-foot climb should be easy. Half a mile."

"Oh, ver-ry easy," piped up Lonnie from the back seat. "And what are you knowin' about it?" he asked rudely.

Amy turned around and faced him squarely, glaring. He didn't like her and she didn't particularly like him, either. Lonnie Dougal, she thought, could easily be the one.

Then Glen and Rob began a conversation about Jay—would Jay freeze up when the time came to cross that bad spot?

"Maybe Del should have gotten someone else," suggested Glen.

"Naw," said Rob from the driver's seat, "Jay'll do fine. You'll see."

I hope so, Amy thought apprehensively.

As they bounced along the rutted, muddy road, the chains on the tires clanging, Amy saw the valley begin to narrow. Snow covered the ground, growing noticeably deeper as they climbed. How deep was it up in Pearl Pass, she wondered anxiously. The mountains seemed to rise on either side endlessly. It would have been breathtakingly lovely land if they'd been out for a joy ride. As it was, Amy felt intimidated by the steep rock faces above them and the narrow, twisting gullies below.

By the time they reached the end of the road and the site for base camp, Amy's bones hurt from all the jostling. And they still had to set up the tents.

"Here's yours and Deborah's." Del tossed Amy a neatly folded blue nylon tent. "Set it up over there." He pointed.

Amy gulped. "Set it up?"

Deborah took charge.

And it was fortunate she did so. Flint dropped off Amy's backback, tossing it casually on the ground with Deborah's. Amy immediately opened it to check her tape recorder; that jerk could have busted it with his rough handling!

When she pressed the Eject button, her heart jumped. The partially used cassette was gone!

She sank down on the hard ground, huddled over her machine. Then her head rose and she looked around the clearing. Everyone was busy at work—busy and innocent-looking.

Who had taken it?

Anyone who'd loaded gear onto the jeeps that morning—or unloaded them just now. Then she remembered that Pereira had been helping that morning.

Quickly, nervously, she felt in her pocket. At least he didn't know about the gun.

She realized with a jolt that all of her suspicions were absolutely valid. She tried desperately to recall what she'd put on tape and how incriminating it was, but her mind was blank, unable to remember a thing.

The whole team was laying out the big tent, pounding in pegs. Had one of them taken the tape? They'd all seen her using it. And yet that made little sense. Why would a team member—good guy or bad guy— bother to steal a cassette he couldn't listen to up there in the woods?

The finger pointed at Pereira. She could envision him, at that very moment, sitting in his cabin, listening over and over to Amy's suspicions. Great. Now that he knew that she knew...

Yes, someone had already been sent along to silence Roger. But how would Pereira get word to his accomplice to silence Amy, as well?

She looked over at the climbers again. Which one was it?

Then Ollie waved at her and she had to go over, smile and admire the tent.

"It's huge," she said, feigning interest.

There was even a reinforced hole in the top of it for the stove pipe. "Stove?" asked Amy.

"So you can get warm and do the cooking," explained Oliver patiently. "Me, I'll man the radio from in there."

"It's just like home," she said dubiously.

Aside from Amy's new worry, she could feel immediately that the atmosphere was different up at base camp, where their goal was so much closer. It was obvious in the undercurrent of expectation. No one could seem to help their surreptitious glances upward, as if they could see the crash site.

Amy knew they were all wondering if anyone was alive up there, each team member pondering the possibility that he would risk his life to climb this mountain, only to find four frozen corpses.

"Pearl Pass is over there," said Flint Smith, pointing, and Amy followed his finger up to where mountains shouldered one another aside to climb far above them.

She felt very puny.

"Twenty-five hundred feet up," Flint was saying. "But it's not really a technical climb—except for the icefall."

"Technical climb?"

Flint grinned. "Sure, like making a climb on a vertical face of rock where you need equipment and know-how. Ropes and pitons and carabiners and so on. A difficult face."

"Or an icefall," prompted Amy.

"Yeah, that, too."

An icefall, thought Amy, picturing big blocks of ice careering out of the sky. Or a frozen Niagara Falls.

"You know what an icefall is?" asked Flint.

"Why, sure I do," replied Amy, shrugging. No reason to seem too ignorant. "Well, see you later." She wandered away from Flint innocently.

If the weather permitted—and the wisps of clouds and plumes of snow blowing off the surrounding peaks were not promising—they would start the ascent that very afternoon.

There was still much to be done at base camp, however, and, as if an invisible hand snapped its fingers, the crew members suddenly dispersed to their chores.

Del and Swede went off to stretch out the brightly colored climbing ropes—eleven millimeter nylon line—and check them one more time. Flint Smith and Oliver Pardee were setting up the radio in the big tent. Amy could hear them arguing about where a certain wire went.

Deborah was making neat piles of climbing paraphernalia and putting them in stuff sacks. Amy would have gone over to talk to her, but Deborah seemed so intent she was afraid to disturb her. Everyone was terribly busy. Amy wandered around aimlessly, then sat on a rock and watched.

Rob and Jay were having a rather loud disagreement about a sleeping spot in their tent. It must have been a serious matter, because eventually Rob stalked away angrily and started chopping at a fallen tree trunk with an ax. Swish, chunk. Amy hoped he was taking out all of his temper on the tree.

Glen was shaking out his sleeping bag and hanging it over a tent support. He whistled idly as he worked, his wool cap pushed back on his head rakishly, his green-and-black plaid shirt rolled up at the sleeves. He looked young and carefree and good-natured, a regular Paul Bunyan. When he'd completed his chore he went into the cook tent, and Amy could hear him ask Ollie if he should start a fire in the potbelly stove. Soon smoke was puffing from the tin pipe above the tent. The smell of it filled the clearing, reassuring and homey, taking Amy back many years to bonfires on the Lake Ontario beaches in high school, weenie roasts, Girl Scouts.

Beef stew, Amy decided, was the easiest thing to make for lunch. As she opened the cans and dumped the contents into a pot, she tried not to think about the stolen cassette or Roger, up there somewhere, helpless, hungry, maybe even injured. Rescues took days, especially in lousy weather; he must know they were coming.

It was shortly after noon when Oliver got the radio working properly and called the sheriff's department. A few minutes earlier, they had all heard the chop-chop of one of the helicopter's rotors somewhere above them, and as Amy stirred the stew, she held her breath nervously.

"Ollie Pardee here. We are at base. Over."

The radio crackled. "This is Nora, Ollie. We have just received news from the chopper. Do you read? Over."

"Loud and clear. Over."

"The pilot made a successful flyby and reports movement. Over."

Oliver sat straight up. Amy froze. "Someone is alive up there? Over," he asked quickly.

"That's an affirmative, base. Over."

"Can he get back in for another look? Over."

"Negative. Too windy. Over."

"The weather report, Nora, what is it?"

"Wind and snow showers. Sorry."

"We'll be in touch at five. Over and out." Oliver jumped from his seat and grabbed Amy, who was crying with joy.

"Did you hear that?" Oliver shouted, surprising Amy with his spryness.

The news was greeted with cheers and backslapping and a few swigs from Swede's bottle.

Glen put his arm around Amy's shoulder and squeezed her to him. "The wind and snow showers are just the tail end of last night's storm. We'll get up there."

"Today?"

"Del is thinking we'll hold till dawn. Now don't look so sad. He's right. We'll make better progress if we don't get snowed in. There's our safety, too, Amy, you understand."

"Yes, I do. And besides—" she tried her utmost to sound bright and cheerful "—we know Roger's alive now. We know for sure."

"That's my girl."

Glen was standing with Amy, facing the big tent, his arm still around her, when Del strode over. "I saved what I could of the stew," he said sarcastically.

"The stew!" Amy cried. "Oh, no!" She raced into the tent. It was ruined. She couldn't even salvage the top. "Darn it!" she kept saying, "Oh, darn it all!"

They ate it, anyway. There wasn't much choice, as the supplies were limited. No one said very much, but several of the team looked at her questioningly between mouthfuls. Lonnie Dougal actually threw down his tin plate in disgust and stomped out.

Deborah shrugged and smiled at Amy. "He's a jerk."

"I like it," said the red-haired Flint. "A little overcooked, but it's okay."

She'd served Del, but he didn't eat and finally walked outside. Amy noticed that Glen got up and followed him.

It was humiliating; everyone could hear their angry voices.

"You're a real sport, aren't you?" Glen was saying hotly.

"Go stick it in your ear, Shepherd," retorted Del. "This rescue is my responsibility."

"Big man," Glen taunted. "But there aren't any *National Geographic* cameras here to play to this time. Your true character is showing, Pardee. You're a bully."

"Mind your own business," snapped Del.

Amy felt her face burn. They were arguing because of her and everyone knew it. She'd scorched the stew and caused Glen and Del to fight and they all must despise her. And Del, the man she'd kissed and caressed and adored last night, despised her more than any of them.

Blindly, her contacts sliding on a film of tears, Amy pushed her way out of the tent.

Eventually, of course, she had to go back and help Ollie clean up. He gave her a crooked, apologetic smile out of the corner of his mouth and patiently continued scraping the bottom of the blackened stew pot.

"Never mind," he said. "They're both varmints."

Tremulously Amy smiled, putting Ollie firmly at the head of the good guys column.

All afternoon she had the opportunity to watch the climbers as they worked around base camp, looking like brightly colored bears in their big parkas and hats and insulated boots. She could hardly tell them apart; somehow they had taken on an otherwordly aura, that of men, and women destined for superhuman effort that put their very lives in jeopardy. And she knew, too, that she was going to be there beside them on that climb. How? How was she ever going to pull that one off?

Amy blew dinner, too. She managed to cook it all right, but dropped the entire pot of spaghetti on the plywood tent floor. Deborah helped her save the mess and somehow they all received nourishment.

"Eat it," said Amy defiantly to Lonnie as she dished it, splattering, onto his plate.

"It's great." Jay grinned at her.

"Goot!" Swede gobbled it down.

Del did eat. Of course, he hadn't been in the tent when the pot slipped out of her hands, and no one told him. Especially not Amy.

This time Glen helped her clean up and Amy was once again listing him in the good guys column. He had been a pal so far through this whole ordeal. He'd helped her to buy clothes, didn't object to her coming on the climb, lent a hand with the dishes, defended her to Del.

She was drying her hands and smiling at Glen, when she saw Del sitting on a tree stump nearby, watching her.

Her skin tingled, just as if it were his hands on her body and not his eyes. It was dreadfully awkward to be around him so much, to pretend disinterest when her heart cried out in anguish at her lover's coldness. It wasn't in Amy to love a man one night and turn her face away in indifference the next day. It hurt, all the way down to her toes.

And still his deep-set blue eyes pinioned her, making her fingers fumble and her heartbeat stumble.

She turned away deliberately. Glen was saying something; she had no idea what. She attempted to smile at him, but her face felt all crumpled. She tried to pay attention to Glen's voice.

"You should turn in early tonight," Glen was suggesting. "Even though it'll be just you and Ollie here in camp, there's plenty to do."

"I wish I could go on the climb. I could cook up there, too," she said suddenly.

He shook his head. "You're a wonder, Amy, a glutton for punishment."

"But who's going to cook?"

"Other than hot chocolate and instant coffee, we eat dried stuff pretty much."

"Oh..."

"Besides, you'll hear everything over the radio."

"Ollie's radio?" asked Amy, bewildered. "But I thought that was for calling the sheriff. What good would that do me?"

Glen smiled patiently. "Del carries a handset, a walkie-talkie unit. When he switches it on he can talk to Ollie here at base camp and let him know exactly what's going on. He'll probably set up certain times that he'll call."

"Oh, I see," said Amy, glancing once again at Del.

"You'll be okay down here, won't you?" Glen was asking. "I mean you aren't scared of the woods or anything?"

"Me?" Amy put a hand on her breast. "Certainly not. I love the woods and nature." What a terrific liar she was becoming. Love the woods?

She'd rather be locked in a closet.

But she needed to be there. And somehow she had to be up on that pass when they got to Roger. Somehow....

Amy looked at Glen appraisingly. She was terribly tempted to confide in him. He was the obvious one to tell, being a law officer. She shivered and hugged herself, uncertain.

In the tall treetops the wind moaned ceaselessly. She looked up into the encroaching dusk toward Pearl Pass and sought an answer. Roger's life, already in terrible peril, depended on her judgment.

"Are you cold?" asked Glen. "You're awfully quiet." He put an arm around her shoulder.

Amy glanced across the clearing to Del. He was speaking to Flint; their heads were lowered. Then, as if he sensed her gaze, he lifted his face and looked at her. His expression was cool and impersonal.

"It is getting cold," breathed Amy, nervously pushing her bangs off her forehead. "I think I'll call it a day."

CHAPTER TEN

Day 3 P.M.

DEL WAS ABOUT TO REACH his boiling point. How in the devil had Amy managed to get invited along? She was creating havoc where none was needed. Climbers had to be thoroughly prepared, mentally as well as physically. They were like gymnasts on a balance beam; they needed to concentrate one hundred percent on the task. She was too much, that one, with all her lies and secrets and furtive glances.

Well, Del thought heatedly, he didn't need the aggravation.

Finally she disengaged herself from Glen's arm and walked to her tent. He watched her crawl through the opening, her little bottom wiggling as the huge red parka got stuck in the entranceway. And some cook she was! Why, she'd lied through her teeth. And, it dawned on him, Hilkka had known it. What was the matter with his mother? Was she trying to throw him and Amy together, having finally given up on Deborah?

He moved away from Flint and stalked around the camp's perimeter, hands thrust into his parka pocket, shoulders hunched. What was he going to do with Amy? Of course, he couldn't have left well enough

alone. Oh, no, not Delwood Arthur Pardee. No, he
had to make love to the poor kid. Darn it, he reminded himself, she was not a kid! Not a bit, he
thought. Amy Slavin was every inch a woman, even if
she was a skinny one.

How had it happened? For an uncomfortable moment Del wondered who had seduced whom. Not that
it mattered. He should have known better. For Pete's
sake, she should have known better.

That woman was nothing but trouble.

Now here she was out in the middle of nowhere and
it was too late to remedy the situation. Or was it?

Del walked along, kicking at stones, his brows
drawn together in a fierce frown. He noticed Swede
upending his bottle, sharing a swig with Lonnie and
Flint and his brothers. Ollie was checking out the radio; Deborah was off on a short hike to limber up, and
Glen was drinking coffee. At least the camp was quiet,
now that Miss Slavin had retired. Del wished there
were nothing more on his mind than tomorrow's mission; he wished he could join the fellows and take a
swallow of burning aquavit and forget everything.

But he really had to take care of the problem that
he'd created. He kicked at a dead branch; satisfyingly
it broke with a sharp crack. A few heads turned toward him, then swung back to their own business.

Del decided he needed to hash it all over with
someone.

"Got a minute, Pop?"

Ollie looked up from the radio, on which he was
adjusting dials. "Sure, what's on your mind?"

"Amy Slavin."

"I should have guessed something of the sort. You've been in one whopping foul mood all afternoon, son. Is it serious?"

Del sat on a canvas stool, nodding. "I think it's painfully obvious that she's a real hindrance here. You can't be watching the radio all day and baby-sitting for her, too."

"Oh, she'll be all right, son."

"Not likely," interrupted Del. "Are you forgetting that yesterday she got lost in Jackson? Right in downtown Jackson, Wyoming? For Lord's sake, she'd be underfoot all day long. And besides, she can't cook. And how will you handle it if we find her brother...dead? She should be home at the ranch with Mom."

"Well," said Oliver, "I see your point."

"And you know perfectly well it was Mom who manipulated this whole mess."

Oliver rolled his eyes. "So what do you suggest?"

"Amy goes back to the ranch."

"But I can't possibly get her back there *and* man this contraption!" He looked at the heavy, military-style radio.

"I realize that," said Del. "So I'll just have to drive her back myself."

"Tonight?"

Del rubbed a big hand over his whiskers. "Looks like it."

"It's a long way. And on that road...at night. I don't like it."

"Neither do I. But when we start up that trail to-morrow morning, I'd feel a lot better if Amy were safe at the ranch."

"I don't know..." said Ollie doubtfully.

Del rose. "I've made up my mind. I'd rather lose a little sleep tonight than spend the next few days worried about her."

"Do what you have to. But if you change your mind, son, I'll be glad to keep an eye on her here. I kind of like that spunky little gal."

Purposefully Del walked toward Amy's tent. He'd just have to have it out with her and make her see some sense. She didn't belong here; she was a liability to them. Surely she'd see the logic of the situation.

He squatted down at her tent's door flap. He heard her talking. To whom? "And it took Ollie and me a half-hour to get the burned stew off the bottom of the pot," she was saying. "And everybody was giving me these pitying glances." It seemed to Del that there was a catch to her voice, and then he felt terrible that he was eavesdropping.

"Amy?"

Her voice stopped so abruptly that it sounded as if she gasped.

"Can I come in, Amy?"

"Yes," she replied anxiously.

He crawled in to find her sitting cross-legged on her sleeping bag with the small tape machine on her lap. Ah, that explained the talking. Her eyelashes were spiky, as if from tears, and her hair stood up in wild curls, as if she'd pulled her hat off with undue roughness.

"What do you want to tell me, how I screwed up dinner?" She started right in.

"No."

"What, then? Didn't I do the dishes right? Maybe one of the men could do them better!"

"That's not fair, Amy," he tried.

"Not fair?" Her expression was incredulous; her pink mouth turned down in anger. There was a smudge of dirt on one cheek that he wanted to wipe away.

Del took a deep breath. How had she changed the subject so drastically? "Look, Amy, you've really tried hard today. We all appreciate that."

"Ha!"

"But I think it's better if you go back to the ranch now."

"What?" She whirled on him, and for a minute he thought she'd begin to spit like a cat. "After I scrubbed my hands to the bone? And...and bought all these clothes? And put up with you...?"

"What do you mean...put up with me?"

"You know." Her mouth set firmly.

He looked at Amy in disbelief—was she referring to last night? Did she think...?

"You little..." he growled. "You're going back to my mother and maybe she can teach you some manners!"

"Manners! You're a chauvinist!" she cried. "Get out of this tent."

"You're coming with me, Amy," he warned.

"I am not," She deliberately turned her back on him so that all he could see was a huge puffy red parka.

Unthinking, furious, Del grabbed the neck of her parka and began to pull her out of the tent. She twisted and gasped and tried to reach him with one hand, but he was too quick for her. "You're coming with me right now!" he said as he backed through the tent opening, pulling her after him. By the time she was in the open, she was sputtering and flailing her arms and kicking.

"Let me go!" she cried.

"Don't make a scene, Amy. Let's go."

"No!"

So he picked her up and carried her, shrieking impolite names at him, to a jeep, where he plunked her in the passenger side and shut the door on her. He was aware, vaguely, of the others staring in stupefaction at him, of Glen Shepherd's rising and saying, "Hey!" to no one in particular. Well, it couldn't be helped. He'd explain later—when he returned without Amy.

He hopped in, started the vehicle up and pulled away from the camp. The jeep's tires spit up loose stones and slush.

"I could have you arrested for assault!" she threatened.

"Try it." He kept his eyes on the winding, rutted track, driving too fast; the jeep bounced the two of them around like peas in a pod.

"Del, please." She tried to calm herself. "I'm sorry. Take me back."

But he refused to acknowledge her words. He was boiling inside. She'd insulted him badly. As if he would use a woman like that!

Suddenly he caught a flurry of motion out of the corner of his eye and heard the door click open. He turned to see what she was doing and was almost too late to catch her throwing herself out of the door. He slammed on the brakes, grabbed at the back of her parka and hauled her back in.

"Hell's bells, Amy!" he gasped, his heart pounding drumbeats in his chest. "You could've got yourself killed!"

"So what?" she cried. "You want me out of the way, anyway!"

The sudden fright had chased Del's temper away. "I want you safe at the ranch."

"I have to go on the climb," she whispered fervently.

"Amy..."

"Oh, blast it, my contacts...." She was fumbling at her eyes, putting the tiny almost invisible lenses in a case in her pocket while he could see her fighting for control.

Del wanted to touch her, to comfort her, but she'd already made her feelings about him quite clear. His big hands opened and closed futilely around the steering wheel of the jeep.

"Amy, be practical. I can't take you along. You'd be in danger every second."

"Roger already is," she pointed out.

"Two wrongs don't make a right."

"I have to go! Don't you understand? Please." Her voice was shrill, desperate. "I have to go!"

Del studied her pale, delicate face for a time. It was growing dark outside and the rustle of branches and snow-covered boughs could be heard all around them, an eerie counterpoint to their own silence.

"Tell me why you have to go, Amy," he finally said, trying his best to sound reasonable.

Tight-lipped, anguished, Amy only shook her head.

"For Pete's sake, trust me for once," he said. Carefully he reached over and touched her shoulder. She jumped like a startled doe but didn't say a word.

"Amy, come on. If you'd just calm down and explain."

"I can't," she said, her voice so low that he could barely hear her. Eventually she took a deep quavering breath. "I guess I'm just, well, overwrought. Don't pay any attention to me. This is all sort of difficult to take." She fixed him with her big, round, smoky blue eyes beseechingly.

"Amy, what is this national security business? You can tell me that much at least."

She gave a little hiccuping laugh. "It's all...just a...misunderstanding."

He sighed. So she was going to be difficult. If only, Del thought, there was a way to wring the story out of her. He'd tried patience; he'd tried everything, for Lord's sake, but truth serum! Why couldn't he gain her trust? Couldn't she bend a little and lean on him for a moment?

It was futile. She wasn't talking. And the last thing he wanted to see was Amy sitting there, lost, broken up. "Are you going to be all right?" he asked carefully.

She nodded.

"Okay, then, I'll take you back to the ranch now and Hilkka will—"

"Del, I'm not going back to the ranch," she said tiredly.

He rolled his eyes and took a deep breath, but before he could reply, she said, "Don't try to make me. Please."

"Aw, Amy, I can't—" But she touched his hand and fixed her eyes nearsightedly on him.

"Don't ask me to do this . . ." he tried once more.

"Del, please," she whispered.

He groaned and ran a hand through his hair, feeling her touch like a branding iron.

Dark silence surrounded them. There was no light in the jeep, but Del could make out the pale oval of her face and feel the soft touch of her hand on his. He wanted, suddenly, to feel her skin again, to savor the warm, springlike scent of her. Last night . . . Images flashed through his mind: Amy's narrow hips, flat belly, small, strong hands touching him. Her mouth demanding, arousing.

He reached a hand out and stroked her satiny cheek. "Amy," he said, sighing. And she was pressed against him, her arms twining around his neck.

"I thought you hated me," she sobbed breathlessly into his ear.

"Hate you? I couldn't..." His lips silenced her, his tongue exploring, probing. Her hands slid under his parka, pulled at the tails of his wool shirt until they were loose, touched his bare skin, stroking, kneading.

He leaned back, pulling her with him. Her parka was in the way, puffing all around her like a parachute. "Unzip it," he breathed. And she did.

She wore no bra. Her small firm breasts jutted up into his chest. He tried to touch them, but the front seat of the jeep was too cramped.

"Damn!" he muttered.

"What is it?" she murmured against his lips.

"I haven't tried to do this since high school," he admitted.

"You're too big," she said gravely.

"Yeah."

"What are we going to do?" She was half laughing, clinging to him with need.

"Come on." He took her hand and led her out of the jeep. Under a huge spruce was a dry spot and a soft cushion of needles. He took his parka off and spread it on the ground.

Amy looked dubious. "Adam and Eve?"

Del grunted. "Tarzan and Jane."

She sat down on his parka and held her arms out to him. "Just hold me, Tarzan." She tried to sound playful.

She didn't seem to notice the sharpness of the night air or the hard ground. He pressed her back and bent over her, touching her neck with his lips. She shivered.

"Cold?"

"No," she breathed. "Not a bit cold."

He kissed the hollow in her throat, inhaling her fragrance, feeling her pulse jump under his lips. Then he nibbled at her neck, all the way up to her ear. Her breath came in short panting gasps. He helped her out of the red parka, unbuttoned her shirt and leaned over to circle each nipple with his tongue.

"Oh, hurry," she cried.

Getting out of their pants and long underwear was not easy. Amy kept shivering and breathing, "It's all right, Del," and he rubbed her limbs with his hands until she gasped and sighed and clutched at him wildly in the cold, dark night.

Finally they lay touching along their whole lengths, warming each other. Amy ran a hand through the thick hair of his chest. "My socks are still on," she whispered, her tongue playing with his ear.

"I don't mind if you don't."

His big hands could span her waist; he pulled her to him, caressing the tight swell of her buttocks. "Amy," he murmured, "you're so little. I'm always afraid I'll hurt you."

"Never," she breathed.

He rose over her, ready, and plunged deep within her. She met him with thrusts of her own, her hands digging into his broad back. She felt like cool shimmering velvet. He lost himself in her, moving in a wild rhythm that drove away all sensations other than those of bodies fused in passion.

In the cold darkness, he bent his head and took a nipple in his mouth, sucking. She cried out and arched up, shuddering, grasping him, pulsing with her reaction. Del kept moving inside her, feeling her spasms, reveling in her joy. He tasted her once more, savoring her flesh, her nipples, the beauty of her cool, woman's skin. Then he felt himself reaching his own climax and he moved within her more urgently. Amy responded to his needs, arching up again to meet his thrusts, holding him to her, running her fingers along his spine and buttocks. Finally his veins seemed to explode, as if sparks flew from every pore in his flesh, and he gripped her to him tightly and felt the soft fusion of his body locked with hers—man to woman, woman to man.

Time passed. There was only the sighing of the wind in the spruce trees and Amy's gentle breathing in his ear. "Are you cold?" she finally asked.

"Well . . . are you?"

"No, I have a very woolly cover."

He sat up reluctantly and began pulling on all the layers of clothes he had shed with such effort, while Amy did the same.

"We seem to be making this a habit." Her voice came from the darkness, disembodied.

"Amy . . ."

"Don't say a word." She got up on her knees and leaned against his back, putting her head on his shoulder. "You'll ruin it."

"But I think we have to talk. It's like we're going in opposite directions."

"I know." She kissed the crisp hair at his neckline. "Del? Why did you decide I had to go back to the ranch so suddenly?"

"I can't believe you have to ask."

Amy sighed. "I do have to. Why, Del?"

"The reason is only too obvious. I'd be worried if I thought you were wandering around base camp with just Pop there. It's a big country. It's easy to walk out of camp only a few yards and get turned around. People do it all the time. And the weather is likely to turn nasty. You're not used to it. And I'm responsible for you. I can't lead an expedition with half my mind back at base camp, worrying about you."

She was very quiet for a time. "But I can handle it, Del. I know I can. And I'm nobody's responsibility but my own."

"Amy, I don't . . ."

"You're treating me like a child."

"You're pushing me again, Amy. Look . . ."

"Del," she said firmly, "I am a grown woman. I'm not a fool. And I do keep my word. Don't punish me because I got turned around in Jackson. I was so preoccupied . . ."

They both fell silent. Amy's head was still cradled against his back. Boy, could she turn a man's thoughts tidily.

He pulled on his boots. "I'll take you back now, Amy."

"Back where?" she asked a little too innocently.

Del began to say something, hesitated, then gave up. "Back to base camp, okay?"

"Okay, Del. And...thank you."

The camp was pitch-black and as quiet as a graveyard. Only a few red embers remained in the center of a pile of ashes. Del led Amy to the tent she shared with Deborah. She stood on tiptoes and kissed him.

"You are an odd one, Amy." Del held her a moment longer.

"It must seem...strange to you. I know...it's just..."

"You make love to me," he whispered, "but you don't really trust me."

Amy was silent for a moment. "I don't trust anybody," she murmured miserably, looking as if all the troubles of the world were on her narrow shoulders. Then she reached up and touched his face with her soft hand and disappeared into her tent.

OLLIE POKED HIS HEAD into Del's tent at 5:00 A.M. "Weather forecast says it'll be clear this morning, but there's wind and snow expected by nightfall." His voice was uninflected, merely reporting, leaving the decision to Del.

"Damn," Del murmured sleepily from his down bag. "But we'll have all day. What d'you think, Pop? Is it a go?"

"It's your move, Del."

He sat up, scrubbing his curly hair with both hands. "It's a go, then."

The word seemed to spread on the air waves. Everyone rose and began pulling down tents and packing up even before it was light out. Ollie started the fire, but Amy had already begun cracking eggs into a bowl by the time Del stuck his tousled head into the main tent.

She never even glanced up at him but went about fixing breakfast, trying to look efficient.

Del wanted desperately to get a moment alone with her. He was not going to see her for days. No one wanted to go on a dangerous climb with unanswered questions left behind. But what more could he say? They'd been over and over the same ground and Amy wouldn't budge. Didn't she realize that as a leader he had to know every facet of the climb? He needed to reach into each one of his climbers' heads and fully comprehend why they were putting one foot in front of the other. For instance, Del would have to watch Jay like a hawk, especially crossing that icefall. Del had to know that his brother wouldn't freeze up, or if Jay did, Del knew he should be able to anticipate it.

The leader of the climb needed to be a manager, a general, sometimes a psychiatrist. Amy had grasped that, all right, but there was something more complex, something mystifying directing her.

For some unknown reason Amy felt she had to go along on the climb. When Del considered it, her reason became obvious: she thought her brother was in some kind of danger.

From what?

He shook his head angrily, confused, frustrated. Then there was that national security business. Were the two mysteries linked somehow?

He became cognizant that he was glaring at her angrily, but she only looked up and smiled good morning to him no differently than she had to any of the others. Except maybe Glen. Was her greeting really more friendly to Shepherd? It was disappointing, but maybe she was trying to spare him embarrassment in front of everyone. Yet last night she'd been so...loving....

He couldn't get her alone while she cooked breakfast because she was trying so hard. The scrambled eggs were passable, he had to admit. The coffee had grounds in it and the bacon was lukewarm, but she was improving. He looked at the furrow clouding her brow and hadn't the nerve to approach her. After breakfast maybe....

"Amy," he said finally, grabbing her arm as she hustled by him with a coffeepot in her hand.

"Just a minute, Del. This is hot." And she was gone.

She was avoiding him. Okay, but he wasn't giving up. A few minutes later, when the team members were giving their packs one final check, Del again tried to catch Amy as she headed across the clearing.

"Hold up," he called.

She turned for a moment. "Won't it wait? I'm off to the ladies' room." She nodded toward a tall stand of trees on one side of camp.

"The ladies' room," said Del under his breath as he watched her disappear. He marched back into camp with his hands shoved deep in his pockets.

The pale morning light filtered through the spruce trees. Breaths puffed in the cold air. Del knew they were all starting to look a little scruffy—especially him, with his heavy beard. No way to shave from now on. He glanced at Jay, who was carefully shaping his sleeping bag into a tiny roll. A moment of doubt seized Del: what if Jay did freeze up there? What if Del, in his attempt to help his brother get over the fear, had made a terrible error in judgment?

But, no, Del thought, he couldn't be that far off base where Jay was concerned. They'd all had the jitters. Jay would make it.

They were ready. The food was packed. All the small tents but two, for Amy and Oliver, packed. Dried food, rope, crampons, pitons, carabiners, pulleys, first aid supplies, sleeping bags.

The eight climbers drew a collective breath, their last free and easy one, and hoisted the heavy packs onto their shoulders. There was a vaguely ominous silence over the camp, as if in salutation to them, a rarified atmosphere, clearer and brighter than ordinary folk breathed.

"See you, Pop. We'll keep in touch at the prearranged times. You know our route." Del shook his father's hand.

"Take care, son. All of you."

"Sure will."

Del caught Amy's glance on him as he turned to lead the way up the faint trail. Her eyes were huge, all iris, and he imagined that they accused him of something. Of what? He waved to her briefly and she returned his goodbye with a mere lift of her hand.

Del turned and began the trek upward, falling into the familiar rhythm, hearing the desultory conversations of his party behind him.

But Del didn't feel like talking. Even after they'd covered several miles and the going got much rougher, he could still feel Amy's eyes burning into his back.

CHAPTER ELEVEN

Day 4 A.M.

AMY WONDERED if Del had any notion of what she was about to pull. He'd been ready to burst that morning with questions; of course, he assumed that they would not see each other until after the rescue.

How wrong he was!

Nevertheless, as she plotted in her mind, guilt hovered over her like bats' wings. She'd deceived him, and when he found out, he would never believe that her lovemaking had been genuine.

There was still another side to the coin, however. Perhaps Del was the real expert at deception. Even so, Amy couldn't help herself from following his every move with her eyes, suffering doubt and confusion every time her breath caught at the mere sight of him.

But Roger was up there and somebody knew she was suspicious. She couldn't afford the time to pine over Del or wallow in doubt. Amy had to act. And quickly.

For Ollie's benefit, she pretended to fuss around the mess tent, but actually she was cramming candy bars and trail mix into her pockets. Then she crawled into her tent, rolled up her sleeping bag around the tape recorder once more and stuffed it into her frame pack. The gun was still safe in her pocket.

Sooner or later, she was convinced, she would need the weapon. No one ever had to know there weren't any bullets in it. Why, if someone were to wave a gun under her nose, she wouldn't dream of arguing with him over whether it was loaded or not.

Oliver made it too easy for her. He retired to the men's room—the other side of a stand of trees. "I might be a while," he said unself-consciously.

So she wrote him a note: "Don't worry, I know what I'm doing. It's not your fault. Amy." She didn't want him to be upset over her departure, or to think that she'd gotten lost or something.

She shouldered the backpack. It felt light as a feather, its weight distributed beautifully by the light aluminum frame. Marvelous, Amy thought. She could walk all day carrying it.

She decided to go slowly, conserving her strength, getting accustomed to the altitude. And besides, she didn't want to come upon Del's crew by mistake. She'd heard them talk about the hiking trail that went directly up to Pearl Pass and how it really wasn't very hard until near the top. By then she would have caught up to them and it would be too late—they'd have to take her along.

The climbing party's plan was to make as much time as possible while the weather held. If they could reach the plane wreck today, they would, but Del had thought it more likely that they would bivouac before they got to the icefall.

What was an icefall, Amy wondered as she tramped upward. How did you cross one? She supposed she'd find out.

It was easy at first, ambling along between snow-covered trees and boulders and little streams running under a thin skin of the previous night's ice. She even got so warm she had to unzip her parka. The trail was unmistakable, what with eight pairs of heavy hiking boots having stomped along it ahead of her, so Amy's worry of getting lost faded. All she had to do was keep walking—up—until she came upon their camp—or the wreck. If she reached the icefall and didn't know how to get across . . . But she'd think about that when and if she got there alone.

She hummed to herself tunes, such as "I've Been Working on the Railroad" and the theme from *Bridge on the River Kwai*, looked around at the wild, lonely, rugged scenery that was so very different from any place she'd ever been. The Tetons were rough mountains and their great, ancient backbone of rock showed through a thin covering of soil. The trees were almost all aspen or spruce, but Amy noticed that higher up the aspen gave way to the hardier evergreen.

It was a spare, dry country, despite the snow. There was no wild profusion of tangled underbrush between the trees; except for some big bushes with berries still on them, the ground was practically clear.

She saw a bird and a ground squirrel. And it was a squirrel—even with her eyes she could see that. Nothing to this climbing business, she told herself. And the wonderful hiking boots! Big and clumsy they might be, but they marched along over rocks and mud and snow as if they were robot feet. Fantastic things.

Amy adjusted the shoulder straps of her pack. It was beginning to feel heavier. She would have loved to talk into her tape recorder, describing the scenery and going over the theft of her cassette, but it would be too much trouble to dig it out. Still, her mind toyed with possibilities. Assuming Pereira could locate a machine to play a tape on, what would he do once he listened to her recording? He would have no way of contacting his support person during the rescue, but what about afterward? Surely Pereira was no fool. Shearing would not have sent a dolt to handle a job as sensitive and difficult as this. What fate was Pereira planning for her?

Her musings were interrupted by a sudden crackling of undergrowth. Amy's head jerked around. What was that? She peered nervously, nearsightedly, into the brush. Two large dark eyes stared back at her. She gasped and stopped dead. There was a long brown head, a roman nose and two huge, flat, branched antlers. The creature was bigger than a horse!

Her mind whirled feverishly, searching the storehouse of pictures in her head until it came to the right one. A moose!

The animal snorted, its big velvety hanging lip quivering. Then it shook its head warningly, its antlers scraping against bare branches.

"Nice moosey," whispered Amy, holding her hand out in a submissive gesture. She backed away, never taking her eye off the brute. A tree stopped her progress. Slowly she backed around it, getting the trunk between her and the moose. Then her nerve broke and she ran, crashing through the bushes, breathing in tearing gulps, her heart pounding wildly, the pack thumping on her back like a ton of bricks.

Eventually she stopped, puffing like a steam engine. The moose was far behind. She was safe. Taking a giant, cleansing breath, Amy went on, looking around uneasily.

It wasn't long after that she realized her legs were beginning to ache with weariness. Instead of resting, she ate a chocolate bar. In five minutes she was thirsty. Oh, my. She'd forgotten water! Never mind. She scooped up some snow and melted it in her mouth. A real woodswoman, resourceful, tough, fearless—that's what she was.

She wondered how far ahead the climbers were. It seemed as if she'd been trudging uphill for hours, but her watch read only eleven o'clock. Strange how her pack seemed to gain weight with every step.

She took the pack off at noon and plunked herself down on a log, munching trail mix and sucking on some snow. She rubbed her sore shoulders, wondered if Deborah ever complained and was thankful that the weather still held.

At around two, Amy felt the cool wet kiss of the first snowflake. She threw her head up and felt faint panic squeeze her heart. The flakes drifted down onto her upturned face, melting, tickling, chilling her insides.

They'd all agreed that snow and wind would make the mission more dangerous and might even hold them up—for days, if the storm was a bad one.

"Why, I remember being holed up on the Flatirons for three days," Flint had said yesterday. "We ran out of food and water. And it was *cold*."

That couldn't happen! They had to get to Roger! Amy picked up her pace, as if she could make the whole expedition get there faster. She pulled her wool cap out of her pocket and put it on, stuffing her hair up under it. Hadn't someone once told her that you lose seventy percent of your body heat through your head?

The snow fell more heavily, building up on her shoulders, on branches and rocks and logs. The path became a fainter line of footsteps in front of her. There was a wide open meadow she had to cross; it was completely, uniformly white. Where did the path disappear into the trees again?

She had to search for the trail, but finally located it.

It was scary. The snow muffled everything: her footsteps, the cheery birdcalls she'd heard that morning, the sound of water trickling downhill. Everything was all covered in marshmallow, deadened. The wind picked up, swirling around her, blowing snow into her face, tugging at her pack, but she just lowered her head and trudged on. How much worse it must be up higher where Roger was!

She came out of the trees eventually, into a broad, tilted open space where only a few scrubby wind-bent bushes stuck up from the snow. Where was the path, she cried to herself in panic. Then she saw a few faint depressions leading across the frozen expanse.

Thank the Lord, they were still in front of her!

The snow seemed to slither beneath her feet, to drag at every step, to actively hold her back. The pack weighed a ton, her shoulders ached, her feet were blistered; she was too exhausted to stop and eat. She took one step after the other, checked the depressions in the snow, took another step, remembered to breathe deeply. Her face was getting raw and cold from the wind.

Surely she'd come across their camp any minute now. They must have stopped. It was nearly five and becoming noticeably dimmer out. The sudden thought of being out—alone—in this storm all night made her shudder. She'd die!

No, she wouldn't! Roger hadn't, and he had no down parka or sleeping bag guaranteed to twenty below zero. She'd dig a snow cave and live in it. She remembered reading about some mountain man who had done that.

Don't panic, she told herself. *Stay calm.* She'd find them. Very soon now. And there would be hot coffee and food and a tent. Del would be absolutely, ferociously furious. Glen would be concerned, of course, but he'd understand. And Del would not be able to spare anyone to accompany her down, nor would he trust her to make her way alone. So—they'd be stuck with her.

And Amy would be there when they reached Roger, no matter what.

Suddenly she realized that the trail in front of her was completely obliterated. She could hardly see in the snow and growing darkness, anyway. She blinked her eyes, looking desperately for those faint, familiar indentations.

Nothing.

She turned slowly in a circle, peering out around her. Even her own footsteps were rapidly disappearing, blending into the vast, silent ghostly expanse around her.

Alarm rose in Amy's breast. Should she go back? But she could hardly tell where *back* was anymore. She felt so dreadfully alone, a minuscule figure in the middle of a snowstorm, lost, fighting panic.

If only her sense of direction were better! She knew she had to keep going up, but it was flat where she was. Which way was up?

She drew in a deep breath, flexed her shoulders and began trudging once more, making a big circle of the level expanse to see where the mountainside began to rise again. The snow blinded her, gusting into her face on one side of her circle, pushing at her back like a rude hand on the other. Images crowded her mind unbidden: bears, cougars, abominable snowmen. A frozen body lying on its back, the snow falling on open, sightless eyes.

No! It couldn't happen to her!

She bent her head into the wind, struggling. In a few minutes she'd just lie down and rest. But she couldn't. She knew, from some childhood tale, that she had to keep going . . . going. . . .

Was the ground rising under her feet again? She thought so. And there were two huge boulders she'd never seen before. In the shelter of one were some footprints. She was on the right track!

"Del!" she heard herself sobbing once, but the wind whipped the words away and the snow muffled the noise. She called out a few more times, but the sound of her voice was so pathetically futile in the storm and the vastness of the mountain that she gave up.

"This is stupid," she mumbled to herself once, her lips half-frozen. "Dead reporters don't file their stories on time, Slavin."

She looked around once in a while, but it was practically dark. And cold. She began to shiver uncontrollably.

There was a light ahead, a part of her mind registered. Another part chided her foolishness. A light out there in the middle of nowhere? Ridiculous!

She stopped short and stared fiercely ahead. There *was* a light!

It was the camp! She was saved! Amy tried to run but could only lumber like a seasick bear. Yes, a light! A fire! And bright red and blue and orange tents! She burst, gasping, panting, half-frozen, into the circle of firelight.

"Hello!" she yelled. "I'm here!"

A head popped out of one of the tents. "Amy?"

Amy dropped in her tracks, rolling onto her back, not even able to shrug off her pack. She felt like an upside-down turtle. "Deborah, am I glad to see you!"

"Amy?" Deborah's long lean body emerged from the tent like a butterfly from a cocoon.

"Where is everybody?" Amy asked, lying on her back, the snow falling in her face while she looked up at Deborah.

"Out looking for you!" said Deborah, stunned, incredulous.

"Me? But how on earth did they know..."

"Del's hand radio, Amy. When he checked in this afternoon, Ollie told him about your note."

Amy hit her forehead with the palm of her hand. Boy, was she dumb! She'd forgotten the radio. "Is he raving mad, Deborah?" she ventured.

"Sure. What'd you expect?"

Slowly, stiffly, Amy sat up and let the pack slide off her shoulders. "I'm in for it, aren't I?"

"Sure are," said Deborah curtly.

Amy put her face in her hands. "I almost died out there," she mumbled.

"That's why they're out looking for you," said Deborah. "It was pretty dumb of you to follow us."

She couldn't bear to have Deborah, of all people, looking at her as if she were some kind of idiotic *worm*. She had reasons for what she'd done. It was just that she couldn't tell anyone her reasons.

"Let me call base camp, Amy. Ollie's worried sick."

While Deborah fiddled with Del's radio, Amy managed to get herself a cup of coffee heated up on the camp stove. She put three teaspoons of sugar in it, sat back and sipped. Oh, my, but that was good!

Now if there was something to put in her growling stomach, she'd be fortified to face Dreadful Del.

"Is there anything to eat?" she asked Deborah. "I'm starved."

"Sure, I'll heat you up some packaged soup."

"Anything..." whispered Amy fervently.

She sat on the floor of Deborah's tent, cross-legged, her fantastic automated hiking boots in a corner, a sleeping bag over her wet shoulders, gobbling soup from a tin cup. Deborah was outside adding wood to the sizzling fire, a necessary signal for the search party. Amy thought quickly. The men would return at any moment. She desperately needed an ally. Deborah was there, on hand. And Deborah would make a strong confidante—if, of course, Miss Brewster was a good guy. Amy's instincts told her she was trustworthy, but there remained that small risk.

Amy thought furiously; her brain was tired and troubled. Should she take a chance on Deborah?

Think, Amy! Decide!

Okay, she told herself, *take a shot at it.* She crossed her fingers and whispered up a prayer and wondered, how would Barbara Walters handle it?

Deborah ducked back in the tent, the snowflakes on her hair and shoulders turning instantly into tiny beads of water.

"I sure hope they get back soon. Del said they'd return by seven no matter what," remarked Deborah, frowning.

She'd better hurry, then. There was a lot of explaining to do.

"Deborah," Amy began, pushing her bangs back nervously, "you aren't going to believe me at first, but will you promise to hear me out?"

"What on earth . . . ?"

"My brother's life is in danger."

"Of course it is," said Deborah in surprise.

Amy put up a silencing hand. "One of the team members is going to try to kill him. . . ."

CHAPTER TWELVE

Day 4 P.M.

WITH EACH DIFFICULT STEP undefined images flashed through Del's mind: Amy out there in the cold white wilderness, stumbling through the snow, lost, frozen, hungry, alone....

Panic kept bubbling up in him, but Del forced it down. They would find her and Amy would be okay. Then, as he trudged along with Glen and Lonnie, the driving snow blinding them, Del thought that he should have turned on the radio and checked in with Ollie sooner; for Lord's sake, he should have realized that Amy was going to follow them!

Guilt and blame and a deadly fear ate at him.

"Let's be facin' it," called Lonnie through a sheet of white. "Best thing to do is radio Ollie and get help sent in from Jackson. We have our-r wor-rk, remember?"

"I am *not* leaving her out here!" Del turned and fixed him with an implacable gaze. "You got that?"

Dusk was falling slowly and inevitably over the mountains. Del's group had found no trace whatsoever either of their own trail or anyone else's. That, of course, did not mean that one of the other search groups had not located Amy.

"We better get to the rendezvous point," said Glen finally. "Maybe Amy is with the others already."

"That crazy kid," muttered Del as he felt a surge of angry futility swamp him. "Why couldn't she have followed orders...?

"You know something?" Glen threw back. "You haven't got a sympathetic bone in your body!"

Del ignored him and led the way through the darkening forests and across brighter, open fields. His thoughts were consumed with only one thing: Amy's whereabouts.

They reached the rendezvous site to find that one group was still not there: Rob and Jay's.

Neither was Amy.

Ten minutes later he heard Jay's muffled voice calling across the white meadow through the sheets of snow, "We're below you! Have you got Amy?"

Glen cupped his hands and called back, "No!"

Del felt sick and utterly helpless. He knew what to do, though; they had to quicken their pace and radio Ollie immediately. No one in Jackson who was sane would commence a night search, but by first light there could be dozens of hikers scouring the mountainside for her.

Could Amy survive a night in the wilderness? She was so damn skinny and inexperienced. Did she even have a sleeping bag with her?

Swede Björkman was walking a little behind the group and off to the side. "Over here!" he yelled suddenly.

Del's heart pumped furiously against his ribs. He rushed through the drifts to the big man. "What is it?"

Swede pointed. "Someone came dis way. An hour ago, maybe?"

Del studied the faint path with a flashlight. Yes!

"Could it have been Deborah?" asked Flint, who had trudged over, too.

Del shook his head. "She would never leave the camp." Hope welled up in his chest.

The tracks, as faint as they were in the deepening snow seemed to head upward, vaguely in the direction of camp one. Amy Slavin sure had a guardian angel!

It was still half a mile to the campsite. Everyone, including Del, was cold and exhausted and hungry. It occurred to him suddenly that Amy could be at camp one already, safe and warm. His emotions did a curious flip-flop, turning from desperate, tearing worry to hot anger. If she was in camp and they'd been tramping around in a snowstorm...!

It was close to seven when the weary search party trudged into camp. The first thing Del saw was Amy's backpack lying in the snow near the fire.

His heart gave a great leap and he broke into a lumbering run across the clearing. "Amy!" he yelled, torn once more between relief and rage. "Deborah!"

Two heads popped out of Deborah's tent.

"Amy," he breathed, squatting down into the snow right where he was, feeling suddenly exhausted beyond endurance. He simply gaped at her. Should he pull her out of that tent and shake her silly for causing them all so much trouble? Or perhaps he should take her in his arms and hold on to her for dear life....

"You crazy voman!" yelled Swede over Del's shoulder. Then everyone was hovering near the fire, greeting her warmly, as if, Del thought, she'd done nothing whatsoever wrong.

Del gritted his teeth and watched the scene unfolding; he saw Glen give Amy a big hug. Oh, she'd pay for this!

"How you ever found the camp," marveled Flint.

"It's a miracle," declared Glen, holding her out at arm's length, grinning with vast relief.

"She's for-rtunate she's alive," mumbled Lonnie finally, but to no one in particular. "Probably didn't even bring a sleeping bag."

"Yes, I did!" piped up Amy.

"No one invited you," he snapped, and Amy wondered, *is it Lonnie?* She looked at Deborah, who shrugged in return, then shook her head as if to say, "No, it can't be him. It's too obvious."

Nervously glancing around, Amy located Del, still squatting just out of the perimeter of firelight. He was glaring at her, his face a thundercloud.

"You'd better tell him, Amy," suggested Deborah, nodding toward Del.

"No! I can't." Then she added solemnly, "Deborah, you have to swear you won't say a word...to anyone. No matter what. This is my responsibility. I have to be the final judge. Promise me, Deborah. I mean it."

"What does Del have to do to prove he's one of your good guys, Amy?" asked Deborah pointedly.

Amy's righteousness deflated instantly. "I don't know. I just don't know, Deborah. But promise me."

"Okay."

Amy shrank into the safety of her puffy down parka as Del finally came toward her. The other team members, Deborah included, discreetly rose and disappeared into their tents.

Oh, brother. Amy cringed and steeled herself, all the while casting her eyes about desperately for help. Was she in for it now!

Then he was there, big and threatening, looming over her. She didn't want to look at him, but found her eyes traveling up to his face, anyway. She blinked as the melting flakes of snow struck her in the eyes and blurred her vision. His anger seemed to radiate out and touch her.

"We're going to have a little talk," Del began ominously.

Amy looked down, fumbled with a contact lens and swallowed hard. "Aren't you hungry? Don't you want to eat first?"

"My tent, Amy."

She crawled into his tent, feeling a sudden rush of claustrophobia in the tiny space. Del followed, then lighted a Coleman lantern. It cast eerie shadows on the nylon walls and on Del's wet, angry face.

He looked demonic to Amy. His clear blue eyes were storm dark now, shadowed holes in his craggy face. His jaw was covered with stubble and his hair was wet and plastered down on his head. Then there was his size, which filled the two-man tent to bursting.

Amy edged back into a corner automatically.

"I just want to know if you realize what you've done," he said gravely. "No evasions, no cute roundabout stories, Amy."

She took a quavering breath. If she told Del, and if her dreadful suspicions about him had any merit whatsoever, she could be signing Roger's death warrant. She'd have to take the flak. He wouldn't...hit her, would he?

"Amy..."

"Yes, I know what I did." She met his hard gaze defiantly. "I almost died out there."

He watched her silently for a time, making her squirm under his scrutiny.

"You're a fool, Amy," he finally said.

Her glance fell away from his face. "All I can say is I have to be there when you find Roger."

He looked solemnly at her again for an unbearably long time. "Let's say I believe you, Amy. Have you considered the fact that I can't spare a person to accompany you back down to base? Do you know what that means?"

"I go up with you." Her heart was beating furiously. He couldn't say no; he couldn't....

"That's right. But before you jump for joy, think of this. You've become a liability none of us can afford. We're professionals. One amateur along can cost lives. You may have cost Roger his."

"No!" Amy cried miserably. "I'm here to protect him!"

Del watched her carefully. "If you had told me in the beginning what there was to protect your brother from, I could have helped, Amy. As it stands now..." He leaned so close Amy could feel his warm breath on her cheeks. "If anything goes wrong up there, you might have to shoulder the blame."

Amy bowed her head, put her face in her hands and felt wretchedness consume her. What if Del was right? But if she hadn't come along, someone, maybe even Del, would have made darn good and sure Roger never got down at all.

"I had to do it," Amy murmured, a sob welling in her chest.

A ponderous silence filled the tent. Outside, voices broke the quiet occasionally, but they were small and lost in the vastness of the mountain.

Del groaned. "Amy, what am I going to do with you?"

She raised her face to meet his gaze squarely. "Nothing. You don't have to do a thing with me. I'll make it. I won't hold you up. I'm tough, Del. I made it up here, didn't I?"

He studied her, and his face appeared so worried, so concerned, that she couldn't believe he'd try to hurt her—or Roger.

"Trust me, Amy," he finally said. "If you don't, you're making my job a lot harder."

She wanted to cry out her terrible fears to him, to be held in those strong arms, to feel his big solid body—

to be as close to him as she'd been last night. His nearness stifled and thrilled Amy; both sensations dragged at her, tearing her apart.

She felt his hand touch her cheek softly. "I sure wish I knew what was going on in that head of yours. There's something awful eating at you, Amy."

Mutely she looked at him, craving his touch, yet dreading it. Her stomach knotted with tension; her eyes closed inadvertently at the sensation of his gentle caress.

When she opened them he was gone.

THE CAMPFIRE BURNED LATE that evening, sending sparks erupting into the night sky. The team members ate and warmed themselves and retired to their tents, replete after the fatiguing day. Amy had fallen asleep where she was. She slept restlessly, having nightmare after nightmare of holding a gun on Roger and pulling the trigger.

She started up suddenly. Her hair was wringing wet with sweat and Del was back. How...?

"You fell asleep," he said, peeling off layers of clothes as Amy watched, still caught in the throes of her dream. "I woke you when I came in...I'm sorry." He sounded resigned to her going along, at least.

"I'll go climb in with Deborah." She began to move toward the opening of the tent, acutely aware of his presence, of the dark curling hair showing at the neck of his long underwear.

"Wait a minute." His tone seemed reluctant. He looked tired and unhappy. Her heart went out to him.

"Deborah's asleep," he said uneasily.

"Oh," replied Amy, equally uncertain.

"Look. I just spent the past hour out by the fire, thinking. You're driving me nuts, Amy."

"I know..." she said under her breath in a very small voice.

"And I don't know what to do about you." He looked at her hard. "No, I don't mean about the climb. You have to go up with us now. I'm talking about *us* and our...relationship."

"I know what you mean."

"I've got you in my head and it's like an itch I can't get at."

"That bad?" she whispered.

"Worse."

"But do you want..." She paused, taking a deep breath. "Do you want me to stay here tonight?"

He looked at her without speaking. Yet words seemed to fly around the small tent, ricocheting off the nylon walls, filling the air with an expectant thrum that made Amy's heart pound. His face was shadowed, almost brooding, but she knew he wanted her. The silence thickened—all those words crashing around, finding no lips to speak them. Then, slowly, his hand reached out and touched her face, moved around to the back of her head and pulled her toward him.

Their lovemaking was violent and urgent. Del couldn't keep his hands from searching every hollow and curve of her flesh, from the back of her knees to the soft roundness of her buttocks, back up her spine to where he lifted her hair and nuzzled her neck. The sinewy, corded hardness of his body pressed to hers drove her wild with yearning. She kissed the swell of muscle above his breast bone, drew her tongue downward, across the coarse hair on his chest, and traced a path along the thin dark line of hair, tasting his male flesh, savoring him, burning deep inside to possess all of him.

"Make love to me now..." she breathed, as a hot fluid torrent writhed in her stomach.

Later, when soft snowflakes tapped the sides of the tent and the clouds were beginning to part above them, Del awakened Amy with warm tender kisses.

The raw virility of his body touching her length aroused Amy from half sleep. "Umm..." She put one bare leg between his knees.

His lips found the sensitive pulse on her neck. Then he moved his head down and drew his mouth across her nipples lightly, until they tingled and grew taut. He teased her belly button with his tongue; her nerves jumped in sweet torment, and she pressed his head to her in longing as Del played on her sensitive skin, licking at the soft flesh of her stomach.

Finally he poised himself above Amy, and she ached and squirmed desperately to feel him enter her. But Del only teased her with his hardness, until Amy moaned unashamedly. Suddenly he filled her, then left her bereft, again and again, and Amy rocked in the rhythm of passion. Throbbing, she lost all sense of time and space, and was conscious only of feeling herself filled with his beautiful body and of seeking that secret pinnacle that loomed over her, beckoning, urging, taunting.

Del whispered in her ear and took her mouth with his until her breath caught. Sometimes he almost hurt her, and then his lips would become tender and teasing and adoring.

They glided together while Del's hands moved under her buttocks and lifted her to meet him. Amy whispered her desire aloud, seeking, seeking, as his hands molded her flesh, kneading her buttocks, crushing her to him with each thrust. Finally she was gasping as if she'd been running a long way. She arched to meet him one last time and cried out her passion against the wall of his chest, muffling her joy as her nails raked across his back. Del's mouth covered hers then. He breathed huskily against her parted lips as he shuddered above her and finally lay, spent, against her damp length.

"Wow," he whispered a few moments later, and Amy felt it, too. No man and woman could have shared more. It was, she thought dreamily, a miracle and a gift, that certain perfection of fulfillment that comes, possibly, once in a lifetime.

"My God, Amy," he said as he held her face in his huge, rough hands and kissed her.

"I know," she whispered.

CHAPTER THIRTEEN

Day 5 A.M.

WHEN DEL AWOKE at four he was alone in his tent. He reached over for a moment, felt the empty space next to him and recalled the way Amy's delicate body had thrashed wildly against his with a strength and passion that perpetually surprised him.

A strange girl-woman. Intelligent and coy, yet naive and sensitive. She was decidedly uncontrollable but fiercely loyal in her convictions. No man would ever pin Amy Slavin—Slavinsky—down. A resourceful man might catch her, but Del sensed that she would always live like a bird, flitting and carefree, an elusive spirit. Nor, he decided, would she hold a man back; she seemed to respect her own freedom too much to ask someone else to give up his.

What had gotten into him? You'd think he were contemplating taking on a mate.

Slow down, he told himself. First of all, Amy Slavin truly was driving him crazy. Second, he wasn't ready to get married. He had too many other responsibilities. And besides, he wasn't even thirty-six yet. There was plenty of time left to think about future and family.

And—above all—what sap would be insane enough to consider marrying a woman who didn't trust him?

Nevertheless, he had gotten several clues to this mystery out of her—inadvertently, of course—and he was starting to put the pieces of the puzzle together.

Amy had flown from Rochester, New York, and climbed a mountain because she truly believed her brother to be alive and in danger from one of the team members. Because of Amy's violent dislike of Frank Pereira, Del could assume that Amy thought Shearing was at the root of her brother's danger. And it had something to do with national security.

As he lay alone in his dark tent, Del's mind began to awaken and click, putting two and two together. Amy must believe that Shearing Aerospace, through Frank Pereira, had somehow bribed or paid one of the rescue team to...to do what? Kill Roger Slavinsky? Good God....

Amy's brother had been on his way to Washington, D.C. A person from the Defense Department had been with him. Was he being escorted by a government representative to Washington with some information Shearing didn't want the government to know? Or was that jumping to conclusions, Del wondered.

He sat up and stretched and switched on the tiny lamp. Amy had grouped them all together in her mind. Villains. And what hurt, what was really chomping at his gut, was the fact that he was right up there on top of her list!

Del dressed in the frigid first light. Whatever was going on in Amy's Machiavellian brain was his problem, too. He had a team to get to the crest of Pearl Pass. And a nasty feeling gnawed at him that Amy's suspicions were going to complicate matters—if they proved true.

He stuffed his lightweight sleeping bag into the small sack and began taking down the mountain tent. Outside, the little camp stoves were going already and Amy and Deborah were bustling around to prepare breakfast. Del's eyes met Amy's meaningfully for a moment. Then he turned back to his task of repacking.

"It's clearing," said Rob as he strode over.

Del looked up. It didn't matter, because they were going, anyway, but the early dawn clouds were breaking up, although some were still lying on the mountainsides. Overhead, there were patches of pale blue sky, a promising omen.

"If it just stayed decent for a few hours," called Jay from the camp stove, "I'd be happy."

Del thought of the climb to come, of the icefall they had yet to cross before the final push. Would Jay freeze up on the crossing? And how in the name of heaven were they going to get Amy over to the other side of the perilous wall?

Before eating, Del checked in with Oliver, who was still below in base camp.

"What's the forecast? Over."

"Clearing this morning. Chance of snow showers by evening. It's iffy. Over."

"It's almost November, Pop. It's expected. Over."

"The chopper is flying again this morning. He'll radio if there's news. Watch that icefall, Del. Over."

"Roger. I'll call in at noon. Over and out."

Amy was standing above him, offering a cup of coffee, as Del was packing up the radio.

"How does it look?" she asked anxiously.

He took the hot tin cup. "Coffee? It looks great."

"No." She shook her head. "I mean the weather forecast?"

"Oh, that," Del teased as his blue eyes roamed her dirt-smudged, waiflike face. "It's pretty good for this morning. But it can change within moments," he said seriously.

"I've noticed," Amy remarked, working on a hopeful smile. Then she began to turn back toward the fire.

Del rose and took her arm gently. "Wait a sec." He saw a frown cross her brow. "No, I'm not going to yell at you, Amy," he said. "I just want to say that ... well ..." he fumbled suddenly. What *was* he going to tell her? Thanks for last night? Or how about the fact that he was strangely reluctant to let her go from his side—even for a moment? Maybe it was, "Trust me. I'm falling hard for you...."

"Yes?" she was saying, her smoky blue eyes searching his unshaven face.

"Nothing, really. Just follow instructions today and you'll do all right."

"I will. Don't worry about me." She looked down at his hand on her arm. "Do you want powdered eggs?"

"I'll get them," he said as she gently disengaged herself.

Glen Shepherd walked up. The deputy's glance went from Del to Amy and back. "Are you going to stand around talking all day, or can we get this show on the road?''

Del shrugged as Amy turned away and quickly sought the others. ''We'll be off in twenty minutes. That suit you, Shepherd?''

Glen glared at him. ''You're pretty confident this morning, Del. Did you have a good rest?''

''Slept like a baby,'' replied Del, wondering just what Glen was up to.

''I can imagine,'' said Glen. ''Some baby.''

''What's your problem, Shepherd?'' growled Del.

''After all these years you still have to get back at me, don't you?''

''What are you talking about?''

''That cute little Indian girl you were so crazy about back in high school. Well, I got her, so I guess it's your turn this time,'' Glen said smugly.

All the disgust Del had felt for Glen Shepherd since that incident came back to him. Had Glen been trying the same line of bunk on Amy? Well, she was too smart for him. Or was she?

He watched Shepherd's handsome, smooth face and hated it, as he'd hated it that time so long ago. He wanted to smash a fist into it, as he'd done then. But now he was twenty years older and the leader of an expedition.

''Just mind your own business. You're here as part of a rescue party. Don't forget it,'' said Del in a hard voice.

''Don't worry about me, Pardee. I'll make it, with or without Miss Slavin's considerable charms,'' shot back Glen, smiling.

Del turned his back on Shepherd deliberately and walked away. He clenched his teeth to force the anger down.

The jerk, he thought as he slung his heavy pack onto his shoulders.

THE GOING was relatively easy but steadily upward as the team traversed the snow-covered mountainside in a file. Del led the way. Then came Deborah and Amy, his brothers, the giant Swede, who hummed a tune, Flint and Lonnie. Glen held up the rear.

By midmorning the late-October sun felt warm on their shoulders and they took off their colorful parkas and tied them on top of their packs. Del had Deborah pass out candy bars and they drank thirstily from their plastic water jars when they took a break.

Del sat beside Amy for a moment. "Tired?" She had her face turned up into the sunlight, and her chest was rising and falling steadily beneath the plaid wool shirt.

"A little," she admitted.

"It's the climb and the thin air at this altitude. The combination gets to even the best of us."

She tipped her head back down. "That's at least reassuring."

"I shouldn't offer but . . . do you want me to carry your pack for you?"

Amy laughed suddenly. "Now that's the nicest thing anyone has said to me since I got to Wyoming!"

He smiled, faintly embarrassed. "Well, do you? I will."

"No," Amy replied. "I'd never be able to live it down. Besides, I'm practicing to get on the cover of *National Geographic*."

"Somehow I don't think you're going to make it. Maybe try for 'Ripley's Believe It or Not.'"

"Can I join you?" Glen pushed himself down onto the fallen log beside Amy.

"Sure," she said, while Del looked at him impatiently.

"It's a great day, isn't it?"

Wonderful, mused Del, the image of the Lear jet suddenly filling his mind.

"It's not snowing," commented Amy, smiling.

"You doing okay?" Glen patted her arm.

"I'm fine. Really."

"All right, then, I guess I'll go tell the others to saddle up."

"*I'll* tell them, Shepherd." Del rose and walked away from them.

As they neared the icefall, Del could hear Deborah chatting with Amy behind him. Amy wasn't answering much, though—she was panting too hard. She should have let him take that pack. As it was, she looked like an ant crawling up the hill with a giant crumb on her back. Poor, determined thing. And he knew, too, that Amy's thoughts were on her brother, because she kept glancing up toward the endless heights above them. Once he even thought he heard her whisper breathlessly, "We're coming."

They each in turn stepped over fallen trees and rocks and depressions in the uneven snow. Del stopped several times and took Amy's arm, half lifting her weight over particularly big obstructions.

"Thank you," she told him with a smile, panting.

They were a quarter of a mile below the icefall, when Del called another rest. "It's noon. I'm going to radio Pop."

They'd heard the chopper somewhere above them at around eleven. Perhaps there was news.

"Spotted movement again," came Oliver Pardee's crackling voice, and the team let out a simultaneous cheer.

Del put up a silencing hand. "More than one survivor? Over."

"The pilot radioed a big maybe. Where are you? Over."

"Below the icefall. Over."

"Go safely. And son, be there for Jay, will you? Talk to you at the rescue site. Out."

Del pushed the antenna down and snapped the radio into its case. He looked at Amy. She was crying quietly.

"How are you doing?" he asked for want of the right words.

She sniffled through a bright red nose. "We're so close now," she said, then met his gaze tremulously.

"Very close," Del agreed, but in the back of his mind he knew only one thing for certain: between Amy and her twin brother lay a perilous icefall that had been made worse by new snow followed by a hot, pounding dose of sun.

It would be touchy as hell...the fresh snow ready to give way underfoot, and the exposure below....

By twelve forty-five they reached the fall. They stood at one side and silently gazed at the wall of ice that spread across a treacherously steep rock face for almost forty yards.

"Now ther-re's exposure!" breathed Lonnie Dougal with excitement as he looked down the wall to where it ended hundreds of feet below.

Amy looked at Del in horror.

"Ah, it's no problem!" boomed Swede loud enough to cause an avalanche.

Del looked to the back of the group, where Jay stood alone. His brother's face was ashen.

He knew exactly what was going on in Jay's mind: this was it, the dangerous spot, the focus of all that fear and wondering. He went to Jay immediately.

"It's a cinch," he said. "Don't worry."

"Sure," mumbled Jay, but Del could feel the fear quivering in the air around his brother.

"We've done these crossings a hundred times. You could do it in your sleep."

Jay did not reply.

"Look, I need your backup. I've got Amy to worry about. There's something funny going on here. I need men I can trust." He could hear someone hammering in an ice screw so that he could start his crossing. Every blow seemed to make Jay wince.

"You can do it," Del said fiercely.

Jay turned fear-glazed eyes on to him. "Maybe I should wait here."

"No! I need you. There are four men up there—dead or alive. I need everyone, Jay. Why do you think I asked you to come?"

"I'll try." Jay's Adam's apple jumped in his neck.

"You'll do it! And you'll do it well. I have faith in you, pal."

"Guess I can't argue with that." Jay tried a shaky smile and Del feinted a punch to his brother's belly. Jay dodged automatically, and his smile broadened.

"Never could hit you in the gut, could I?" Del grinned.

Fastening on his complicated climbing harness, hung with dozens of dangling pitons, ice screws and carabiners, Del clanked like an automated Christmas tree. But every item was absolutely necessary to his safety.

Glen had pounded in the piton and knotted one end of the bright red nylon rope to it. He handed the neat coil to Del and nodded to him. Their eyes met in cold challenge.

Del tested the piton, then gave it a couple more blows to be sure. "Never trust a piton you haven't put in yourself," he'd always taught. He tested the knot and the rope, aware of Shepherd's smug smile on him. But Glen's piton and knot were good—he had to give him that.

It was Del's job to carry the rope across the practically vertical wall and fix it solidly with ice screws. This fixed rope—which they would all use to cross— would be the party's lifeline. Del's task was the most dangerous; it left him exposed to a fall, as he would be connected to a rope only at one end.

He strapped on his crampons, the spiked foot gear, got out his ice ax and edged out onto the wall. He clung like a fly, supported by the ice ax and by the points of the crampons that he could kick into the wall. Every few feet he would brace himself, lean backward out over the abyss and hammer in another ice screw, securing the trailing rope to it. Thus he could only fall a few feet.

Use a rope for safety, but climb as if it weren't there. That was the climber's principal rule. It reverberated in Del's mind as he inched his way across the forty yards of ice. The expanse was like the ocean, constant, yet always changing. In one place a screw stayed in as if welded; in another the sun caused the ice to crumble as if rotten, and he had to try again. A wall such as this one was inflexible in its demands. Yet if a man approached it with knowledge and courage and care, it would accept him and relent in tribute to his struggle.

Suddenly a chunk of ice broke off under his ax and he swung outward, losing contact. He hung there, suspended for a moment by one hand and his crampons. He heard someone watching him gasp. Rob yelled out, "You're belayed, don't worry!" but he hardly heard. He dug the ax in again and it held. He went on slowly, doggedly.

Del had no real fear of falling. Even as loose snow drifted from above in airy sheets, as rocks clattered below him, as his hand felt and refelt for a practically nonexistent hold, he was sure.

Climbing gave him the ultimate freedom to be himself. It provided the supreme challenge.

"Why did you climb Mount Everest?" a reporter had once asked him.

And Del had replied, "Because I had it in me to do it."

Today, too, was a challenge for Del, but he was not consumed with it. No. His body was merely functioning like a well-tuned motor as he slowly and steadily crossed. His mind was elsewhere; it was back across the deadly ravine with the others, with Amy and Jay and the rest.

He reached the other side and stepped onto level ground. Relief and regret filled him. He'd won this round and it had been a good one, but there was always next time....

"Okay," he called back across, his deep voice reverberating off the mountainside. "I'm secured over here. Start out, Swede."

Everyone had been issued a two-inch web belt, called a swami belt, with a carabiner attached. The carabiner, an oval metal ring, could be clipped on to the fixed rope that now stretched across the steep icefall. No one could fall farther than the slack in the fixed rope, a few feet. Swede clipped himself onto the rope, then slid across sideways, using his crampons to practically walk on a vertical surface.

"Too easy." Swede smiled, slapping Del on the back, but Del could see the sweat that was making thick rivulets down the big man's leathery neck.

Rob was next. Then came Flint, whose face was beet red when he reached Del.

"I hate icefalls!" he rasped, panting. "Gimme a loose rock slide anytime!"

Then Lonnie crossed. About halfway one of his feet caused a small avalanche of snow, and he slipped several feet before the belt around his waist caught him up. Pulling himself back up to the route, he made it the rest of the way easily.

Glen had smoothly insisted on helping Amy.

Del tried to read the expression on her sheet-white face as she watched Deborah cross skillfully. Then Glen was by Amy's side, his hand at her back, urging her closer to the edge of the icefall.

"I'm not moving a foot!" she cried to Glen. "Not a foot!"

Jay, who would be last to cross, was no help, either. Del stood there debating. Should he try to coax her with words, or go back across himself and get her?

"Come on, Amy!" he called. "You can do it!"

"Don't look down!" shouted Deborah, and Del shot her a scathing glance. No point in reminding Amy of that!

Finally—and it wasn't by the book—he crossed back about halfway. "Come out this far," he said in a reassuring voice. "Come on, Amy. Nothing's going to happen."

She stared in horror at him. "I . . . I can't," she moaned.

Glen put a hand on her shoulder. "I'll help you, Amy. It'll be easy."

She looked at him frantically, then at Del. "Come on, Amy," Del coaxed.

Glen helped her put on a pair of crampons and her swami belt, then guided her into position and snapped her carabiner onto the fixed line.

"Kick the points in, Amy," said Glen. "Harder. That's it." He followed her closely, urging her on step by step.

She groaned occasionally as she went and gasped and muttered to herself. Del felt grudging respect as Glen talked her across. He was good, perhaps more patient than Del himself would have been.

When Amy had nearly reached Del, a clump of snow gave way under one of her feet. If she hadn't been so terrified, Del might have considered her position ridiculous. She was spread-eagled, and upside down, hanging on to the rope for dear life, looking straight down the icefall.

"I'm falling . . . I'm falling . . ." she gasped.

Del reached her quickly. "You're all right. The belt is holding you. Give me your hand." He reached down to her.

"I . . . can't . . . let . . . go . . . of . . . the rope!"

"Of course you can," he coaxed softly, gently. "The belt around your waist is clipped on to it, Amy. You're safe. Now give me your hand."

"No!"

"Give it to me," said Del with resolve, "or you won't get to Roger."

Her eyes snapped up instantly. "Oh, God . . ." she moaned, still not moving.

Del caught her horror-stricken eyes and tried to hold them with his own confident ones. "Now just loosen your fingers slowly."

"They . . . won't . . . move!"

"Do it!" She obeyed finally, very slowly, her gaze locked with his. Then he leaned down and took her one trembling hand in his and pulled her quickly up against him. It was pointless to try to talk her across on her own. He'd seen this happen a hundred times—she was lost in a bottomless pit of fear.

He looked down into her eyes. "Amy," he said carefully, "wrap your arms around my waist...there, that's it...now put your foot where mine just was...okay, good, that's my girl." Over and over.

When she'd made it across and Swede reached out to take her from Del, she collapsed in his big burly arms.

She was laughing and crying and threatening. "Never again! Never!"

"You going to stay up here forever?" asked Swede as he winked over her shoulder to Del.

"Yes! I'll build a house up here! You can go down, but I won't!"

Glen crossed the rest of the way without incident, showing his confidence and experience.

"Good job," commented Del in a professional manner.

"Thanks," acknowledged Glen, grinning before he walked over to comfort Amy.

Jay alone now stood at the far side.

"All right, Jay," Rob yelled. "Let's get a move on." He looked meaningfully at Del.

They all watched, holding their breaths, as Jay began to make his way over. Each person on the far side of the dangerous fall, even Amy, was quite aware of Jay's bad experience and the fact that he had since then carefully avoided any really technical climbs.

Del, when he'd all but forced Jay to accompany the team, had a dual motive: first, he needed Jay, and second, if Jay didn't get over his fear soon, his climbing days would be history.

Del stood motionless and watched Jay put hand over hand, foot after foot, one in front of the other, making his slow but steady progress across the fall.

"You're okay," whispered Del. "You're going to make it, little brother."

Then suddenly, when it seemed Jay's crossing would pass unmomentously, he lost his footing in the exact place Amy had.

"Blast it!" swore Del under his breath as he watched Jay struggle. Then abruptly, Jay slipped again. Only this time, the rope didn't hold; a piton popped out of the ice. Jay dropped, dangling and flailing, a few more feet.

Instantly Del hooked back on to the fixed rope.

"No!" Jay cried, his face turned to Del. "I have to do it."

Del froze. Jay was right. He drew the cool air into his lungs, trying to calm himself. "Can you get a footing?"

Jay shook his head; fear was blazing from his blue eyes.

"Try to get one foot fixed in." Jay knew the proper procedure, Del thought, but at that moment his kid brother was not thinking straight.

"Shake it off, Jay, come on!" Rob cupped his hands and shouted. It was Oliver's old line—shake it off—get rid of the fear or it'll kill you.

They stood together then as a single silent unit, praying at the edge of the icefall, "Let Jay make it!"

Agonizing minutes later, Jay moved his right leg and kicked his crampon in. Then the other one. Above him, snow dislodged and slid over him. He began to pull himself up with the rope, hand over hand, very, very slowly, kicking in his toes. Above his head was the ice-ax, still buried in the wall. "Look up," called Del carefully.

Jay strained his neck. "I see it." He could barely be heard.

Then his fingers reached the handle and he grasped it. The muscles of his powerful arms worked and flexed beneath his shirt, and sweat poured from his brow as he lifted himself, straining and panting, back up onto the route.

The fixed rope looped down below him with the piton hanging at its deepest arc. Jay looked at it, then slowly pulled on the rope until the piton was in his hand.

If he slipped now, thought Del, the rope would be under such a strain that the other pitons could very well pop...one after another...until the last one gave and Jay plummeted to earth, far, far below.

"Get it hammered in," whispered Del.

"Lord..." breathed Flint, "*hurry*."

Jay pulled out his hammer and raised it cautiously. For a brief moment he froze on the perilous wall as his eyes swept the abyss below. Then he braced himself and began to strike the piton with sure, steady blows until it was once again fixed in the ice.

Breaths were expelled in a long, collective sigh. In minutes Jay was over safely. There was no more sighing; instead the men slapped his back and cheered uproariously. Swede yodeled, the sound echoing through the valley far below them.

"Congratulations!" Deborah said, beaming. "Good work." She gave Jay a big hug, while he grinned and blushed.

"I knew you could do it," boomed Del, laughing, and more relieved than he had thought possible. "But you didn't have to do it the hard way."

"I was plenty scared," admitted Jay, "but I guess that's all part of it. I'd forgotten that for a while." A bemused expression crept over his big, square face. "I guess I was more afraid of failing than falling. It was the failing that had me there for a time."

A slow smile gathered at the corners of Del's mouth. "When you climb, little brother, there is no other fear worth having."

CHAPTER FOURTEEN

Day 5 P.M.

EVERY MUSCLE IN AMY'S BODY was throbbing, every nerve ending screaming for rest.

One step at a time, she kept telling herself. Onward and upward. Oh, my, how she was suffering! How could muscles hurt so badly? And her poor, poor little feet. The blisters—ooh....

Every so often Deborah turned around and gave her a reassuring glance, but Lonnie, who was right behind Amy, kept mumbling, "Amateurs."

The team snaked upward until finally, mercifully, they came to a flat meadow where they took a short break. Stumbling behind a boulder, Amy used her last bit of energy to go to the bathroom. She wasn't even sure she would have cared if anyone had seen her; modesty didn't exist at survival level. When she emerged from behind the rock, she lay down on her back in the snow. She didn't even bother to remove her pack—nothing mattered. She needed to rest. As she looked up wearily, Amy could see the clouds massing, hanging all around them like thick white clots of mist. Was it going to snow?

"Amy," came Del's voice, "you're going to break your back lying that way."

"I don't care..." she groaned.

"Poor kid." He rubbed the thick, stubbly growth on his neck. "Are you beginning to see why I wanted you to stay below with Pop?"

Mulishly she refused to give him the satisfaction of an answer.

"Well, we're just below the site now."

Her eyes grew big and round and she sat up instantly. "We are?"

"Yep. Another hour, I'd say."

Fear suddenly grasped at her. "What if . . . what if I'm wrong about . . . Roger? Oh, God."

"We'll find out shortly, Amy. We're all praying along with you," he said soberly.

The weather began to close in again, and the snowfields and jagged-edged peaks became indistinguishable from the leaden sky.

The rest stop was over. Amy was sure she wouldn't be able to stand up, but somehow she did. She knew the others were watching her, just waiting for a show of weakness, expecting it. She had to keep going!

She leaned into the mountain. One step after another. . . . If she thought only about one step at a time, she'd make it.

Then the sun began to set, gilding the tall peaks around them. The air was turning frigid; Amy's breath was puffing out in plumes. Her mind was ceasing to function properly. They had ascended to nearly ten thousand feet—almost two miles high. The air was oxygen poor up there. Amy fell back a few yards, just to rest a little, to catch her breath.

She bumped into Swede's broad back. Stunned, she bounced back and her legs quit moving. Her thoughts were forming sluggishly. *Swede must have stopped*.

Amy looked up. A few yards beyond the party, she saw a tilted silver wing. Large black figures on it read 6-1-C, Amy registered blankly. Her mind ground on torpidly. *An odd thing to find up here,* it noted in oxygen-starved detachment.

The exhaustion drained out of her on the heels of the thought. "It's . . . the plane!" she gasped. She began to race ahead like a long distance runner sprinting with her last ounce of strength to the finish line.

"Roger! Oh, Roger!" she kept panting.

The small plane was nosed into the snow, its one wing broken, its doorway a black, empty hole. It was practically buried in new snow.

She could not see anyone.

"Roger!" Amy screamed, gasping and floundering in the piled up soft snow as in a nightmare in which she tried and tried, but couldn't move.

She reached the plane finally and stuck her head into the open door. There were three huddled figures in there, covered by a single blanket.

"Roger?" But she knew even before she recognized one of the unshaven, pinched faces. He was one of them—he was alive.

Faces crowded the open door behind her. One of the men in the plane struggled to rise. "You found us," he rasped weakly. "I thought we'd never . . ." And then he began to weep quietly.

They couldn't get much more out of him just then, beyond the fact that he was Ted, the copilot. The pilot, who had miraculously landed them in one piece, was unconscious. So, it seemed, was Roger. They were all three suffering from exposure and starvation.

"Take care of Grant first," said the copilot. "He's in bad shape. Roger here has a broken leg, I think. God, I can't believe you're really here."

They were all still crowding around the door of the airplane, hardly able to believe there were three men alive up there.

"Move over, Amy," came Del's grave voice at her shoulder. Then someone's gentle but firm hands were pulling her aside.

Everything happened so quickly from that moment on that Amy was only seized by impressions. After the men had been moved into the open, she stayed close to Roger, however, cradling his head when they would let her, hating how useless she felt.

Someone—it was Lonnie, Amy registered—found a snow-covered pit of ashes. "At least they made a fire," said the dour Scot.

Jay looked down at the scratched-out pit. "Yeah, but I'll bet they were too weak to get one going during yesterday's storm. And there's not much wood up here, anyway. We're practically at tree line."

Deborah and Swede opened packages of food, while Lonnie built a fire near the three men. Del held each of their heads in turn, trying to get water down their throats, while Rob and Flint pulled out medical supplies and sleeping bags.

"I think he's got a couple of broken ribs," said Del as he worked on the copilot.

Flint rubbed the man's hands in his own warm ones, then wrapped his torso tightly in tape.

"Thanks..." Ted mumbled.

"Have you had anything to eat in the past few days?"

Ted tried to smile through blue lips. "Grant," he began nodding to the unmoving figure next to him, "eats like a pig, so we were well stocked. But not for...this. We had a bunch of sandwiches, but they were gone days ago."

"Okay," said Del, pulling the down bag up around the man's neck. "You just rest now."

Ted's eyes began to close. "Grant's...pretty bad off...."

Amy tried not to look as she hovered over Roger, but nevertheless her eyes strayed to the pilot as Del examined him.

Del glanced up at Flint. "He's bleeding internally. Radio my dad immediately. Tell him we've got three men alive up here and we need those four litters as soon as possible."

Amy gasped. *Four?* But of course. There had been a representative from the Defense Department in that plane, too. Where was he?

Cautiously, a lump growing in her throat, Amy glanced around the crash site. Glen and Jay were kneeling down beside an elongated drift of snow. *No,* thought Amy, *that's a mound...*

A sad knowledge settled on her. She took her eyes from the men and their task. "Del?" she said, "is that...the other man?" Amy nodded behind them.

He didn't bother answering, but she knew just by the way his thick brows drew together in a frown. Then he turned his attention back to the pilot, although there was little he could do for the severely injured man except make him warm and more comfortable.

Flint strode over from where he'd been using the radio. "It's gusting pretty bad on top of the pass, Del," he said. "Neither the chopper nor a plane can make it up this high right now."

"Damn!" swore Del. "And it's getting dark."

"They're going to make a definite pass at first light and try to land. If they can't, they'll send a plane to drop the litters."

Roger was still out cold but breathing evenly. Amy tried not to worry about the weather and kept her eyes on her brother, pushing his dark wiry hair away from his brow, checking the color in his lips.

"Why won't he wake up?" she asked Flint as he unzipped the sleeping bag and tore away Roger's right pant leg.

"Exposure and shock, Amy. Put it this way, his brain is half-frozen."

"Oh, dear God . . ." Amy whispered.

"He'll be okay. He just needs to be warmed up. Right now all three of them are beyond the point of feeling cold, but their core temperature is very low. Once we get them warmer, they'll start shivering. Then they'll get even warmer and stop. So don't worry if you see your brother shivering. It just means he's warmed up." Flint smiled through his red stubbly beard, trying to reassure her.

She looked over at the copilot; he would be okay, too. But the pilot...Del was still working on him, bundling him into a sleeping bag, taking his pulse, pulling up his blue-veined eyelids and checking his pupils. Could the poor man take another night in this frozen wilderness?

Camp finally settled down. It had grown bitterly cold as dark drifted over the high snowfield. Two fires were going, and the brightly colored mountain tents circled around them like wagons seeking protection from Indian raids. Del bunked in with the pilot and Flint with the copilot, as they were the team members with the best medical training. Lonnie of all people was supposed to sleep with Roger. Fat chance of that! The Scotsman was still right up there near the top of Amy's list. Either he didn't like her, or there was some other more sinister reason for his sour looks in Amy's direction.

Regardless, Amy insisted she sleep with Roger in her tent.

Del protested. "If Roger needs attention during the night," he said, "Lonnie can see to it."

"Oh, no," Amy shot back stubbornly. "No one but me is going to see to Roger."

Del finally, reluctantly, let her have her own way.

Deborah poked her head into Amy's tent at around ten. "How's it going?"

Amy shone her flashlight on Deborah's face for a moment. "It's fine in here. But I couldn't get much food in him. I'm worried he'll starve. He can't seem to wake up, either. And he keeps shivering. It's scary."

"That's normal. His body is sluggish, Amy. He doesn't need much nourishment right now."

"He doesn't really know I'm here."

"I'm sure he senses it, Amy." Deborah smiled. "You just keep watching and I'll back you up, okay?"

"Yes." Then Amy thought a moment. "Can you stay in here for a sec? I've got to visit the girl's room."

When Amy crawled back through the small opening, she was shivering. "It's freezing out there!"

Deborah nodded and then began, "I think you should tell Del the truth. The weather's not any better. It's a long way down, Amy, and a lot can happen."

"You didn't tell him anything, did you?" Amy asked in a panic.

"No, but I've been tempted. I mean, now that we all know Roger is alive, this person is really going to try something." Deborah looked at Amy assessingly. "*If* you're right, that is. After all, Mr. Pereira is far away in Moose. And as for the team—boy, I'd trust my life to any one of them. I already have, for heaven's sake."

"It's not your life that's at stake here. It's Roger's. Please, Deborah, don't say anything. Not yet." Her dark blue eyes implored the taller woman.

"Okay." Deborah sighed. "But you're wrong." She shrugged her strong shoulders. "Del and you . . . well, it's pretty obvious. . . ."

Amy looked down.

"How can you still not trust him, Amy? He's a wonderful guy, and believe me, I do know our man." She raised her brows at Amy apologetically. "I suppose you guessed that already, though."

"From the instant I saw you two together at the airport."

Deborah laughed lightly. "Yeah, and it was written all over your face, Amy. 'Who is this woman!'"

"Sorry."

"No problem. Del and I called it quits ten years ago. We're buddies."

Amy nodded and looked away. "I realize you trust him completely," she said, "but I've got real problems with the way he kept trying to keep me from coming along. It seemed more than just a protection thing."

"It was a double protection thing. You're a danger to yourself and to all of us." Deborah paused. "Theoretically."

Amy flushed uncomfortably. "I didn't believe all that stuff. And besides, what about his money problems? Wouldn't a hefty 'donation' help him out there? No one's above temptation."

"Del is when it comes to murder," said Deborah positively. "And besides, he hasn't got any money problems. Not serious ones, anyway."

"Hilkka said he needed a loan for expansion."

"Del, my dear Amy, has been grumbling about that ever since I met him. His dad was never much of a manager. It was Del's grandfather who ran things smoothly. Del himself," explained Deborah, "is a great manager. And I'm sure no matter how prosperous the climbing ranch is, Del will always worry. He's real, real conventional that way."

When Deborah left, Amy lay awake with thoughts batting in her head like wings. They circled, flitting, restless. She was almost afraid to go to sleep lest they land and consume her.

Inside the tent she could hear Roger's soft breathing next to her. Several times she switched on the flashlight and checked his coloring. He looked better, except that he was shivering uncontrollably. But Flint had said he would. And his leg—it was splinted for now. He'd be all right, she told herself.

Outside, it was silent save for the occasional burst of an ember. Was everyone fast asleep?

Amy thought about morning, when a helicopter might arrive to airlift the wounded man to safety. At the very least a plane would drop supplies and litters for the three injured men and also, she trembled to think, for the one who hadn't survived.

But even if they had to descend the whole way on foot, Del had said the trek down would go much more quickly than the climb up—providing that the weather held.

So if it didn't snow and if the helicopter could pick them up somewhere safe for everyone, they might have the injured men in the Jackson hospital by tomorrow. *If!*

Stop tormenting yourself, Amy thought. What would be would be. She had her job to do—watch over Roger like a hawk. And soon she would have her big story. She tried to tell herself that the story was important, vital, exciting. But the truth was that Amy really didn't give two hoots about exposing Shearing anymore. What she wanted desperately was to get Roger safely off that mountain.

She would have sold the story to the devil in a second if he'd promised to get them down unharmed.

Midnight came and went. Amy checked Roger once more. He mumbled something in his sleep. She poked her head out of the tent opening—just checking. The three stars of Orion's belt shone above her. And the Big Dipper. Those were the only constellations she recognized from Girl Scout camp. The thin air quivered with coldness. Somewhere far overhead she heard an airplane pass; the people in it were warm and safe, she thought wonderingly.

It was then that she heard a footfall in the snow nearby. The sound came closer.

Amy sat up and quickly snapped on the flashlight, every muscle in her body tense with fright as she searched her pocket for the gun.

She waited. Her heart was playing havoc in her chest. The footsteps neared.

Suddenly the tent flap moved. A hand appeared. Amy held her breath. Would he go for her, too? He'd have to...

"Oh, my God," she whispered in terror.

Then a wool-capped head appeared. Who was it?

"Amy?" A man's hushed voice.

She gulped down her fear, but it stuck in her throat. "I'm...here." Surely, she thought frantically, no one would try anything like this—why, if he did, she would scream. The whole camp would come running.

Then, as the man's shoulders appeared from the womb of the darkness, visions flitted in her head. He could use Mace or a hypodermic needle filled with poison or one of those chemical knockout drugs.

They'd find her body along with Roger's in the morning. Frozen. Dead. No one would know who did it.

The man's head turned up into the beam of her flashlight. "You all right?"

It was Glen! She glared at him as her fingers in her pocket tightened around the butt of the gun.

"I saw your light go on and off and I thought you must be lying here going nuts."

"I am." She breathed slowly and cautiously.

"You've got to get some rest, Amy."

Her narrowed eyes held his. "So do you."

"Oh, I will. Four or five hours is all I need. How's Roger?" He glanced over at her brother.

"He's fine." Make your move if you're going to, Glen Shepherd.

"Is . . . something the matter?"

"No. I just need some rest. Good night, Glen." If he didn't leave, what in God's name would she do? Scream? Pull the gun?

But Glen did begin to back out of her tent. "You know," he said, smiling disarmingly, "you look more like your brother than you said you did."

"Oh," she replied blankly.

"And I just want to tell you, Amy—" Glen shook his head admiringly and the flashlight's beam glinted off his clean-cut features "—I think you're a real sport. Climbing all the way up here just for your brother."

"I had to, Glen," she said carefully.

"We would've got him out, Amy. You can see that now. I don't really understand why you felt you had to come along. But I have to give it to you. You've done well.''

Her heart swelled with gratitude. ''Thanks, Glen,'' she murmured.

Roger stirred and mumbled. Amy turned the flashlight on him; he subsided, shivering in his sleep.

''What I really wanted to say was...'' He paused and cleared his throat. ''Well, gee, Amy. I know it's none of my business, but I really like you. And I sorta hate to see you hooked up with a guy like Del Pardee.''

''What kind of guy is that?'' Amy queried, trying to cover up her discomfort.

''I told you about that incident in high school. He's not such a nice person. I hate to see him deceiving you as to his intentions.''

''Don't worry about me, Glen,'' said Amy softly.

''Now Amy, I hate to bad-mouth another guy, but I like you and I don't want to see anyone hurt you, you know?''

''Thanks for the thought, Glen,'' she murmured.

''Well, good night, Amy. You sure look cute in that parka.''

''Good night, Glen,'' she managed.

When he was gone, Amy sat back and took a couple of deep breaths.

Finally she settled back in her sleeping bag, and she saw Del in her mind's eye as he'd crossed the icefall that day—powerful, sure, a man in his element. She could hear his breathing and see the muscles working under his shirt. He'd moved with utter grace and perfect concentration.

He excited her. She wanted him terribly as she lay in the dark. She wanted his strength and sureness and those calloused, skilled hands on her body, awakening her, making every nerve ending quicken with pleasure.

She wanted him to come to her through the dark, cold night.

But if he did . . . if he did, what would he want from her?

Half-frozen, with one arm wrapped around Roger, Amy awoke in the morning with a start.

She'd actually, somehow, slept!

She was checking Roger, when she heard a noise, a dull roar somewhere above her tent. Quickly Amy poked her head through the flap. Yes! There it was! A plane!

The whole team was out, too, waving, shouting, as if the plane's occupants could hear them. Then there were three parachutes gliding toward earth, and the plane tipped its wings. The barely risen sun flashed off its body in a burst of radiance that nearly blinded her. Immediately it veered away, disappearing into a cloud, and the sky was empty except for the ragged white plumes of snow that streamed like pale wind socks from every mountain peak.

Wouldn't the helicopter be coming soon, then?

Amy put her hand to her breast in joy. Last night, in the wee hours, it had seemed as if they were the only people alive on earth. The loneliness and the fear beating in her ears had been almost unbearable. Now, as the bundled supplies fell, drifting to earth, Amy thought, *we're going to make it!*

She dressed quickly and allowed Swede and Rob to carry Roger outside to the campfire. Her brother was still incoherent, but he did open his eyes and gaze at her for a moment before subsiding. If he would just eat something....

Amy squatted in the trampled snow and got herself a cup of coffee, cradling it in her hands, sipping, while Deborah helped Roger drink some hot chocolate.

"When is the helicopter coming?"

Deborah shrugged. "Soon, I guess."

The men were retrieving the supplies that had fallen downslope. Gusts of wind blew snow in whirling spirals, making the fire sizzle, stinging Amy's face, obscuring the men as they went about their tasks. Storms were still hanging in the air.

Amy kept looking up, checking on the weather. There were patches of blue, but the clouds were ominously gray, scudding across the sky before the wind, as if they were on some predestined errand.

Suddenly Deborah stopped what she was doing and cocked her head. "Do you hear something?" she asked.

"The plane again?" suggested Amy, listening.

"No, it doesn't sound like a plane."

They both strained hard to hear. There it was again, a thudding noise.

It appeared off to the west, a tiny speck, its rotors flashing a regular signal as they reflected the sunlight.

The other members of the party had stopped their work and were all standing watching the helicopter.

Del ran up to the radio and called base camp.

"Ollie, come in."

"Ollie here. Glad you called. They're going to send in a chopper and try to land. Over."

"It's here, but the wind is pretty bad. I think it's too dangerous. Over."

"It's your call, Del. I can't help you. Over."

Del put the radio down. Amy watched him carefully. It was his decision. But surely he'd let the chopper land; it was so close! At least to take out the wounded men! He couldn't turn it back when it had come this far!

A particularly strong gust of wind sent snow rattling against the nylon sides of the tents. A door flap pulled loose and cracked sharply, like a flag. A lone mitten rolled across the snow, a colorful tumbleweed.

Del was looking up at the helicopter. It hovered over them now a couple of hundred feet up, bucking the wind. Snow blew around wildly as the turbulence from the rotors reached the ground.

Amy thought she could see the pilot, and she could make out the big red cross painted on its belly. The chopper lurched as a vicious gust caught it, and the pilot tilted his machine and made a wide circle above them.

Del looked at the three men lying on the ground; he looked at his climbers. Amy could sense his mind working at top speed, sifting all the permutations and combinations, making his decision.

Then, as the chopper came around again, Del stood out in the middle of a clear area. The backwash flailed at him. Snow whirled around his motionless figure.

What was he going to do?

He raised his arms finally. It was going to land any minute. It was so close!

Amy sucked in her breath in a sharp gasp. What was Del doing? His arms were waving, slowly, reluctantly, but definitely. The helicopter rose, pulling away from them as if tugged by an unseen string. He'd waved it off!

He couldn't! Amy's mind wailed.

But he had.

CHAPTER FIFTEEN

Day 6 A.M.

SO IT WOULD BE a descent on foot. How long would that take, Amy wondered despairingly. Could any of the three injured men stand another day in the cold—or possibly another night?

She bent over her brother again and searched his face. Normally he was thin and hyper like Amy, but the ordeal of this last week had made him gray and dreadfully gaunt. His mind wandered when he was awake. Once he'd called Amy "Mom."

"It's normal," responded Flint to her frightened query. "He's just out of it. He'll come around."

But would he?

Ted, the copilot, was terribly weak, although still the most lucid of the three. His feet were frostbitten, so he'd have to be carried down, too. The pilot, Grant, was big and silent, barely conscious. Deborah forced some hot tea into his mouth, but most of it dribbled back out. Deborah tried again, holding his mouth open, her eyes filled with tears of frustration.

They would need all eight members of the team, then. Two to a litter, for the sad, blanket-draped form would have to come down, as well.

Del was on the radio to Ollie again. Amy fed Roger tiny sips of soup and tried to listen to the radio conversation.

"We'll be leaving soon. What's the weather report? Over."

Ollie's voice came in, weak with distance and obscured by static. "Snow showers again this afternoon. High winds. Get your butt moving, son. Over."

"We may have to stay at camp one tonight. I'd like to know the advisability of a helicopter in the morning at camp one. Repeat, can a chopper get to camp one tomorrow? Over."

Her heart sank. Tomorrow. And just minutes ago that helicopter had been only a few hundred feet away. Why couldn't this have happened in the summer?

Roger stirred and opened his eyes. "Enough," he whispered.

"But you have to eat something," she kept urging.

"It makes my stomach hurt. Too long without food, I guess...." Then he shut his eyes, apparently exhausted once more.

Amy carefully tucked the sleeping bag around his neck. At least he wouldn't be cold on the descent. The climbers had packed in four extra sleeping bags, just in case. Thank heavens they had, thought Amy fervently. As a matter of fact, the rescue party had remembered everything they could possibly have needed—the extra bags, the medical supplies, the food that starving men could digest, plus all the climbing gear.

No wonder Del had spent so much time going over and over those lists. Each man and woman had carried packs weighing at least fifty pounds, crammed with essential items.

Amy looked across Roger to Del, who was talking on the radio. He'd organized the whole thing, from hot chocolate to toilet paper. She was impressed, despite herself.

Finally Del signed off. He sat by the radio for a time, arms resting loosely on his knees, head hanging between his shoulders. When he looked up, Amy suddenly became aware of how much he'd changed on this climb. His face was covered with a four-day growth of whiskers; he appeared drawn and tired and older. There were deep frown lines etched in his forehead.

The extent of his burden struck Amy then: this entire expedition—now consisting of thirteen people— was Del's responsibility and his responsibility alone. If one single person was hurt or lost he would bear the brunt of the guilt and pain.

She looked down at Roger, then raised her glance to catch Del watching her. She felt herself blushing, an odd reaction for Amy. But his gaze had the power to make her recall his touch and the strength of his big hands and the raw power of his body. She tore her eyes away with difficulty.

Damn it, Amy thought, anger roiling within her. How could she have fallen for someone she couldn't trust?

How in God's name could Del really want Roger dead? After Del had gone to such pains to keep everyone alive? It was hard to believe. But, then, perhaps he was diabolically clever at appearing innocent.

Amy practically groaned in torment. She had to know! She had to! The doubt was killing her.

She pulled out her tape machine while she waited for the camp to get organized for the descent. With Roger's head pillowed in her lap, she spoke quietly into the hand recorder, giving her impressions of the downed plane, of Pearl Pass, of the campsite. She might need these details for her story. But dictating was a habit, in any case, and regardless of her big exposé, she would have done the same. Curiously, it seemed more important to record her impressions for herself than for the story. She wanted to remember every moment of this experience.

"Why did Del wave the helicopter off this morning?" she demanded softly into her machine. "Was it really unsafe, or did he need more time to complete his contract? Darn, I wish I knew!"

"Gabbing again?" asked Flint, coming around to check Roger's pulse.

"A habit," Amy said nervously, stuffing the tape machine into her pocket. Why was Flint Smith interested?

But he was kneeling by Roger, explaining that they would be strapping him into a litter to carry him down. Amy wasn't sure Roger understood.

Deborah was devastatingly strong and efficient, lifting the wounded men with Rob's help, strapping them into the lightweight metal mesh litters so they looked like mummies. Amy felt helpless and could only watch, ruing her inexperience, slowly munching on a granola bar. She thought, miserably, that despite her denial, Deborah would make a fit mate for a man like Del. The two of them could go on climbing into the sunset until they were old and gray.

Lonnie cleared up the camp. Jay folded the tents into tiny, compact squares. Glen helped Deborah and Rob with the litters. Flint checked vital signs on the three men. Everything was so *efficient*.

They divided up the litters, two climbers to carry each one.

"Can I help?" asked Amy as they lifted the wounded. She was well aware they were carrying their own heavy packs, as well.

Lonnie gave a short harsh laugh.

"It's okay," said Jay kindly. "We'll be going real slow."

Somehow Roger's litter fell to Del and Glen. Was this some kind of prearranged deal? By Del . . . or Glen . . . or *both* of them? She shook her head in confusion but said nothing to Del. She'd just have to watch Roger like a hawk.

DEL'S ARMS ACHED with the weight of the litter. It was exhausting work—even going downhill—to carry the injured men. The terrain was rough, and the new snow was making it terribly difficult to get a steady footing. It was backbreaking labor, even for eight fit, experienced climbers.

Del called rest stops often.

Every time they had to pick up those litters again it hurt worse. And the loads seemed to get heavier. . . .

They stumbled over buried rocks and logs. Swede cursed in his native tongue loudly and often. Once Deborah tripped and dropped the end of the litter. Ted, the copilot, couldn't help crying out.

"I'm sorry," Deborah panted.

"Lady, I'm not complaining." Ted tried to grin.

Del was aware of Amy dogging his footsteps, hovering over her brother like a mother hen, casting furtive glances at every team member.

The whole situation galled him. Amy would sleep with him, all right, but confide in him? Apparently not. Didn't she know that he was on Roger's litter, not the heavier one containing the pilot, so that he could also keep an eye on Roger Slavinsky? He guessed Amy didn't realize that, either.

Del was aware, too, that the weather was worsening, socking in for yet another storm. The blue was gradually being chased across the sky as clouds moved in from the west. A fresh wind swirled around them in ever stronger gusts. Far up on the peaks, curtains of snow slanted in from the crest of Pearl Pass. Soon visibility would be lessening down here where the climbers struggled along. He had to weigh their exhaustion carefully against the danger of being caught in a blizzard.

"Rest!" he yelled, putting his end of the litter down and shaking his arms out. Hell's bells, this was hard work!

He saw Amy drop in her tracks. He had to admit to himself that she was doing pretty darn well for a rank beginner.

Amy Slavin. Cute, wiry, stubborn, all angles and wild gestures and flashing thoughts. A tornado. It was impossible to keep his eyes off her, to get her out of his head. He wanted to throttle her, and perversely, he wanted to take her in his arms and let his pent-up desires blaze.

He sat in the snow, trying to relax, to gather some precious bits of strength. There was little talk around him. Everyone kept looking uncomfortably up at the darkening sky, at the black spruce trees whose branches swayed and hissed in the wind.

"Lousy storm coming in," growled Swede for want of conversation.

Deborah sighed.

"We'll make it," said Glen, irritatingly even tempered. "Not too far now."

"There's the icefall," reminded Jay.

Lonnie grunted his agreement.

Del was silent. He desperately needed to rest, mentally as well as physically, but his mind remained too active. Why had Glen gone to Amy's tent last night? To say good-night? Hardly. No, it would be more like Glen to have gone in there to try to seduce Amy!

Jealousy and anger shot through Del, just as in the old days, back in school, when Glen had always pushed the limits and they had ended up like two bulls, horns locked. Then handsome young Shepherd had taken the notion that that Indian girl had to be his. Well, Glen never had known how to take no for an answer.

They should have called what Glen did rape.

And how in the name of decency could Glen run into her and her child now on the streets of Jackson and look her in the face?

Del had thought last night of going over to Amy's tent and dragging Shepherd out by the heels, but Glen had left before the urge got too strong.

Was Amy blind? Couldn't she see what Shepherd really was? Why did she seem to trust him?

He shook off the unsettling thoughts. There was work to be done.

"Let's go!" Del straightened and nodded to Glen. They lifted the litter. The rest of the crew stood, some groaning, and prepared themselves. Del set a fast pace, maybe too fast, but he felt as though he had to run away from something that was stalking him.

Whatever it was, it walked just as fast as he did.

The fixed rope across the icefall was still in place, glaring bright red against the white snow. Del didn't even have to give orders; they all knew what to do. Lonnie crossed silently and agilely, like a brightly hued monkey. More ropes were fixed on pitons. Pulleys were dug out of packs; ropes were attached to litters and knotted. The webbed belts were handed out.

Finally they were ready.

Jay and Rob crossed. Then the ropes were tested for safety. Deborah and Flint went next. Three of the litters were attached to pulleys and dragged across with tag lines. So far so good.

Swede crossed, slipping a little, but pulling himself up.

"You go next, Amy," said Glen, checking the pitons once more.

Amy looked around, as if to say, "What . . . me?"

"You did it last time," Del said. "It'll be easier now."

"I won't go until Roger's across." She folded her arms stubbornly.

Del looked at Glen in exasperation. Shepherd shrugged. "Okay." They waited until Jay tested the pitons on the far side of the icefall.

"Ready?" yelled Jay.

"Okay!" shouted Del.

Roger's litter was hooked on to the pulley. Jay caught the tag lines that were thrown to him and started to tug. The litter edged, bumping and scraping, across the glacial wall.

Del wasn't even watching when it happened. He heard Amy's sharp gasp and sensed Glen straighten up quickly beside him.

The litter seemed to sag a little. Jay stopped pulling instantly.

"What's the matter?" Amy was asking. "What is it?"

Then one of the fixed ropes tied to a piton near Del's feet snapped, slithering away just out of reach to hang down from the far side. Roger's litter lurched, its tail end suddenly hanging over the thousand-foot drop.

"My God!" he heard Deborah yell. Jay was securing the tag line to a piton. But the strain on the remaining lines—and ice screws . . .

Del couldn't do a thing! He was on the wrong side!

"Help him!" Amy was crying.

It was only a split second, but it seemed like hours that the litter had been dangling, swaying sickeningly above the abyss.

Did he dare cross on the remaining rope? No, the strain would be too much. Del's mind raced. The litter was closer to the far side.

Suddenly he noticed Jay edging out from the other side.

"No!" he wanted to yell. "Not Jay!" But it was too late. All he could do was watch helplessly as his brother reached the litter. *Quick, Jay,* he thought. *The strain is too much.*

Jay was trying to attach another line to the litter but was having trouble. What was taking so long?

Del prayed. *Hurry, hurry. Let it hold.*

Abruptly an ice screw on Del's side pulled out of the ice with a wrenching noise. He lunged for the rope, but it jerked out of his hands.

Amy screamed.

The litter was dangling vertically now, held only by a single line, the same one that supported Jay.

Del swore, his heart pounding. *Let it hold, let it hold!*

Flint and Swede had already grabbed their end of the crucial rope and were struggling, yelling to Jay.

"Hold on!"

"We'll try to pull you up!"

"Oh, my God."

"Throw him another line!"

Lonnie was crawling out, hammering in screws with great ringing blows, his expression intent on the work.

But Del could see it was up to Jay alone. Slowly, carefully, deliberately, Jay hammered in a piton.

Never trust a piton you haven't hammered in yourself.

Standing with the points of his crampons dug into the ice wall, he hooked his carabiner to the piton and braced himself. "I'm going to push the litter from underneath," he called up. "Grab the slack, guys." His voice was cool and professional.

Slowly the litter rose; the others pulled at the rope, helping.

Del held his breath.

Finally Swede grabbed the end of the litter and gave a great heave, his veins popping. The litter slid onto a level surface.

Roger was safe.

Lonnie, perched like a gecko lizard on a wall above Jay, threw him another rope.

"Hook it on!" yelled Flint. "Hurry, man!"

Methodically Jay secured the rope to his carabiner, then to the ice screw. Habit. He began inching his way up the ice wall, finding holds where seemingly there were none. He got to ten feet below the outstretched hands of the others; someone tossed him another line. He grabbed the end, and willing hands heaved, pulling him up until he stood on level ground.

"Good Lord, you had us scared silly," said Rob, slapping his brother's back.

"Roger okay?" was all Jay asked.

"Sure, sure."

Swede yelled something indiscernible.

Deborah kissed Jay's cheek.

On the other side, Amy had sunk onto the snow, her face totally drained of color. Her eyes were huge in her small face.

"He's okay," Del said to her. "They're both fine."

She raised her eyes to him, but couldn't seem to answer.

He stood there over her, watching her thin form huddled on the ground, trembling. He wanted to gather her up into his arms and comfort her, to brush the curly bangs back from her forehead, to wipe the smudges of dirt off her face, to kiss away the fear and anxiety. She'd just seen two men nearly fall to their deaths. It was harrowing for anyone, but for Amy...

He touched her bowed head with his hand. "He's all right, Amy," he repeated, not knowing what else to say.

Then she turned her face up to his and he saw that she was desolate, filled with terror and awful, tearing doubt.

CHAPTER SIXTEEN

Day 6 P.M.

AMY CROUCHED ON THE PATH, trying to still the pounding of her heart. Someone had just tried to kill Roger. She'd expected it all along, but somehow the actual act was as shocking as if she'd never suspected a thing.

She looked up at Del, sensing his eyes were on her. Was he the one?

Then, before she even had time to collect her thoughts, she realized that it was her turn to cross the icefall. A knot of fear twisted in her stomach. She'd never make it this time.

A hand touched her gently. "Go on, Amy," Glen was saying. "It's safe now."

She turned and looked into Glen's reassuring eyes and almost said, "That's what everyone told me about Roger." Then Amy glanced across the span of vertical ice. Roger was over now, tied helplessly in his litter. She had to get across to him!

"Remember," said Del, "keep your mind on the other side and just move one foot at a time."

She had to go! Slowly Amy clipped herself to the line and stepped out onto the fall; she was shaking from head to foot, which only made each move more difficult. But Roger was over there, waiting.

Come on, Amy, she kept reminding herself. *You have to get there.*

For a moment, when she was just past halfway, she glanced down and was overcome with dizziness. *You're going to fall!* her mind shrieked. She took a deep, controlled breath and then made herself move onward, hugging the wall, ignoring her strained, quivering muscles. All she needed to do was keep moving and trust the ropes—she was nearly across. *Don't look down, Slavin.*

There were outstretched phantom hands down there, beckoning. But she could escape them if she kept moving.

Then, amazingly, she was on level ground. She sagged, unable to stand, sure that her heart was going to burst right out of her chest.

"Is Roger all right?" she managed to gasp to the others.

"He's fine," said Flint. "To tell the truth, I think he was unconscious the whole time." He patted her bowed head affectionately.

"Jay? Where's Jay?" She looked around, too weak to get up.

"I'm here," he called, smiling.

"Jay, you were wonderful," Amy breathed. "I've never seen anything like it."

"He vere pretty darn good!" boomed Swede.

"Nice technical maneuver-r" Lonnie put in grudgingly.

Amy mustered some strength, pushed herself up and tottered over to where Flint was bandaging a rope burn on Jay's hand. She put her arms around him and gave him a big hug. "Thank you," she whispered.

Jay just ducked his head.

When realization finally settled over Amy that both she and Roger were safe, her heart began to slow down and she looked across the icefall to the two men on the other side. They were talking and Glen was hooking himself on to the line.

She narrowed her eyes and watched them. Suddenly, curiously, Del looked down at something and froze. Amy could almost feel the tension emanating from his big body. She strained to see what held his concentration: a bit of red. It looked like a piece of bright red rope still knotted to a piton.

Glen was very still, staring at it, too. Slowly Del's head rose to meet Glen's gaze. The two men stared at each other for what seemed like an eternity. Then Glen bent over, too, and seemed to be studying the end of rope. She could see them both fingering the knot, talking about something, but she couldn't hear and they were too far for her to read their faces.

Finally Glen straightened, shrugged and snapped himself on to the fixed line.

And as Amy squinted, trying to see across the wall of ice, Del turned to look at her, fixing her with his gaze. Her heart thumped woodenly with awful apprehension, but she could not decipher his expression.

The rope had been tampered with—that much was obvious. Amy could have told them that. What confused her was Del's reaction. Was he truly surprised to discover that the crossing had been sabotaged? Or was he merely wondering whether she suspected him?

She tore her eyes away and knelt beside Roger. It couldn't be Del. She would not *allow* it to be him.

Then who was it?

She scanned every face around her, even Glen's as he stepped onto level ground after his crossing. How did a guilty person look? Could you tell? They all appeared shaken by the near accident, but was one of them merely disappointed?

Jay, of course, had moved into the good guy column. And Lonnie, despite his abrasiveness, had risked his life to help Roger.

Flint—well, he'd had lots of chances to do something such as slip the wrong drug into Roger, what with his paramedical training. He probably wasn't the one, then.

That certainly narrowed the field. And for the guilty one, time was growing short.

Del was crossing the icefall easily, quickly. He unsnapped himself from the fixed rope and went straight to Jay. "You idiot," he barked, but the honest concern on his face belied his harsh tone.

"Come off it, Del. Somebody had to do it," said Jay.

Del had no answer to that; it was absolutely true. He put a big hand on his youngest brother's shoulder and stood there, mute, for a long time.

Thank heavens they were going down, Amy thought a hundred times during the descent. Her shoulders ached increasingly from the heavy pack and her feet felt more like clumsy, sore blocks of cement with every step. And then, to top everything off, the long threatened storm came in, bringing with it wind-lashed sheets of snow.

They were finally approaching the site of camp one, when Rob stopped and announced that he smelled smoke.

"There's a campfire somewhere," he said. "I can't see anything, but my nose never makes a mistake."

"Camp one? But no one's there," breathed Deborah, struggling to lift her end of the litter over a fallen tree.

Swede shouted as loud as he could. Then they waited to hear an answer. But the snow deadened sound very effectively.

Swede yelled again. Faintly, from out of the dim, snow-obscured distance, a voice emerged. They picked up their pace and moved toward it.

It's the police, thought Amy, *coming to meet us! Or Ollie, perhaps, tired of sitting at base camp.*

A lone figure materialized out of the murkiness below them. "Hello, folks!" Amy heard as she strained to identify the person. That voice was familiar. . . .

"Frank Pereira," she heard Del say, and she sucked in a breath of horror.

"Am I glad to see you!" the Shearing man called jovially. "You've done a great job, just terrific! I spent yesterday at base camp. Heard all the news on the radio."

Del was carrying the front end of Roger's litter; he kept moving while Pereira walked alongside. "What are you doing up here?" Del asked in between even laboring breaths.

"I, for one," Glen interrupted, "am real glad to see him. Smell that fire! There's bacon cooking!"

Amy heard Pereira's reply. "I'll tell you all about it as soon as you're warm and rested." He dropped back a few feet and offered to take Deborah's end of the copilot's litter.

Deborah blinked the snow off her lashes and shot him an incredulous glance. "*I've* got it."

Pereira! Amy's mind tried to fit itself around the reality of his presence. Pereira was there....

Then he was talking to Del, and she strained to listen. His smooth, friendly voice nauseated her. "Why, Ollie and I were watching the weather like two hawks yesterday. When it cleared, he agreed that I could hike up to camp one. I couldn't bear sitting around doing nothing."

Sure, Amy thought heatedly. She just bet! She watched him carefully and saw his glance fall on her helpless brother. She clenched her teeth in anger.

Of course, Amy thought, she should have known Pereira would have to meet the team sometime before they reached safety. He must have made his decision to hike up to camp one the minute he played her cassette.

Stupid! She should have realized!

Amy twisted her head to look at the team, struggling along with their litters. Who was Pereira's man? Who, her mind shrieked in desperation.

By the time they entered the clearing of camp one Amy was exhausted, mentally and physically, tired of being wet, cold, dirty and hungry. Tired of the continual anxiety, of being afraid, of not being able to trust anyone. And now she had to worry about Frank Pereira!

"I'm proud to be associated with you wonderful people," Pereira was saying. "It's a miracle, a true miracle." He bent over Roger. "Mr. Slavinsky, I can't tell you how happy I am to finally meet you. Mr. Gerhunt sends his very best."

Roger opened his eyes and stared up at him blankly. "Who're you?" he mumbled.

But Pereira was turning away. "Fine people, all of you. Your Dad," he said to Del, "told me he'd talked to the sheriff, and there's a clearing a mile below here where they can land helicopters. They have two machines ready for tomorrow morning if the snow stops."

Amy looked over the team members. Was anyone exchanging knowing glances with Pereira? She couldn't tell. One thing she knew for certain, though. Whoever it was had one night left to complete his unfinished business. Now there were two would-be murderers—Pereira and his accomplice. She'd have to watch Roger twice as carefully.

The rest of the tents were raised quickly to shelter the wounded men. The climbers devoured the bacon and warmed up dried beef stroganoff on noodles. Not exactly Maxim's, but it was nourishing and hot.

Amy ate, her eyes flickering around nervously, expecting the worst. She never let Roger out of her sight. If only her brother were coherent enough to understand. She wanted desperately to explain to him the danger he was in. He had to know.

Deborah sat with her as she tried again after spooning food into his mouth. "Do you know where we are, Roger?" Amy began.

He didn't move. Deborah made an attempt. "Roger." She shook his shoulder lightly. "Wake up." Then she looked doubtfully at Amy. "I don't know...."

Slowly Roger opened his eyes and mumbled, blinking.

"Roger, it's Amy. Come on."

"Amy," he murmured, "it *is* you." Then he subsided for a few moments, trying to gather a thought. "So confused...."

"Try to listen," urged Amy as she looked at Deborah for help. "There's a man from Shearing here, Roger. Do you understand?"

"Why," he slurred, "are you here?"

It was hopeless. Amy felt like crying and raging and taking out her frustration on him, but she knew how ridiculous that would be.

"I know," commiserated Deborah. "Give him time, Amy. By morning I'm sure he'll be coherent."

"By morning," Amy said with a sigh, "I'm not sure I'll be coherent. And to think, all this so he can be a hero and I can get my stupid story."

As darkness fell the snow began to abate; the well-fed climbers retired to their tents to rest, to take off their boots and massage aching, blistered feet, to dry out damp sweaters and socks.

One more night, Amy thought, drunk with fatigue. Automatically she felt in her pocket for her gun. Her fingers wrapped around the cool metal almost reverently as images crowded her weary mind.

How would they come at Roger? Silently, the flap of her tent opening without her noticing until it was too late? Or would an erstwhile friendly head poke itself in? "Just checking, Amy..."

She knew without any doubt that whoever it was would have to kill her, too. How would her death be explained? Oh, Roger's was simple enough. They could smother him and it would be attributed to exposure. INJURED SURVIVOR OF CRASH DIES. But what about her? Heart attack? Not at her age. Sleeping pills? Had Pereira brought some kind of drug up with him just in case?

Amy could picture the headline: SISTER OF SURVIVOR OVERDOSES. But her boss, Ken, wouldn't buy that, or... would he? Kenneth had no idea what was going on. She shouldn't have just bragged about her big story. She should have leveled with him.

Deborah, yes. Deborah would know that Amy had been murdered. Then a terrible sinking sensation swept Amy. By the time Deborah told the police that Amy's and Roger's deaths were not accidental it wouldn't matter!

Amy would be dead. And Roger, too, along with all the jargon in his head.

One piling on the other, the thoughts kept beating at her, beating and pounding and driving her crazy. She didn't dare fall asleep. Del's face kept materializing in her exhaustion-drugged mind, his blue eyes at first soft and loving, then narrow and cruel, as he was choking her, forcing pills down her throat.... Oh, Del! It couldn't be him!

Soft voices drifted into the tent occasionally. Footsteps crunched on snow. A log in the fire cracked like a pistol shot, making Amy jump.

She was almost dozing again, when she realized that there were footsteps approaching her tent. Suddenly alert, Amy felt for the gun in her pocket once more and scrambled to the tent's opening.

"Who is it?" she asked, peering out into the darkness. If only she could see better!

"Frank," came a voice. "Just wanted to check on your brother, Miss Slavin. After all, that's why I'm here."

"He's fine," she said coldly, "but I don't want him disturbed."

"Of course not. Wouldn't dream of it. The poor fellow. He's been through an ordeal, a real ordeal." He nodded, agreeing with himself.

"Good night, Mr. Pereira," said Amy firmly, pulling her head back into the tent and thinking, he wouldn't dare try that ruse again, would he? All she had to do was scream, after all....

But, she recalled with a tremor, Pereira was not in this alone...

THE PIECE OF CUT RED ROPE sat like lead in Del's parka pocket. And there hadn't been a moment to be alone with Amy, to show it to her, to pin her down and get some answers.

Until now.

Pereira a few minutes earlier had worried him. However, Amy had apparently handled Frank just fine. But, then, Pereira had not been up there on the icefall, which meant that one of the climbers, horrifying as the thought was, had tried to kill Roger Slavinsky.

"Damn," he swore under his breath as he rubbed a calloused hand over his bristly jaw. She'd slept with him, cried on his shoulder.... Blast it all, she seemed to really care about him! So why wouldn't she trust him?

Del began to walk toward her tent. He promised himself to keep a lid on his temper, but he could feel it bubbling up inside of him like a mud spout as he bent down to enter.

"Who is it?" came Amy's small, tense voice. "Someone's there. Who is it?"

Del opened the flap. "It's me. Put on your coat and come on out here." His voice was a harsh whisper.

She came out all right, but very, very slowly, eyeing him as if he were Jack the Ripper.

"Del." Amy's voice was frightened. "What do you want? Please don't ..."

Seeing the fear of him written so plainly on her face abruptly infuriated Del. His tenuous control snapped.

"Don't what?" And then he grabbed her arm, much harder than he'd intended to, and pulled her up against him. He forced himself to keep his voice down, but the anger and frustration were almost too powerful. "Don't *what*?" he said again. "Tell me!"

Amy began to struggle, and if he hadn't been so confounded and furious her futile twisting might have been comical. Then suddenly one of her arms was free—how?—and she was reaching into her pocket and...

The realization of what she held in her hand hit him like a hammer blow—instant and utterly shocking. He reacted without thought, instinctively knocking her hand aside. The force of the blow caused the gun to fall to the snow-packed ground.

"You little..." he gasped. Then he held her easily with one hand and reached down, picking up the weapon.

"I'll scream," came Amy's quavering voice as she recovered and began to struggle again.

"Don't bother." He was holding her against him tightly, trying unsuccessfully to unload the little weapon with his free hand, all the while grumbling, "I don't believe this. A gun!"

"It *is* you!" Amy's voice whispered fiercely. "Why? Oh, why, Del?"

"Whoever, whatever, for God's sake, it is *not* me! Now quit thrashing around before this thing goes off."

"It isn't loaded. I don't have any bullets for it."

He let go of her abruptly. They were both standing there facing each other, their chests heaving, when Del became aware of Jay's head poking out of his tent. Then, like a jack-in-the-box, Deborah's popped out of hers. Del rolled his eyes in exasperation; he and Amy were making too much noise. Everyone must think they were having a lover's quarrel. Hell's bells!

"You mean to tell me," Del began, immediately realizing he was still too loud. "You mean to tell me," he tried again in a raspy whisper, "it's not..."

"I don't have any bullets," she repeated.

He was finally able to check the chamber in the gun. "I can't believe it," he said. "You brought this along to protect yourself and you don't have any ammo."

"No. And I don't have any way to stop you, either. Oh, Del," she choked out, "why? Why must it be you?"

"Stop the theatrics," he ordered, his surprise gone. He looked around, hoping no one could hear their conversation. "And keep your voice down." He reached into his pocket and pulled out the rope, dangling it in front of her face. "Quit standing there like a scared rabbit and explain this to me. It's been cut, Amy, but I guess you know that."

"Yes," she breathed.

"Why? Why is someone trying to kill Roger?" But he got the same response as he always received from Amy—silence and stubbornly pursed lips.

"I'm so damn mad," he growled, throwing both the rope and the gun at her feet. "Keep them. They'll make nice souvenirs." Del began to stride away before he did murder someone, then suddenly spun back around to her. "Answer me one thing," he said in a harsh whisper. "Tell me why it is you think Glen Shepherd is such a swell guy and I'm dirt?"

He could see her lick her lips and swallow hard. "You tell me about . . . the girl in high school. The Indian girl." Amy's gaze fell to her feet.

"How did you . . . ?" Of course, Glen had told her— probably some twisted version of his own devising. *I don't believe this,* repeated itself over and over in his head. *He* was being accused! Glen, that son-of-a . . .

Del could barely contain his temper. "What exactly did Shepherd tell you, Amy?"

He could see her swallow hard. "It was just some things about high school. About an Indian girl...."

"Specifically, Amy!"

"Something about her having a child."

"Mine?"

Amy nodded miserably.

"That..." Del swore under his breath. "The fact is—if, of course, you're interested—that her child belongs to Glen."

"Del...I don't know what to say. Why, why would Glen tell me that?"

"Because he hates my guts and wants you to hate 'em, too."

"He said that you were the one who always goaded him. Competition, all that stuff."

"Sounds like our fine, upstanding deputy." He turned away from Amy, pausing in thought. "I've never known why, but right from the very first year at school, Glen felt he had to compete with me. Oh, sure, I egged him on at times over the years, but only because he was always breathing down my neck. Then he had his revenge."

"The girl."

"That's right."

"But couldn't you have helped her?"

"You don't understand Indian clannishness and pride, Amy. No. By the time I found out, she had dropped out of school and fled to the reservation. No one would tell me anything. I finally had to give it up or cause her more humiliation."

"It's all so crazy," whispered Amy then.

"What is?"

"You, Glen, everything."

"And someone trying to kill Roger. Don't forget that." Del watched her reaction carefully. Her eyes grew big and round in the darkness and she shrank from him slightly. A horrible silence settled between them. Del's emotions were in a turmoil. He kicked at the snow with a boot and stalked back and forth in front of her. Then he stopped and faced her. "You are the most aggravating female I have ever met!"

"Del..."

"No!" He put up a hand. "I'm mad as a hornet right now and I don't know how to handle it...or you. Frankly, all I'd like to do is throttle you."

"You wouldn't dare."

Del's eyes narrowed and he shook his head in wonderment. "Believe whatever you want, Amy." Then he turned on his heel and walked away.

CHAPTER SEVENTEEN

Day 7 A.M.

AMY ROLLED OVER in her sleeping bag and groaned. Every muscle in her body ached. Then she realized it was morning and Roger was talking to her and everything inside the tent was bathed in muted blue brilliance.

The sun was out! It was shining through the blue nylon walls of her tent, turning everything into a cheerful munchkin world. She was alive. Roger was alive! Today was it; they'd be airlifted out, home free!

"I'm starving," her brother was saying. "Could you...?"

Amy smiled at him; Roger was coming around. Thank the Lord! "Sure, just a sec. Oh, Roger, we made it! Just a little while now. He has to let the helicopter land now. He has to!" She talked, explaining everything to her brother as she pulled on her hiking boots, the only articles of clothing besides her down parka that she'd removed for five days.

Ugh, she must look like a witch, Amy thought as she crawled out of the tent and straightened up. At least women didn't sprout beards, but she would love to wash her hair.

Wow, mused Amy, just to be thinking about things such as washing her hair must mean life was getting back to normal.

The sky was frosty innocent blue, a traitor, a turncoat, as if it had never been a howling nightmare yesterday and the day before and the day before that. The snow was already melting, dripping from branches.

Deborah held the coffeepot up to Amy, grinning. "Good morning! The sun's out!"

Amy felt like dancing. She was filled with a vast, lighthearted relief.

Frank Pereira was eating breakfast. She even smiled at him archly and said "Good morning, Mr. Pereira. Lovely day, isn't it?" He couldn't get to Roger, not today. It was too late.

Del was on the radio. Just seeing him made Amy cringe inwardly, but she wouldn't think about last night; she wouldn't wonder why, after the camp slept, he had not returned to do his dirty work. It could be— it really could be—that Del wasn't the one. After the helicopters got the wounded out, after she'd washed her hair and slept for a hundred years, then she would decide what to do about Del Pardee.

She took up a bowl of dried oatmeal and looked at him. Del was not talking—who could blame him—yet she couldn't help but notice the way his heavy beard lent him a primitive look, the way his muscular thighs strained at his pants as he sat hunched, talking on the radio. Yes, she could look him over all she liked, for he was sure not paying any attention to her.

She ducked back into her tent quietly, not even yelping when boiling hot coffee slopped out of her mug onto her knee. *You klutz,* she chided herself.

"I'm starved," Roger was saying as she hunkered down beside him.

"Literally," Amy said with a laugh.

"Not funny," Roger retorted.

He was so much better! It was like magic. Food and warmth were all he'd needed. She wanted to sing with joy and relief.

"I sure hate to be so much trouble," he said, wolfing down the oatmeal that Amy fed him a spoonful at a time. "If my leg weren't broken . . ."

"Roger, was it awful? Were you scared?" Amy asked suddenly.

"When the plane crashed? Terrified. I know I blacked out for a while." His face was still haggard; he looked even worse when he spoke of the crash.

"Sorry for dredging it up," Amy said quickly.

"How are the other guys?"

"Ted's okay. Grant is . . . well . . ."

"Not so good. We knew . . ." Roger's face drew into harsh lines. "And to think I was curious about the scenery down here."

Amy considered a minute, then decided to ask. "Roger, is there a possibility that the plane was sabotaged? By Shearing, I mean."

He was silent for a moment. "I thought of that. But Ted and I had hours—days—to talk, and he went over the crash. You can imagine. He decided it was a problem with the fuel readout gauge. It was a new electronic one. Anyway, it gave them the wrong reading.

Ted said they should have checked it manually, but they'd been assured the tank had been filled in Portland. And Shearing never knew about the plane, as far as I know."

"I see," Amy said thoughtfully. "So you're pretty sure the accident was due to human error."

"Yes. And pure rotten luck."

Outside her tent she could hear Del's voice. "We have to walk out a mile or so."

Lots of groans, but good-natured ones.

"A mile, that's all. To that big meadow. They're sending two choppers for the wounded and any other casualties."

"Me," somebody yelled, "I'm a casualty! I can't walk!" Laughter and catcalls followed.

"The heck you are," somebody replied.

"Pop's still at base camp," Del continued, "and the rest of us are going to have to help him pack and load up the jeeps. Then we can put our tootsies up, folks."

There was cheering.

"So let's get a move on. They'll be there in an hour."

An hour! Only one more hour! Amy grinned to herself. "You haven't forgotten the story you were going to tell the Defense Department, have you?" she asked Roger playfully.

"Not likely." He smiled back then, sobered. "I sort of remember meeting that Frank Pereira in Portland. I think he gave a talk on company security and industrial espionage or something like that."

"I'll bet he's an expert," said Amy dryly.

"You don't really think," ventured Roger, "that he was actually sent here to...to..." He obviously couldn't say it.

"Kill you? Of course. I'm convinced of it. And me, too, probably. And any other witnesses. It's pretty easy to have accidents on a climb. Like the one you had yesterday."

"It's hard to believe, Amy. I mean, sometimes that imagination of yours goes a little wild."

"Well, we aren't going to find out if I was wrong or right on, baby brother, because Mr. Pereira and whoever he's bought waited too long," she retorted smugly.

"Nothing like self-confidence," replied Roger sarcastically.

Amy took a minute to feel in her big pockets and pull out the small mirror she'd brought along—one of her essentials. It was cracked right down the middle. She looked at her reflection, slashed crazily by the crack. Oh, my! There was dirt smudged on her forehead. Feathers from her sleeping bag perched in her tangled hair along with a few twigs and a dead leaf. Her fingernails were broken and dirty. A street urchin in climbing clothes.

"Disgusting," she muttered, combing her fingers through her hair to pull out the bigger pieces of flotsam. If she used her comb she'd likely break its teeth.

"Come on out, little Amy," boomed Swede's voice. "Ve're going to load up your brudder."

The litters were readied once again. Amy insisted on taking down her own tent, folding it up and carrying it along with her sleeping bag in her pack. After all, it was only a mile.

Del came up to her as she was swinging her pack to her shoulders. He reached out to help her get the straps on, but she did it by herself.

"We're almost there, Amy," he said carefully.

"Has this been a successful mission for you?" she couldn't resist asking.

"Yes, very. No injuries. Three men rescued. I'd call it successful." He watched her face closely; his cobalt-blue eyes, narrowed in the sunlight, were boring into hers. He looked mean with that dark, stubbly beard of his and the stern lines on his face.

"No thanks to me, I suppose," she managed to say.

Not a step of the way down looked familiar to Amy. She'd climbed that part of the trail in blinding snow, in the dark, wandering in circles. Today it was a pleasant hike down a path between huge sheltering spruce trees. By the time they reached the clearing, patches of mud and grass were showing through the rapidly melting snow.

The two choppers were already waiting for them in the wide-open, slightly slanting meadow where Amy had become lost that awful night. She only recognized it from the two large boulders on either side of the path.

"There they are!" yelled Flint.

Everyone seemed to pick up his pace, stumbling, laughing, making jokes. The pilots walked to meet them, grinning, shaking everyone's hands. One helicopter was from the sheriff's department; the pilot knew Glen. The other was from the Jackson hospital, a Flight for Life chopper with its own paramedic on board.

Amy stared at the two pilots and the paramedic in amazement. They looked so clean, so well groomed and smooth shaven. Their uniforms were neatly pressed. How must the motley crew of climbers appear to these men?

They loaded the litter with the body on it first—into the hospital chopper. Next were Grant and Ted, who was grabbing everybody's hand, saying goodbye, thanking them over and over.

"Hey, Swede, bring me a bottle of aquavit in the hospital, will you?"

"Sure t'ing," agreed Swede.

"And Deborah, my love, promise me you'll come fly with me sometime?"

"After what you just did to an airplane?" She laughed, patting his arm.

Flint was also going with the wounded men, to help the paramedic relay their conditions to the hospital.

"Those helicopters sure look tempting," said Rob ruefully.

Lonnie grunted. Did that mean he disagreed? She never could tell with Lonnie.

They started putting Roger's litter into the Flight for Life chopper. Amy followed, assuming she'd be going with Roger.

"I'm sorry, miss," said the pilot, "but my machine won't carry any more weight. You can go in the other one."

She looked at Roger, who was disappearing inside the whirlybird, then at the pilot. "But I have to go with my brother."

"I'm really sorry. But I can't endanger my machine. That's why we brought two along. In case there was more than one load."

"But I have to go with him!" It was all coming back—the fear, the uncertainty, the paranoid suspicion of everybody and everything.

"Amy," said Del, "go in the other one. Roger will be all right."

She whirled on him. "The only reason he's all right now is that I was with him. And I'm going with him now!"

"Ma'am," said the paramedic, "you're delaying the transport of critical patients. We'll take real good care of your brother and you can come see him in the hospital later."

"I will not let him go without me!" she cried again stubbornly. She was aware of the glances exchanged among the people around her. She didn't care.

Deborah came up to her and put a hand on her arm. "Amy, take it easy. I'm sure—"

She shrugged Deborah's hand off. "Why can't Roger and I go in the other helicopter? It's empty."

"It isn't going to the hospital," said the pilot of the Flight for Life machine.

"But it could," insisted Amy.

Glen stepped forward, clearing his throat. "Look, Terry, I'll take the responsibility for this. You carry Miss Slavin and her brother and I'll come along to explain it all to the sheriff. Besides, he'd probably like to hear my report as soon as possible. Is that okay with you?''

"Sure," said Terry, "as long as you take the responsibility."

"You mind, Pardee?" Glen turned to Del.

Del said nothing; his face was filled with an odd tension.

"Okay, then. Amy, that suit you?" Glen smiled reassuringly.

She threw him a dubious glance, feeling distinctly uncomfortable with this turn of events. "Well, I guess so. If it's the only way I can go with Roger."

"Say there," interjected Frank Pereira, "if you have room—I'm not in great shape these days. I'm all done in. Think I could bum a ride there, Deputy Shepherd?"

Glen hesitated for a moment, then shrugged. "Sure, why not? There's room, isn't there, Terry?"

The pilot nodded.

Amy couldn't believe what she'd just heard. She stood there, rooted to the spot, horrified, while they went to transfer Roger, and thought, *how did this happen?*

She and Roger in the helicopter with Pereira? She hadn't meant for it to work out this way at all. And now, if she wanted things changed back, after all the fuss she'd made, why, they'd think her truly insane.

Pereira. She'd felt so smug earlier, but now... Now she and Roger were in danger again.

Oh, stupid, stupid! Amy cried to herself.

There was, of course, the pilot. He couldn't be involved, not a sheriff's department helicopter pilot.

And surely the presence of Glen and him together
would stop Pereira from attempting anything.

She was aware of Deborah looking at her questioningly. Amy smiled to reassure her. She couldn't put
Deborah in danger, as well.

The rest of the climbers were shouldering their
packs, getting ready to walk down to base camp.

"See you!" yelled Jay, waving.

"Ve'll have a trink tonight," called Swede loudly.

"Just her luck to get a ride," muttered Lonnie.

Rob poked Lonnie in the ribs. "Shut up, Lon," he
said genially.

Amy's eyes searched out Del, who stood solidly, silently. He looked at her as if from an untold distance.
Yet every detail of his appearance impressed itself on
her mind with absolute distinctness, from the bright
blue of his eyes to the harsh vertical lines on either side
of his mouth to the way his head was cocked expec-
tantly. His expression seemed vaguely puzzled, his
arms crossed as if he were considering something sig-
nificant.

Her heart swelled with the misery of her distrust and
with the severing of her last ties to him. Oh, how she
wanted to tell him everything. Maybe she'd be able
to—soon. And then again, it was possible that she
didn't have to tell him—perhaps he already knew.

"Well, Amy, let's go."

"Sure, Glen." But her eyes were drawn, as if by a
magnet, to the rest of the climbers, who were moving
away from the whirlybirds. The team members seemed
suddenly to be old friends, practically family. They
were her only salvation, and they were walking away

from her with their bright puffy parkas and stubbly faces and clumsy, scuffed boots. She was abruptly, unequivocally positive that not one of them—except possibly Del—was Pereira's man.

The pilots climbed in and started their machines. The rotors revolved slowly, then more quickly—thud, thud, thud. Glen pulled at Amy's hand. He mouthed the words, "Get in," but she couldn't hear over the racket. Snow whirled up around them. The Flight for Life chopper lifted off.

Jay raised his arm again from across the meadow. Amy waved back, wanting to cry out to him, to run and beg them all to take Roger with them.

But she couldn't. She began to climb in—Glen helped her, attentive, smiling. She turned again, craning her neck to see her friends. They were there, bright figures obscured by the helicopter's maelstrom. She couldn't bear to leave them.

But the rotors whirled faster, beating at the air. The pilot spoke into his helmet microphone and touched his controls. Amy could feel the machine shudder. Surreptitiously she felt the hard outline of the gun in her pocket.

She leaned out of the open doorway. Del, strangely, was still standing there, his hair blowing about wildly from the rotors' backwash. He was staring, as if in a trance, at the machine that was already tilting.

Suddenly he seemed to snap out of his odd stupor. Amy could see his head turn. He was shouting something to the others, but she couldn't hear what it was. Then he dropped his pack and sprinted toward the helicopter, ducking beneath the spinning blades, grabbing the rim of the doorway and swinging himself aboard.

CHAPTER EIGHTEEN

Day 7 A.M.

"DEL," BREATHED AMY, astonished. But it took no more than a second for her to realize why he was there. So it was Del, then.

"What the devil?" Glen was saying.

"Thought I'd come along for the ride," replied Del coolly, with a curious smile.

Amy stared at him blankly, wanting desperately not to accept the obvious truth: he needed to finish the job.

She looked around the crowded cabin. *Think, Slavin,* she cried inwardly.

What would Del do? Her eyes snapped to Frank Pereira—he must have a weapon on him. To help complete the job. This was the contingency plan; the climbing accident had failed, so now Pereira was on hand to make sure.

Her mind spun with conjectures: Pereira and Del would have to kill them all; they were witnesses. How? A helicopter crash, destroying all evidence, with only two survivors. But couldn't Glen and the pilot stop them? Her eyes switched to Glen. He smiled at her reassuringly as if to say, "Roger's safe, it's okay now. Relax, Amy." But he didn't know! Her glance flew to the back of the pilot's head; he couldn't see anything behind him, and besides, he had to keep the blasted thing in the air.

If one of them tried anything, she could pull her gun. Oh, great, she remembered suddenly, Del knew she didn't have bullets for her weapon. She closed her eyes for a split second, feeling sickening, paralyzing terror well up in her.

Del's face was a study in concentration, as implacable as the rock he climbed; he was watching each person in the helicopter. Was he judging their weaknesses?

Amy shrank against the rounded wall of the vibrating machine, trying to make herself inconspicuous. If no one noticed her, she still might be able to help.

When would it happen? Her eyes darted from Del to Pereira to Glen. She willed Glen to be ready to protect them. He was a sheriff's deputy. Surely he'd been trained to react in this sort of situation. If only he had his gun with him!

Below them the black spruce stands flitted by like giant shadows on the white snow. The ground undulated, falling away lower and lower to the valley. They'd be there in minutes!

Del seemed to flex his broad shoulders as if readying himself. Amy's stomach lurched. The noise in the helicopter was steady and practically deafening; there was no way to warn Glen.

Glen rose from his seat then and went forward to talk to the pilot. Amy closed her eyes in relief. He suspected something! He was telling the pilot to watch out or to radio his base.

The chopper dipped sharply. Someone was shouting. Amy's eyes flew open. Unbelieving, she saw Glen standing there, his long lean legs braced, holding a gun to the pilot's head! A swarm of thoughts shrieked instantly in her head. *Wrong, wrong!* she cried to herself. *You had the wrong man!*

Her gaze lunged to Del. All her instincts had been right. But Glen—so deceptive, his insinuations smoothly delivered with just the right amount of truth. The Indian girl . . . Del *had* told the truth. Glen—ambitious, stifled. Why hadn't she seen?

Remorse filled her in a black engulfing flood. If only she'd told Del what was happening, as he'd begged her to do! His eyes met hers for a charged instant. He was trying to tell her something. What?

Pereira stood, smiling grimly, and joined Glen. The pilot craned his head around, staring, horrified, at the two men behind him. He said something—Amy couldn't hear it—and got Glen's gun jammed in his ribs.

The helicopter started descending. Her mind churned with images: they'd land and then everyone would be killed and the machine set on fire as if it had crashed. And two lonely survivors would walk out. Amy was frozen with awful, bottomless dread. It couldn't be happening.

Del mouthed something to her. She could hardly concentrate enough to decipher it. "Get down," she thought it was.

Then everything went haywire. The pilot pulled hard to the left, causing the chopper to lurch and throw everyone off balance. Del launched himself across the cabin at Glen, tackling him. Pereira stumbled to the floor, along with Amy, and groped for support.

Suddenly there was an explosion—Glen's gun had gone off. For an instant Amy was paralyzed, waiting in terror to see if anyone was hit. But evidently the bullet had gone awry. Then the pilot went into another series of fancy maneuvers, tossing them all around like kernels of popcorn.

Think!

She began searching in her pocket frantically, cutting her hand on the broken mirror. Yes! There it was!

Amy pulled the gun out, feeling sick from fright and the lurching of the machine. Pereira was almost on his feet now.

"Hold it!" she cried, bringing the empty gun up with her two hands. "Hold it right there, Mr. Pereira!"

He stood unmoving. The chopper lurched once more and she staggered backward. Frank reacted instantaneously and knocked the gun out of Amy's hand onto the floor.

"Get it!" Roger was yelling from his litter. Then she saw that Del had somehow gotten Glen's weapon and was holding it on the deputy. "Get the gun, Amy!" Roger kept urging helplessly.

But Pereira reached it first. "Freeze! And steady this machine," he hollered to the pilot, "or this little lady has had it!" He turned to Del. "Drop it, Pardee, or I'll shoot her right here on the spot."

Suddenly, wonderfully, Amy felt like crying in joy. Her gaze met Del's with shared knowledge.

"Drop it!" commanded Pereira again.

Del shook his head.

"You son-of-a..." rasped Pereira. He clicked back the trigger a notch and fixed his eyes on Amy. She knew a moment of unreasoning horror, even though she realized the gun wasn't loaded, and she closed her eyes.

Click! Another click!

Her eyes flew open. Pereira was staring at the gun in disbelief. His expression was one of such stupefaction that Amy found herself giggling in nervous reaction.

"I never use bullets," she breathed. "They're too dangerous."

AMY STOOD ON THE TARMAC near the rear of the hospital and watched the flurry of activity. Flint, who'd been on the first helicopter, scurried around efficiently, helping to transfer the patients to the emergency ward. Del stood close to the second helicopter, holding the gun on Glen and Pereira. Amy could hear a siren wailing somewhere out on the highway as the police car neared the hospital.

She walked over to Roger's side as three men lifted him onto a gurney. "The pilot radioed for the sheriff," she told Roger. "Everything's going to be okay now. Guess you're about to be a hero."

"Didn't think I'd have to go through this!" he said, looking up at her and smiling weakly.

Amy tried to still her trembling, and gave Roger a shaky smile in return. "Neither did I."

After they'd wheeled her brother into the emergency room, she turned to look back at the helicopter. Del was still there. The sheriff, however, had arrived and relieved Del of Glen's gun. They would, of course, want the complete story from her. She felt suddenly drained, barely able to stand there and watch them as Glen was handcuffed along with Pereira and led away to the Blazer.

Glen Shepherd. *The poor guy,* popped into her mind unbidden. A man whose ambitions were greater than his possibilities. She pitied him. Then Amy wondered, would he really have pulled the trigger on any of them? Or was she only trying to believe the best of him? She'd probably never know.

Her gaze rested on Del. How could she ever have thought him the guilty one? Del Pardee was everything that was good and kind and strong and wonderful.

He must despise her. She didn't blame him. And what if he hadn't jumped on the helicopter at the last minute like that? They'd all be dead. She saw him glance over at her, his eyes shadowed, his brows drawn together. Someone had put a bandage on his cheek where Glen had hit him. She tried, unsuccessfully, to smile, but his face remained taut.

He couldn't stand even to look at her.

Finally it was Amy's turn to talk to Sheriff Conger. "You're a TV reporter?" he asked.

"Yes."

"Well, you sure have yourself a story here, don't you?"

"I guess so."

"Mind telling me your version?"

Amy did her best, leaving out, of course, her suspicions about Del. Even if he hadn't been still standing there with her, she couldn't have admitted it.

"Your brother is going to get the VIP treatment," said the sheriff. "A Mr. Kirklaw telephoned from the Defense Department for the hundredth time this morning and he's sending some men to watch Mr. Slavinsky."

"That's good," Amy agreed. "And by the way, part of my story is missing."

The sheriff quirked an eyebrow.

"It was on a cassette," Amy explained. "It was taken out of my backpack."

"We'll search for it," he said offhandedly.

"I really need it," Amy emphasized. "I'm sure Frank Pereira took it. If you look through his cabin at the Pardee Ranch..."

He smiled then. "We'll get it for you, miss."

"Good," said Amy firmly.

Sheriff Conger went on and on asking questions. Amy kept wondering how many times she would have to explain the whole thing over and over. Then there was her story, her great and glorious exposé. If someone had told her a week ago what she'd have to go through to get it, Amy would have laughed in his face.

Barbara Walters, indeed!

He finally finished with her and explained that at some future date, Amy would be called on to testify at the trials. It occurred to her that she could perhaps send in a sworn deposition. To return to Jackson, to have to face Del again...Amy didn't know if she could handle it.

She checked on Roger, who was still going through the emergency room procedure but would be transferred to a private room shortly. Del called the ranch while Amy promised Roger that she'd be back that afternoon to visit.

"Okay, sis." He squeezed her hand from his bed. "Go get some rest."

Del strode up to them then. "Take it easy, Roger. Amy," he said, "a deputy's waiting to give us a lift back to the ranch."

She merely nodded, unable to meet his eyes.

The ride was awkward. Del was in the front, while Amy sat in back with a mystified Flint. The red-haired climber asked as many questions as the deputy, but Del merely grunted monosyllables in reply and Amy said nothing at all. She couldn't talk to Del there, in front of the deputy and Flint. She had to explain it all to him alone. Her heart broke at the thought of how disgusted he must be with her. And he'd saved her life—hers and Roger's. She owed him everything and she couldn't even tell him, not yet.

Everyone had arrived back at the ranch from base camp. They all were waiting in front of the lodge with Hilkka, who stood, her hands on her hips, shaking her head. "You two all in one piece?" she demanded.

Del kissed her cheek. Amy nodded mutely. Then the whole crowd closed around them and everyone was talking at once, while the dog, Sally, barked with hysterical joy.

"That Shepherd. I always..."

"Can't for the life of me figure..."

"How'd you do it?"

"No wonder that rope broke..."

"Poor, poor thing..."

Just then a small car roared up the drive and came to a grinding halt. A young woman with long blond hair hopped out. Who?

She sped across the path and leaped into Jay's arms. Sue-Ann, thought Amy.

"You did it!" the pretty girl cried. "I was so worried, babe, and I wanted you to go, but I didn't and... Oh, Jay! I'm so proud of you!" She finally disengaged herself from the blushing Pardee brother and grinned widely at the team members. "Hi," she said brightly, "I'm Sue-Ann."

Then they all began to talk at once, and Sue-Ann kept staring at Amy in wonder. "Oh," she said, "how did you ever manage to do such a brave thing?"

Amy couldn't answer. She clung to Hilkka's hand, overwhelmed, hearing Del trying to explain the whole thing. She felt her eyes filling with tears; a contact lens began sliding out. She fumbled for it.

"Now why did Pereira do it?" Ollie asked, and Del had to start over again.

"Amy's *gun*?" Jay was astonished.

"She had a gun," Del explained dryly, "but no bullets."

"But Pereira thought she had bullets in it. I see," said Flint.

Then Del looked at Amy. She flinched at the severity of his expression. "Of course," he said pointedly,

"Amy will have to explain why she suspected Pereira in the first place. She never confided in me."

She wanted desperately to tell him how sorry she was and beg his forgiveness, but his grim gaze never wavered, and everyone was asking her questions and demanding answers. Later...

"It all started when Roger called me the night before his plane crashed," she began, "and he told me why he'd quit his job at Shearing...."

When she was finally through, they all stood in silence—a sort of solemn, respectful silence—and looked at Amy.

"Holy cow," said Rob in awe.

"I'll be damned," Ollie breathed.

"I wish I'd been there!" Hilkka snorted.

"Serves them right," Deborah said with a grin, embracing Amy. "I almost died when I saw you go off on that helicopter, but, then, thank goodness, Del jumped on."

Amy grinned weakly.

"She's a good sport." Jay patted her on the back.

"She's a bloody her-roine," said Lonnie, opening his mouth for the first time.

It seemed she was indeed a heroine. Swede broke out a new bottle of aquavit from his inexhaustible store. Hilkka went to cook a celebration dinner. The rest of them retired to the big living room, sat Amy in front of the fire and bombarded her with more questions.

"Come on," she said once, "I only did what I had to."

Gradually, under the influence of aquavit and the companionship of her friends, Amy relaxed. The strength of their caring warmed her. She was accepted.

They got into a discussion of the crossing of the icefall and Roger's rescue by Jay.

"That piton must've been loose...."

"The ice was rotten, anyway...."

"Get my darn ice ax in..."

"Too much exposure..."

"I'd rather use a different knot next time...."

Amy was one of them, a climber who'd just completed a tough job. She felt the stirrings of a great wonder at what these people had done—and would do again. It was all part of the myth of the climber.

And it had touched her.

They discussed Glen Shepherd endlessly, his motives, his character.

"He was very nice to me," Amy put in, "at first."

"Only to t'row you off guard," Swede replied.

"How much do you think Shearing was going to pay him?" wondered Rob.

"A whole lot." Flint's look was faintly regretful. "A hundred thousand? Two? It'd have to be that much to be worth murder."

"I'd be tempted myself," Lonnie muttered.

"Glen Shepherd." Ollie shook his head, disbelieving. "Why, I've known him since he was born. Such a nice boy."

"He helped me buy all those climbing clothes," Amy concurred.

"Real nice guy," grumbled Rob.

"Oh, my gosh." Amy clapped a hand to her mouth, remembering. "He cosigned my check when I bought that stuff."

"So?" asked Ollie, puzzled.

"That check is going to bounce," confessed Amy.

"Good!" said Deborah.

Amy giggled. "I guess he deserves it. Glen Shepherd bought my climbing clothes. Nice of him, wasn't it?"

Swede laughed so loud he spilled aquavit on his lap.

It suddenly occurred to Amy that Del had been chillingly silent. Anxiously she sought him out. He sat in an armchair, a little apart from them all, one muscular arm draped across Sally's back. His blue eyes were on her; their gaze met across the room, hers questioning, tentative, his remote and cold.

Her glance was the first to give way. Pain swept her, along with regret and love and a deep sadness.

It was only too obvious that Del would never forgive her.

CHAPTER NINETEEN

Day 7 P.M.

AMY WAS STILL WEARING her bedraggled climbing clothes that afternoon when she stopped by the nurses' station in the Jackson hospital. She'd just left Roger's room, spoken to the deputy who was guarding his door and had decided to check on the condition of the pilot and copilot.

Ted, the copilot, Amy was told, was coming along fine, but Grant, she was saddened to learn, was still in intensive care—his prognosis was only fair. They'd gotten him to the hospital none too soon.

She pushed open the door and stepped out into the sparkling, champagne dryness of the late Wyoming afternoon.

Jay, who had driven her back into Jackson, was waiting for Amy in the van. "How is he?"

"Great," she said as she climbed in, "until he fell asleep on me."

"Just the medication." Jay smiled as he started up the motor.

"Well, Roger was on the phone this morning and he spoke to the Defense Department. They're sending their own men to watch over him and get his statement. The FBI is getting in on the deal, too. When Frank Pereira came from Oregon to Wyoming and hired Glen to do the dirty work, the crime fell under federal jurisdiction. What a mess this is going to be."

"For you as much as Roger, I suppose, Amy." He looked at her assessingly.

She nodded. "But I asked for it. Meet the new Barbara Walters."

"Mom told me that you called your boss in Rochester and he's sending camera crews and everything out here."

Amy sighed. "Yes, they should be here tomorrow morning."

"You don't sound happy."

"Oh, I'm pleased as punch. I'll get offers from all over the country, Jay. This is the breakthrough that only comes once in a lifetime."

"So smile."

"I am." She did try.

They drove the route back toward Moose in silence for a time. Amy kept looking out of the van's window at the way the majestic, snow-covered Tetons pierced the sky like jagged sharks' teeth. Had she really been up in mountains like that? The WSYU camera crew would want them as a backdrop, naturally.

What a story! PRESIDENT'S STAR WARS PROJECT BROUGHT TO STANDSTILL. COVER-UP AT SHEARING AEROSPACE. BILLION DOLLAR HOAX. It wasn't, of course, Watergate, but it would do.

Amy Slavin, investigative reporter, would make that giant leap from small-town nobody to nationally recognized celebrity.

So why wasn't she happy?

"I'll miss it here," she said pensively. "Moose, Wyoming, has sort of grown on me."

"It does that." He gave her a sidelong glance. "Roger's going to be stuck here for at least a week. Why don't you stay, too?"

"I don't know..." Amy said, and left it at that.

They fell silent once more. As the van passed under the now familiar archway at the entrance to the Pardee Climbing Ranch, Jay said quietly, "You know, when I made it across that icefall the other day, I had built up the accomplishment so much in my head that it seemed like it was all I dreamed about for months. Making it...you know."

"Yes," mused Amy, "it was like waiting for the big break all my life, but now that I've got it...well...it isn't as great as I thought it was going to be."

Jay pulled up in front of the main lodge. "What else would you be looking for?" he asked, not so innocently.

Amy laughed suddenly. "And I thought you were shy!"

"Nope, only when I don't know a person. You're one of us now, Amy. You've made a climb, and a good one at that." He held the door open for her. "You haven't answered my question. What do you want out of life?"

She glanced up into his handsome square Pardee face. Amy shrugged. "A station wagon and kids and a lop-eared dog like Sally."

"That's not half as exciting as climbing," Jay replied, grinning.

"It's exciting enough for me," she said firmly.

It was nearly dark, reminding her of that first evening she'd arrived. It seemed terribly long ago. But this time there was no Del walking out of the big log house and into her life. He was angry and wounded and avoiding her like the plague. She hadn't been able to talk to him yet because she'd insisted on going right back to Jackson to see Roger and get a ship to shore message to her parents. They'd probably call as soon as they landed somewhere. Thank heavens she had only good news to tell them.

She went straight to the kitchen.

"Oh, you're back," said Hilkka, smiling warmly at Amy. "Sheriff was here for a spell and left you a present." Hilkka strode over to a cabinet drawer and produced a cassette.

"My tape!" Amy took it from her gratefully. "Boy, my little habit nearly did it this time." She put it in her shirt pocket and tapped it carefully. "Guess I've got the entire story, after all."

"Sheriff Conger found it lying conveniently on the path in front of your cabin."

"The creep."

Hilkka shook her graying head. "Takes all kinds, Amy. Some okay ones, some real nasty sorts."

"Good guys and bad guys," mused Amy.

"My Lord," Hilkka complained, "that boy Del is in a foul mood."

Amy said nothing, but she cringed inwardly.

"Guess he's tired," Hilkka decided. "That was some rescue. I'm so proud of my boys, especially Jay. And didn't you all have a spell of bad weather?"

Amy agreed gratefully, sinking onto a kitchen chair.

"When will you be on TV?" asked Hilkka, handing her a cup of coffee.

"Tomorrow. Ken doesn't want anyone else to scoop me."

"And there'll be pictures of the ranch? That's always good for business."

Amy shrugged. "Maybe they'll interview you."

"Me?" Hilkka gasped.

"Maybe they'll interview everybody." She couldn't join in Hilkka's excitement. Now that everything was over, she felt exhausted, dead inside. And decidedly filthy.

"Boy, do I need a bath," she said.

"That's where everyone else is, in the bath. Go on, Amy. You've done enough. Relax for a change."

"I will. Look at me. Lord, I'm a ragamuffin. My hair..."

"You'd better shape up. You need to look good when your boss shows up tomorrow and you're on prime time television," warned Hilkka. "And if you need a new outfit to wear, I'm sure one of the boys can drive you to town."

"Yes..." But Amy just sat there at the kitchen table, staring into space, her dirty hands clasping the coffee cup.

Tomorrow. She'd buy some new clothes—on Ken, of course—and look spiffy and sharp, write her piece, answer a million questions. Then she'd most likely get on the chartered plane with Ken and the film crew and fly back to Rochester.

She could stay, using Roger as an excuse, she supposed, but it would be a ghastly mistake. No use torturing herself.

She wished she had the courage to search out Del and finally face him, but he wasn't making it easy. She would do it before she left, though. Amy didn't like to leave loose ends dangling. It would be hard and he'd say lots of things that hurt terribly. He'd be right, of course, and that would make her feel even worse. But she owed him that much before she left.

If only things had worked out differently. If only she'd trusted him and confided in him. She brushed her dirty bangs out of her face with an impatient hand. Oh, what was the use, she thought, sighing.

"Penny for your thoughts," said Hilkka.

"They aren't worth even a penny," Amy mused.

When she got to her cabin she began to peel off her layers of clothes. They practically stood by themselves. She ran the bath and soaked in it for a long time. The water was so dirty by then that she had to drain it and start over. Twigs and pebbles and feathers clustered around the drain.

She washed her hair and scrubbed her neck and fingernails and shaved her legs—only nicking her ankle twice. Back to civilized living. And yet, something vital was lost with the last of the hard-earned dirt that swirled down the drain. Maybe it was her memories: the view of the storm-swept peaks surrounding Pearl Pass, the clouds racing in from the west in layers of ominous pewter, the wide, tree-lined Snake River Valley that was dotted with elk herds. Perhaps she'd been affected by the type of people she'd met, the wonderful breed who conquered the heights on their own terms, whose familiarity with the very mountains that defied them shaped their characters. Warm Hilkka, softhearted Ollie, Deborah—a true friend—sour Lonnie, garrulous Flint. Rob and Jay, larger than life Swede. These were people she'd never forget; they were as close to her as anyone had ever been.

And Del. As sincere and good and exciting as they came. Thank heavens he had one failing—his truly awful temper—or he'd be perfect.

Images teased Amy's mind. What would it be like to live in Moose, Wyoming, with Del as her husband? What would their children look like? Del? Her? Would they live in his cabin, build an addition for each new baby or maybe build a whole new house?

To have Del forever, Amy thought, would be like having Prince Charming slide that slipper onto her foot. Her career? She could finish the Shearing exposé—she'd have accomplished the ultimate goal of all reporters. In reality it would all be downhill from there.

Oh, well, Amy decided, she'd get over him. Hadn't she gotten over many another man?

Not like Del, her mind fired back.

She dried her hair and put on her jeans and hippopotamus sweatshirt and high-heeled boots. They hurt her ankles. Looking at her red parka with distaste, she pulled on her camouflage jacket and walked out into the night. It felt good to breathe in the fresh, cold air. The stars were out, pinpricks of light in the black velvet sky. It was perfectly clear, utterly dark. The Tetons were solid gray masses that Amy could sense rather than see.

She walked to a corral fence and leaned back on it, her hands in her pockets, her face upturned to the firmament. She wished with every ounce of her being that she could be a part of Del's life, that she could share the beauty and peace of the Tetons with him. Tears brimmed in her eyes, dimming the stars' glory into a thousand haloed circles.

Somewhere in the darkness footsteps crunched. A figure materialized before Amy, dimly seen. Yet she knew who it was without asking. Tension and anger radiated from his body, an unseen aura.

She began to say something to him, but the words caught on the lump in her throat. She tried to swallow her tears, but they came despite everything.

"Don't think crying's going to help, not this time." Del's voice emerged from the darkness, inflamed with exasperation.

"I'm sorry, I can't help it," mumbled Amy. "Oh, Del, I'm so sorry."

His shadowy form paced the ground in front of her, boiling with temper and indecision. He kicked at a stone; Amy could hear its hollow thump as it hit a fence post. She cringed as if the projectile had been meant for her.

"Please forgive me," she said. "You have to forgive me."

"I do?" he asked gruffly. "Why?"

"Because…" Her mind spun in neutral, blank and full of futility. "Because I love you and I can't bear it if you hate me," she said shamelessly.

He stopped his pacing abruptly and peered at her through the darkness. Amy's heart caught, stopping dead in the middle of a beat.

"You make me so damn mad," he growled. "Crazy kid."

Misery-laden tears burned in her eyes. "Please, Del," she whispered brokenly.

"Hell's bells, Amy! Don't beg!" he rasped. "All right, all right! I forgive you! Blast it all, I love you, too!"

Her heart gave a great glad thump. She put her hand out to touch him; he was there, warm and solid in the night. The moment hung suspended in time, his breathing audible in the darkness, her heart turgid with hope. Then he took her into his arms. They were strong and comforting and welcome. She leaned against him and buried her head in his broad chest.

"I don't deserve you," she murmured.

"The Lord knows I don't deserve you." Del laughed ruefully. "But I couldn't live without you."

Amy looked up at his face. "I'm so sorry," she said again.

"What for this time?" he asked.

"For not trusting you. For being a terrible pain in the neck."

"Yes, and I'll bet it's not the last time I forgive you for being a pain in the neck."

"It isn't?"

"I'll bet you're going to be a pain in the neck an average of once a day for the next fifty years." His voice was filled with suppressed laughter. "I'll never forget you on the floor of that saloon with drunk old Fred.''

''You won't?''

''I think that's when I fell in love with you, Amy,'' he said simply.

She tried to see his expression in the darkness, but he was all fuzzy to her, except for the white slash of the bandage on his cheek. His arms felt good, though. They felt like home.

''Del, I don't ever want to leave here,'' she whispered.

''You don't have to. You can stay if you want. But Amy, there's your career to consider. I can't ask you to give it all up.''

''Yes, you can. Go ahead, ask me.''

He was silent for a time. ''Amy, will you marry me and live here on the ranch?'' he asked at last, turning her face up to his.

''Yes, I will!'' she cried. ''Oh, I will! I love you so much, Del Pardee!''

''That's my girl!'' He laughed and swung her off the ground and kissed her hard on the lips.

She was breathless when he put her down. ''We're going to have a dozen children,'' she gushed. ''And if I still want to be a reporter I'll do it in between having them, okay?''

''A dozen, Amy?''

''Sure, and they'll all be climbers, like you.''

''And are you going to come climbing with the thirteen of us?'' asked Del, kissing the top of her head.

"Me? Oh, my, no. I've had my fill of climbing. No. I think . . ." She turned her face up to his and smiled to herself in the darkness. "I think I'll just stay home and cook."